Angel of God

Paula Kempler

Contents

CHAPTER ONE

I tried to steady my hands as I reached for the bow tied to my spine. Making minimal noise was my top priority at this moment. The thankfully oblivious fawn a couple feet in front of me continued to graze at what was left of the grass as I positioned the bow and took aim.

The fawn, although small and scrawny, could possibly feed my small family for a few days. We could sell the skin and even manage to freeze half of the meat for the following week. My mouth watered at the mere thought after having not eaten for almost three days now- the dreadful consequences of this severe famine which had struck my village.

I took a steadying breath and double checked my aim, the forest silent.

Come on, Adeline. Just shoot.

I pulled back the arrow, mentally marking the centre of the fawn's body as my target and was just about to shoot when-

"Adeline!" I heard a female voice shout from behind me, "Have you caught us anything yet?!"

I watched in nothing but pain as the deer's head snapped up, it's russet eyes widening and staring deep into my own. Before I could gather my thoughts, it was gone.

"Are you crazy?!" I growled, throwing my crossbow to the ground as both an angry and surrendering gesture. Turning, I met the bored face of my younger sister, who was merely sixteen at the time.

"What?" She frowned, obviously unaware of the fawn I had under perfect target. If only I'd just shot my arrow - if only.

I rolled my eyes, shoving her chest, "We could've eaten tonight if you didn't have such a big mouth. We could've even had new cloaks weaved!"

Elena turned to look over my shoulder in an attempt to find the animal I was preying upon. When she didn't find anything, she looked back to me.

"What was it?"

"A fawn. The size of a miniature pony too!"

"No way," she whined, tilting her head back, "Why couldn't you just shoot it?"

My facial expression reflected my confusion, "I was about to, if you hadn't spoken so goddamn loudly!"

Elena threw up her hands, "Well, you're supposed to be one of the best archers in our village. No - you are the best archer in our village. A minor inconvenience like me shouldn't have thrown you off."

I snorted, "You're being too nice to yourself with the 'minor'. Try major, maybe". I bent down to retrieve my crossbow from the ground, sliding it into its sheath across my back.

Elena directed a sarcastic smile my way, ignoring my remark, "Besides, we aren't even meant to be in the west of the wood. You know what the people back in the village say about this place, plus Papa would kill us. It was you who was dying to come hunt in here."

I started to walk back out of the forest, following the path I had laid out for myself on the way here by tying red handkerchiefs to trees, "You really believe the people back in the village when they say there's immortal creatures in here?" I rolled my eyes, my tone skeptical, "Come on. Let's get out of here."

Elena followed close behind as she let out a huff,

"Yet another lovely night without food."

"You can thank yourself for that."

*****

Approaching back to the house, I could see papa waiting outside from a distance. His aging face was twisted in anxiousness as he watched villagers pass by the road, searching for myself and Elena's familiar faces.

Elena remained a step behind me, "You're going to come up with an excuse to save our asses, not me."

We neared the house, Papa's coral eyes meeting my own emerald ones. He and Elena shared eye colours, however I had my mother's eyes. Papa would often say he saw mother in me - something I found to be a compliment. Based on Papa's description, the image I had conjured in my head of her was truly a beautiful sight.

"Where were you?!" Papa let out a sigh of relief as we made our way up the steps of the porch, the elderly wood creaking beneath the strain of Elena and I's combined weight. She nudged me in my rib - a gesture to signal me to reply.

"We were trying to hunt, Papa," I replied, indicating to the crossbow strapped onto my back.

He tutted, shaking his head. His eyebrows were furrowed in worry, his eyes glistening, "It's past sunset. You know I don't like it when you are out past sunset. Who knows what sort of...sort of things roam the outskirts of the village at this time. Where did you go?"

Both Elena and I fell silent. I hated lying to Papa but he took my word over anyone else's and Elena knew that, probably why she was relying on me to form an excuse.

"I..." I began, chewing the inside of my lip. Goddamn it, Adeline. Pull yourself together and say something!, "We were just-"

"We were using Uncle Howard's hunting fields down the road, Papa," Elena quickly interjected, "We lost track of time though. We're sorry."

Nice save. Useful for something at least.

Papa sighed and ran a creased hand over his face, nodding slowly, "Very well. Just make sure it doesn't happen again." He then gestured for us to enter the house.

Elena gave me a smug look - a sort that said 'thank me later' - before entering the house ahead of the rest of us. I was just about to follow her in before Papa blocked my way with his walking cane. Confused, I looked at him for an explanation.

He avoided eye contact as he spoke slowly in a low tone, "You didn't really go to Howard's hunting field, did you?"

I chewed the inside of my cheek - a habit for whenever I was anxious or under pressure. I didn't know what to say, but it was clear he had doubted us from the start.

I sighed, my eyes flickering towards the wood of the porch beneath us, "No, Papa."

"Then where did you go?"

I hesitated for a couple seconds.

"The west wood."

My voice was just beyond a whisper. I noticed Papa's body stiffen and before I knew it two large hands were on each of my shoulders, shaking me into reality, "How many times have I told you not to go in there?! You took your sister too! I didn't expect this from you, Adeline!"

"How else were we to find food?!" I placed my hands on his own in an attempt to calm him down, "The famine has sent all the animals west ways - that wood was the only shot we had to have a decent meal in three days!"

He shook his head frantically, "No! You know what the legend of this town says, daughter. That wood is somewhere us humans should never tread or tamper with."

I rolled my eyes, throwing my hands into the air in frustration, "How do we even know this stupid legend is true? Do you really believe that forest connects the human world to an immortal realm?" I scoffed, "It sounds ridiculous, father, and you know it. Old folks here just make up every other story to stop their children from going into that forest and getting lost."

Instead of shooting back with a response in his defense, Papa sighed - perhaps in defeat. He pushed the door to the house open and entered without another word.

I followed behind him almost as quietly.

CHAPTER TWO

Our home was a two-story house with small and narrow windows - meaning sunlight indoors was limited. It wasn't like that before... before everything went downhill. Our house and the village it was in were once bright and delightful like our family. Now everything was cold and dead.

Papa slowly climbed the stairs, making sure he was gentle on his weak limbs. My eyes were fixed on the photo on the wall - the only photo we had with mother- as I followed behind silently.

In the photo, two year old Elena was hugging mother's right side while I stood to her left - five years old and proudly showcasing my missing teeth. Since Papa was the tallest one amongst us - he stood behind, his both hands on either of his daughter's shoulders.

I wish you were here mother. Everything would've been so much better with you.

Papa took a seat on the edge of my bed, the wooden bed creaking under the pressure.

"Adeline, dear," He began, "You know that I love both you and your sister very much. I can't lose you or your sister after I lost her". His sad eyes wandered to the corridor and I knew he was referencing mother.

I took one of the spare pillows from my bed and hugged it to my chest before sitting down next to him.

"Papa I-"

I was suddenly interrupted by aggressive shouting coming from outside the house. Papa mirrored the frown of both concern and confusion written on my face as we stood, rushing to the closest window.

It looked like chaos. Men in torn clothing ran back and forth while screaming the same two phrases repeatedly, "The time has come! We need to make a sacrifice!"

We already lacked food and water, what other sacrifice did we need making?!

"Papa," I tore my eyes away from the scene outside the window for a second to glance at his face, "Why are there men looking like Jesus in front of our house? They look like the Jehovah's Witnesses or something to me."

After receiving no reply I turned to look at Papa again and I noticed - noticed how the blood had drawn from his face and how his eyes glistened with fright and concern. Sweat gleamed on the collar of his neck, " It can't possibly be time already? It can't be."

I continued to stare him down for an explanation. My mind was growing impatient with every continuing second while the screaming outside seemed to progressively get louder and louder. Next thing I knew I was running down the stairs and out onto the porch.

It seemed I wasn't the only one confused. People from the village were watching the group of men from their front doors with expressions of both horror and concern. By now Elena had joined me on the porch after being disturbed by the commotion.

"Brother Zakariath!" A middle-aged woman called out to one of the men from the group. I believed I recognised her as the owner of the local farmer's market. She was well dressed before the famine hit, and now she was clad in brown rags with dark bags of anxiousness and restless nights staining her under-eyes. "Is it true the time for the legendary sacrifice has arrived?!"

The man Zakariath replied with an unsettling excitement laced in his voice, "The Father of Hila said - quote on quote - 'those who experience the severity of a famine for over 40 days shall sacrifice a beautiful daughter with talents in combat to the west of the wood. In return, the Legend promises bounties and food in plenty."

I felt Elena take a step back so that she was now standing in my shadow.

Such bullshit - I could honestly say humans were one of the stupidest things to exist in the world and, ladies and gentlemen, this was one of the cases to demonstrate that.

"Why should we throw away one of our beloved sisters?!" I snapped, my mouth working before my brain could even think, "You're all selfish bastards to sacrifice actual humans for something that won't even happen!"

People's eyes now turned towards me. Some gasped and some looked at me in disgust as though I had danced naked in the middle of the road. None of the young girls dared to voice their approval of my outburst, even if they did agree.

An unfamiliar man shouted back in reply, "You females belong under our feet! We can't go to sleep with an empty stomach again when the Legend demands something so simple of us! We need to sacrifice someone and we must do it now!"

The first suggestion arose. "We should sacrifice Amelia Fitzpatrick. She's beautiful - the Legend will enjoy her!"

Elena took another step back, her fingertips lightly gripping my wrist for protection. Her voice wasn't beyond a whisper, "A-Adeline, what're they doing?"

"Fitzpatrick can't fight to save her life!" another male objected from the crowd, "Elizabeth Castille can run a gun or two and is sexy, why not her?"

He was interjected by another, "The Legend don't want no sexy girl with a gun, it wants skill!"

The crowd continued to argue over who to sacrifice while I watched as mothers one by one started to hide their daughters from sight. Papa from behind had attempted to grab my arm and drag me into the house multiple times but on each occasion I had freed myself from his grip. I wasn't prepared to stand by while a helpless girl would be thrown into the woods because a damn fairytale said so.

"Elena," I whispered to my left. My fingers clenched and then loosened, "Take father inside before he-"

"What do you think of Adeline Blanchard?"

My mouth ran dry when I was interrupted by my own name. I knew that voice, and I knew it well.

Uncle Howard.

"She's the perfect sacrifice, gentlemen! She is the village's best huntress and a gorgeous sight, what better could we offer?" He stood with his wretched wife, smug smiles dancing on both their lips.

From beside me, I heard Elena's breath stifle.

No no no. That bastard. I had known there was something wrong with him - and he was fucking smiling! Never in my nineteen years of existence had I seen him smile.

Murmurs of approval began to emerge from the crowd. People were turning from each other to me, nodding in agreement. Women were looking at me with hopeful eyes - like I was their only hope to end this famine.

I scoffed.

"Nice joke. There is no way I'm performing slow suicide for you all so-" before I could protest in my favour any more, a loud thump caused me to spin around behind. Papa had been pinned against the front door by a man who must've snuck onto the porch while we were distracted. My eyes widened as I instinctively reached to grab my pocket knife, but I was pulled back by a strong grip on the length of my brown hair before I could do so.

I tried to kick and scream but whoever held me possessed overpowering strength. Elena was pushed to the ground by a group of unfamiliar women - a scene I watched helplessly from my peripheral vision as I tried hard to resist against the strong grip the men held around me.

My teeth dug into my bottom lip, a habit that I had inherited from my mother as I tried to come up with some form of escape. There seemed to be none. Goddamn it.

Suddenly, the unfamiliar texture of a cloth was clamped onto my mouth and from its strong scent I had already realised what it had been dipped in - chloroform.

No, no, no, no.

I desperately tried to resist while my heart hammered in my chest. Blood rushed to my ears and my eyelids became weighty. From the faint hearing I still had left I listened to Papa and Elena's painful, helpless wailing of my name. It was as though it was a funeral and I was the unfortunate corpse.

And then all vision and sound drowned out into darkness.

———————————

thank u sm for reading! pleaase do leave a vote and comment if you enjoyed!

- jen <3

CHAPTER THREE

My senses slowly returned to me.

The sound of dripping water first, then the echo of rustling leaves in the wind. A lingering coppery taste coated my mouth - blood. Wincing, I opened my eyes, but could only manage to widen them a little in an attempt to focus my vision and take in my surroundings.

I was in the woods. Probably within the deepest, darkest western caverns of the woods. It must've been past midnight - there was no source of light at all. My already weak body ached as I slowly hoisted myself to my elbows using whatever strength I had left. As my eyes adjusted to the intense darkness around me, I began to make out the outline of an object which had been left on the ground beside me.

My bow.

Frantically, I tapped the ground with an open palm in an attempt to find the arrow to go with it. "Come on, come on," mumbles of desperation passed by my lips as I searched the ground closest to me. Finally I felt my skin come into contact with the hard, slender body of the arrow as I let out a sigh of relief I didn't even realise I was holding in.

Resentment bubbled in my blood - resentment for my village, resentment for its people, resentment for this forest and even resentment for myself. They had sworn this 'sacrifice' was necessary. They had also sworn to kill me the moment I came back - if I came back.

Carefully rising to my feet, I realised I was hopelessly lost with no sense of direction. There was no turning back, even if I tried. I started to take a couple steps north, holding my hands out in front of me to stop myself from banging into anything. Every whisper of the wind or any small movement caused my heart to beating frantically - my head was so dizzy I felt I was going to black out again.

I couldn't panic. No. Adeline, you're not going to panic. I had to keep my wits about me.

Stumbling through the woods at a painfully slow pace, I was able to steer my way into one of the more open sections of the woods with less trees. Here, the full moon provided a source of light. A full moon. The sun had only just set when I was taken from the village - how long had I been unconscious down here?

Think, Adeline, think.

Maybe I should wait till the morning to move. Argh, but what if something predatory finds me in the meantime? Maybe if I slept under an oak tree with a great shadow, I could potentially camouflage into the night. Or maybe I should-

A shadow scuttled across one of the branches of the tree above me. I froze, gripping my bow and arrow tighter and tighter with every passing second. I squinted to focus my vision onto the branch, and the moonlight illuminated the shadow of a small creature.

A squirrel. Thank god.

Relief filled my veins and the grip I had on my weapons loosened as a result. "It's a squirrel," I reassured myself, "Nothing but a goddamn squirrel."

And then there was another dark blur from in front of me.

My breath hitched in my throat as I tried to brush it off, "Get over it, Adeline. It's probably a deer." It didn't take me long to realise how the air had suddenly become a lot colder - a lot more chill and eerie with the wind whistling into the night. I was about to take another step when I heard the crack of a twig, my heart now pounding in alert.

What the hell.

I quickly pulled my bow and arrow to my chest while my eyes examined the dark depths of the trees around me. I hadn't heard any footsteps - surely a human didn't have that much stealth. The sky in the moment caught my eye. A small moment ago it was a dark blank canvas of blues and blacks, void of anything. Now it was packed with small iridescent stars, more than I had ever seen in the sky in my life.

Again, another twig. Straight in front of me. Closer this time. I could've sworn I thought I was going to throw up my heart from how hard it was pounding. I tried to steady my breathing. It wasn't like I hadn't ever hunted an animal like a wolf before - if it was a wolf - I just hadn't ever done it in pitch blackness.

Before I could even gather my thoughts, a dark blur passed by in front of me at immense speed - such speed I could feel the harsh breeze it gave off through my hair. Frantically I began to stumble backwards, feeling beads of sweat trickle down my temple and my breathing so fast it sounded like pants.

You're going to die. Use your bow and arrow or you're going to die.

The ground welled up beneath me as I reached for my arrow to position it within my bow, but that effort was cut short once my back hit something sturdy.

It was sturdy yet smooth against my back, nothing like how the trunk of a tree would've felt. And as I focused, I realised it was slightly warm and moved - moved like the rhythm of lungs within a chest, rising and falling. I kept my eyes straight in front of me though, bracing myself for a knife to slice my throat or another rug of chloroform to clasp my mouth or-

"Now, now. What's a girl like you doing in a wood like this?," said a deep, sensual male voice from behind me.

The accent was clear - classy, like someone from the privileged areas of the city of London. His words were smooth and I could hear what sounded like a smirk in his tone - a teasing tone.

I didn't even try to control the trembling of my hands which were at my sides, my body so tense my muscles ached. Calm warm breath from behind rose hairs on my nape.

Death at the hands of a wolf or any bigger beast would've been a better way to die - but death at the hands of what sounded like a sadistic killer? Only God can save me now.

Look him in the eye, a voice in my head screamed at me, maybe he'll pity you and let you go.

I swallowed hard and turned around painfully slow.

Standing almost a foot taller than me, with the moon illuminating half of his face, was the most attractive man I had ever seen.

And behind him at either side were two large dark wings.

omg no one understands how excited this bitch was writing this chap bc i got to introduce my fave boy :') first impressions of him?

3 updates in one day i'm on a roll ;)

please vote and comment if you enjoyed! thank u!

- jen <3

CHAPTER FOUR

He radiated grace.

Dark, black, nape length hair and skin the colour of honey and milk, almost golden. From the half of his face which was illuminated, I was able to trace his strong, pointed jaw and the curve of his structured cheekbone with my gaze. His eyes sparkled with amusement, and were a colour which was unworldly - golden, the colour of dancing flames with specks of brown. My face had become heated by his stare alone.

I tried to take in the sight of his wings. Great, mighty, dark wings - like that of an angel but concealed in black. I couldn't comprehend anything, my mind simply feeling limp and numb. My head seemed to spin and everything was a motion blur except him.

I had to be seeing things. There was no way.

The way he stood with absolute stillness, the way the moonlight radiated off his skin and how he seemed to stand out in the dark - even when wearing all black - made me want to drop everything and run in the opposite direction.

I blinked again - perhaps he'd disappear. He didn't. I took a wary step back and he mimicked my movement, taking a small step toward me into the full spotlight of the moon, his full features now clearly highlighted.

The corner of his lips tugged into a small playful smirk, "You're scared."

"No shit," I blurted out without thinking. I could hear my heart drumming in my ears now, "Are you real?"

"No shit," His smirk widened - amused and entertained, "Is my beauty so beyond this world you'd think I am unreal?"

I retreated another step backwards. If I wasn't in a possible life or death situation, I would've probably rolled my eyes at his arrogance.

He slipped his hands into his pockets in one smooth, graceful motion. His clothes were black, sewn with threads of dark metallic blue which sparkled in the moonlight.

When it became obvious to him that I wasn't going to answer his question, he began to circle me - a predator playing with its prey. "So you're not going to cure my curiosity and tell me what a mortal woman like yourself is doing here during a full moon?" he prowled around me slowly, "Aren't you supposed to stay on your side of these woods?"

I swallowed, my eyes darting around the forest for possible quick-time escape routes. What caught my attention instead was how the multitude of stars in the sky looked like they were moving - floating in whatever direction the stranger would walk.

Either that or I was going utterly crazy.

When I remembered his silence meant that he awaited a response to his question I quickly mumbled, "I was t-thrown in here."

His circling paused behind me, "By who?"

"By my village," I took a deep breath to try and stabilise my breathing while I was coolly interrogated. I was terrified of him, but I wasn't prepared to let him know that, "They said it was a ... a sacrifice written in the Legend. To end the famine in my town."

The circling resumed. When he again passed by in front of me his smile had widened and his gaze was fixed on the ground he tread on. I noticed his side profile, his nose impeccably straight and sharp. I noticed his wings, black feathers with tips of vivid silver. I hadn't ever seen someone so handsome. It really was beauty beyond this world, and maybe that's why my mind was screaming at me to escape.

"Why," He began. A lover's voice. Sensual, rich and seemed to send shivers down every muscle in my body, "Why did they choose you?".

My eyes flickered down to the bow and arrow I still held in my hands. They felt useless now. I felt useless. "Because the Legend required someone who was skilled in combat." My voice was a trembling whisper.

He hummed as though I had confirmed something he already knew. When I looked up from my bow and arrow, I was met by his stare as he towered over me - gold eyes twinkling with interest, "And are you skilled in combat?"

My breath hitched. I tried to tear away from the intense eye contact he held but the striking gold of his eyes seemed to perform a hypnosis on me. They were addicting - like something I couldn't stop staring at no matter how hard I wanted not to, "I-In archery, I guess."

His hand tilted my chin, his fingers cold - so cold, but soft and slender. A half smile tugged at his lips, "That's perfect."

Before I could process it, both my body and eyes began to feel weighty - weight which wasn't forceful and uncomfortable, but instead gentle and soothing. I was trying to mentally resist against it but it was almost as though the force overpowered my own mind.

I heard one last tender drawl before slumber overtook me completely,

"Goodnight, darling."

****

I had woken up to a stabbing pain in my back, something which I realised had happened because I'd fallen off the bed I was on.

I was on a bed. What the hell.

I pushed myself up from the cold tiled floor slowly while attempting to ignore how my muscles were burning. The room was dark but I was able to catch sight of some of the furniture thanks to the moonlight gleaming through the window. My eyes widened at how much bigger than usual the moon seemed to appear through the window of the room - surrounded by an insane amount of stars.

It didn't look real.

This was far from the standard working class bedroom I was used to. It must have been almost three times bigger than my room back home- if I could call it home. The bed - the bed which was far too big for it to be normal, was enrobed with layers of mahogany drapes dangling from the ceiling, finished off with tassles to complete the classy theme which seemed to be prominent in this room.

Where am I?

I was drowning in my disoriented thoughts and the sound of my racing heartbeat when I was interrupted by three loud knocks on the door. "Miss, are you awake?" asked an unknown voice - a female voice, sweet and light.

I froze. I couldn't be sure whether whoever was on the other side of the door could be trusted, and so my eyes began darting around the room in an attempt to find my bow and arrow for defense. The knock came again, and my weapon was nowhere to be found. I swallowed hard, eyes fixed on the door.

"C-Come in."

Through the hefty wooden doors entered the silhouette of a tall woman, carrying a tray of something which was unidentifiable due to the dark.

She's going to drug you. She's going to drug you or something Adeline.

The woman approached me which gave me an opportunity to get a better look. As she got closer, my eyes widened at what I saw. Her copper brown hair was half up and half down, secured with a pearl hairclip. Her ocean blue eyes looked at me like she was confused to see me just as much as I was to see her. Something white and feathery behind her caught my eyes.

Wings.

"Oh my god," I accidentally blurted my thoughts out loud, taking a step back from her.

Is she an angel?! An actual goddamn angel. Am I in heaven?!

She placed the tray down on the table and I was able to catch a glimpse of what was inside. Food. A whole array of food - from juicy in-season fruit to different types of bread. My stomach pained at the sight.

When my eyes finally tore away from the tray, I locked eyes with the woman in front of me - who was staring back just as intensely.

Why isn't she talking? Is she deaf or mute? Maybe both.

"So-" We both began at the same time. She's not deaf nor mute then.

"Who are you and can you tell me where I am?" I quickly demanded, not realising that my voice was evidently shaky - trembling out of fear.

"Good afternoon to you too. You are in Velastille, the capital of Pandaemonium." She smiled. I paused.

Pandaemonium. I'd heard of that before. Multiple times. In Church. De scribing...hell.

I took yet another couple steps back from the unknown woman frantically, my back hitting the wall. My eyes were wide with shock, my brain was racing with unimaginable thoughts and I couldn't control my tongue, "Am I dead? Did I go to hell? There must be a mistake, I did nothing wrong! I swear, please let me speak to God - I know there's been a mistake!"

She stared at me with such confusion, opening her mouth multiple times to speak but then clamping it shut as I continued my frantic rant. She quickly interjected,

"You are not in Hell. Pandaemonium is the central district between Heaven and Hell," She explained slowly, concern evident on her sweet features - but my mind was not comprehending any of it. I couldn't even form a coherent thought.

When I didn't reply - mainly because I couldn't think enough to form a reply to what she'd said - I suddenly began to hear chuckling from her, gentle and bubbly. I frowned.

"Forgive me, your face is quite funny. Has anybody told you your features look earthly?" She mused, but upon receiving my silence and frown of confusion in return she straightened, "I am Cirse, by the way. I will be at your service here."

My maid? I thought I was in Hell. Maybe God felt bad for me and put me in what He thought was a luxurious version of Hell.

"Uh, it's nice...it's nice to meet you, I guess," I mumbled, my back still pressed against the wall. I had questions. So many questions, "How did I end up here? Am I dead? I remember seeing one of you before my eyes closed - a man! Was he the angel of death!?! I knew it! I can't believe I-"

"I am not sure why Master brought you here - to his room, but anyhow you must be worthy of it," she shrugged, placing a bag onto the foot of the bed.

What 'Master'? And why was I in his room? Was she talking about that angel? That angel of death? The strikingly handsome angel of goddamn death?

Stop it Adeline! Breathe!

"Master told me to bring you food and on the bed is your change of attire. You must change into it," She passed me a look from head to toe, "I'm not sure if the dress will fit you. If not then let me know, Miss." She said, doubt clear in her tone over not knowing what to call me.

My stance against the wall eased a little and for some reason I even felt bad for her. "I don't know what's going on, but you can just call me Adeline. Believe me, I'm not worth the title," I confronted her. She hesitated but I quickly shot her a comforting smile - when I was the one who needed it.

Her ocean eyes gleamed with what looked like gratitude and without saying another word she left , leaving me alone in the unlit unknown room. I approached the food platter slowly, my eyes taking in the sight of the delicacies which could have fed my family at least for a week. My mouth watered as I played around with the platter's contents, but I didn't dare eat anything. I couldn't trust anything here. I couldn't even tell what was real and what was simply a facade..

My attention turned to the bag of clothing waiting for me at the foot of the bed. Out of curiosity I opened it, unfolding the pieces inside. There was an ankle-length black dress - plain and simple beside the bell-bottom sleeves and chest area studded with silver jewels of various shapes and sizes. I dug deeper into the bag, fishing out a wide glittery-black leather waist belt which I presumed went with the dress. I tossed it to the side in a pile and looked back into the bag, now pulling out an unfamiliar piece of clothing. It appeared to be a fighting suit - black, leather and tight.

Why did she get me a fighting suit? Again, I flung it to the side dismissively and sighed at the now-empty bag.

My attention shifted back to the room I was in again, and I happened to catch sight of a huge mirror on the left wall of the bed. It looked like the ones I had seen in Elena's French fashion magazine, and so I felt myself walk towards it -entranced.

I stared at my reflection. At my ghastly pale face which once had colour and at the purple which had developed beneath my eyes. At my thinning waist and my protruding collarbones. Malnourishment has done a great job making me weak. At my patchy, rough clothing and my lifeless brunette hair - lifeless brunette hair which had once been voluminous. I tucked a piece of hair behind my ear in disgust and was about to tear my gaze away from the mirror when it caught my eye. I did a double take while running a trembling hand over my ears.

My ears. My once rounded, human ears were now pointed - pointed in a way elves and fairies in fairy tales were described as having.

No way. No way is this happening to me right now.

I stared long and hard at them, maybe I was hoping that they would disappear and it would turn out that I was imagining things due to my extreme hunger. Nothing of the sort happened.

Thoughts were racing in my head but I couldn't make sense of a single one. My head was pounding in a combination of pain, frustration and confusion and my body felt freezing cold and aflame at the exact same time.

I couldn't take it, and before I knew it I was sliding down against the wall - mid meltdown as hot tears slid down my cheeks.

I pulled my thin legs to my chest in an attempt to provide myself some closure. "W-Why do the w-worst things happen t-to m-me?!" I questioned the universe aloud, barely able to get my words out between my uncontrollable sobs. My head pressed between my knees, tears staining my already tainted pants.

And that was when I heard someone enter unannounced through the door.

---

it's already chapter 4 omgy'all like Adeline? Azriels kinda hot, right?□remember to comment and vote, if you liked this chapter!

CHAPTER FIVE

"Why is the little girl so sad?" an elegant voice mused tauntingly, "You're acting as though I have you shackled to the floor in a cell."

I knew that voice.

My head snapped up to see the same man from the forest, his wings now nowhere to be seen. The room was still dark and so I was only able to make out his slender outline, straight and tall. Wiping my tears from my cheeks roughly with my sleeve, I barked in frustration, "What happened to my ears?! Was this your dirty doing?!"

I watched him stalk closer with that regal grace, and he slowly dropped down into an easy crouch in front of me. I tensed against the wall in an attempt to back away from him as much as possible. The light provided from the window now shone directly on his features, allowing me to see his intense amber eyes which sparkled with amusement.

The corner of his lip tugged into a smirk, "I thought a hello would be nice."

"Just answer!" I snapped. It was as though all the fear and confusion I had experienced in the past however many hours had bubbled into nothing but frustration and anger.

He shrugged passively, a beautiful and easy gesture, "You needed to fit in. Wings weren't an option because you probably couldn't handle them, so I decided to give you the classic fairy look."

"Why the hell do I need to fit in?!" I wailed.

"Angels of my type despise mortals - an inner hatred they can't get rid of. If anyone was to realise you were a human, the results wouldn't be pretty."

I shuddered at the thought, tightening the grip around my knees as I stayed sat on the floor, "W-Why did you need to bring me here? Just tell me - am I dead? Did you take my soul?"

"No, you're not dead," He began, examining his nails, "In fact, you're probably more alive than ever - with all the food, clothing and personal care that's available here." His eyes flickered away from his nails to give my seated body a quick look, "You're bones and no flesh. Didn't they care to fatten you up before they threw you into those woods?"

Dickhead.

Before I could open my mouth to reply, he swiftly continued, "And no. I didn't take your soul because I'm not among the angels of death," He locked eyes with me again, his voice now a smooth murmur, "Besides, taking out the souls of pretty little girls like you isn't my thing."

I felt my cheeks heat up as I tore away from the eye contact between us, focusing my attention on examining him instead. His whole persona combined with his shadowed appearance screamed that he belonged to something dark or fearful.

"Then what are you?" I chewed my cheek in anxiousness, "And why am I here? What do you need me for? Who even are you?"

He cocked his head to the right, a sensuous smile appearing on his lips again, "So many questions for a little teeny human."

"Can't you ever just be straight up?!" I asked irritably, my voice beginning to sound like a desperate plea.

"Ah, see, for that you'd have to make me straight up first, darling."

It took me a couple seconds to process his innuendo and while groaning in frustration at his response, my head fell back between my knees in defeat. What an absolute prick.

He laughed a lover's laugh - smooth, rich and gentle before saying, "Alright. First thing is first - let me get an introduction, and then perhaps I'll inform you regarding all the details as to why you're here."

I kept my head buried between my knees with my eyes clamped shut, a desperate attempt to just block out his existence before my blood began curdling in rage. After he realised I wasn't intending to respond, he mused, "My offer expires once I leave this room."

Regardless, I kept my head down and knees pulled into my chest. Peering through a gap through my knees I watched him as he placed his hands on his thighs, ready to stand up from his crouching position. When I still didn't react, he rose - a fluid, graceful motion.

"I presume you wouldn't enjoy your stay if you were left completely unaware as to what your future here holds."

"You're bold to presume I'd stay long enough to have a future here, prick," I spat, my voice muffled between my knees.

Again, a low laugh, before I began to hear the echoing click of his dark boots against the polished floor. His footsteps were slow - almost lingering, as though he was giving me enough time to rethink my decision. My head stayed pressed to my knees - I would do far worse things over revealing my identity to a threatening stranger.

He was getting closer to the door, his footsteps growing distant. When I heard the first creak of the door as he opened it, my mouth quickly opened.

"Wait."

The creaking of the door paused. Hesitantly, I lifted my head from between my knees and let out a sigh. Telling a threatening stranger my identity would be difficult, but being held in this unknown place without knowing why would be far far worse.

"Wait," I repeated again.

The man slipped a hand into the pocket of his dark pants, turning to face me with a grin, "Yes?"

The stupid grin itself was probably the root of all my anger and frustration right now, but I attempted to ignore it.

I rubbed my arm slowly - a comforting gesture to myself, "My name is Adeline. I'm nineteen. I have a younger sister who's fifteen called Elena." I paused. "Now tell me who you are and what you want from me."

His smirk grew wider as he held the door open for himself with one hand, "And I will have all the answers ready for you tonight, when you attend dinner."

Dinner. Was he mentally okay?

I growled, ready to remind him of the terms of our agreement - but I was swiftly interrupted. "As for now though, rest up Adeline."

And with that he was gone, the door shutting behind him.

****

Hours passed with me stuck in this same goddamn bedroom.

I had tried the door multiple times, but it had been locked from the exterior. What seemed to confuse me to hell was how the sky outside the window had not changed at all after however many long hours I had been in here - it was still a dark canvas of blues and blacks packed with glittering stars, almost identical to how the sky had been back in the woods before I was...'kidnapped'.

I had paced around the room for what felt like forever in an attempt to calm my nerves, and now found myself sitting in the window seat, observing whatever view I could make out in the dark. That was when I heard the lock click, and with a slow groan the double wooden doors opened to reveal the same young woman from earlier - Cirse, I believe it was. Her feathered white wings were absent, her long copper hair in wavy tousles down her back.

"Good evening, miss," She nodded, her soft pink lips curving into a gentle smile. Her hands were bound in front of her in both respect and submission.

I swung my legs off the edge window seat and faced her, both my hands gripping the crushed velvet material of the seat padding. Clueless as to how to reply, I just sent her a hesitant smile back.

She gestured to the door, "Dinner is ready."

I shook my head and shifted my attention back to the view outside the window, turning my back towards her, "I'm not hungry, thank you Cirse"

"Master would like you to come to dinner," I heard her from behind me. Her tone was soft-spoken and kind - perfectly matching her features.

I scoffed, "He doesn't own me. It doesn't matter to me whether he wants me there or not - I'm not hungry."

Cirse fell silent for a couple minutes as though she was attempting to form a decent reply, and I did begin to feel a tinge of regret for lashing out at such an innocent soul in that way. However to my surprise, when she did eventually reply her tone had become increasingly firmer.

"He suggests you come for dinner if you would like any of your questions answered. Beyond this point, he will refuse to enlighten you and you will have to remain here against your will - without knowing why." she paused for a couple seconds as if in thought and then added, "If I were you, I would just go. It benefits you more than it does him - you'd get a full stomach and all the answers to your questions."

I rested my head against the cold pane of the window, my warm breath causing a cloud of fog to appear on the glass. In my heart I knew Cirse was right - it was a simple request and all I needed to do was fulfill it, and then have all my confusion cleared. Sighing, I turned to face the young maid again, "Okay, Cirse. Let's go."

She passed a disapproving glance over my torn clothes and shook her head, "I can't take you to dinner in that attire. I'll first bathe you, and then dress you in fine clothing."

I had to bite my lip to prevent myself from letting out a frustrated groan, but I trailed behind her to the bathroom without arguing anyway - the warmth of the bath could provide a huge benefit to my aching muscles.

After Cirse had helped me bathe and washed my hair with soaps of milk and honey, she had lathered rich lotion onto my dehydrated skin before handing me a robe - a black robe made of what felt like the softest cotton to exist. Bundled into it, I sat on the edge of the bed while Cirse left the room for a few brief moments. The chattering of small crickets beyond the window were the only sound audible, no hint of torture or slaughter or anything to fear.

Church sessions when I was younger had taught me that Pandaemonium was the capital of Hell where Satan and his right hand men resided. It was engraved in my mind as a place overpowered by fire, chaos and suffering - but this place was nothing of the sort.

The door creaked and Cirse returned, a couple of clothing hangers with dresses attached to them gripped in her small hands. She lifted the first one up, a plain black maxi dress with a huge plunge down the neck. "How is this?"

I took one look at the clothing and wrapped my dressing gown tighter around me, pleading Cirse not to make me wear a dress. It had been years since I had worn a gown, dress or anything non-practical for that matter - it felt like a joke that she was expecting me to be so dressed up for dinner.

Cirse ignored my pleas and held up the next option - a black halter neck, super tight jumpsuit with a gold belt to cinch the waist. I shook my head, trying not to cringe at how revealing it was. "Why is everything black"

Cirse shrugged, folding the rejected dress and placing it down onto the bed beside me, "It is Master's favourite colour after all."

I would've guessed - his clothes, his hair, his wings had all been black.

I was beginning to feel bad for the amount of rummaging I was making Cirse go through, and so I pointed towards the bag she had left for me earlier. "There's a black dress in there that doesn't show my ass and tits, how about that?"

She huffed a laugh, pulling out the same black ankle-length dress from earlier - plain and simple beside the bell bottom sleeves and chest area studded with silver jewels of various shapes and sizes. "This will look good on you," she passed me the glittery black waist-belt from earlier too, "And wear this, it'll accentuate your tiny middle."

She led me to a chair in front of the darkened fireplace, and I didn't fight back as she ran her long fingers through my brunette hair and began to plait small random strands.

"Why is dinner such a huge event here?" I asked, trying to hide the judgmentalness in my tone, "It's just food."

"I'm not sure," Cirse murmured, her fingers feeling lavish against my scalp, "This is how Master likes it, and that is how it's always been."

I bit my lip to try and suppress the urge to roll my eyes - it was as though this whole place ran under the click of his finger, including the people in it. And when I went to ask some more questions about 'Master' so I knew what I was dealing with tonight, Cirse had already finished my hair and opened the door to the hallway.

"Wear your dress and then meet me in this hallway. I will escort you to the dining room."

And so I did, trying to avoid my reflection in every mirror. I couldn't' bare to see myself dressed up like this while my sister and father starved at home, but most of all - I couldn't bare to look at those stupid pointed ears. They made me feel alien.

As I stepped into the hallway after Cirse, my mouth physically fell open in awe - the corridor alone had outdone the bedroom. The walls were a pale cream outlined with rich gold and had been complete with towering pillars of white alabaster going down the hallway. In the middle of the hallway was a break where the wall ended on both sides and was instead replaced with tall, black-framed rectangular windows which provided a view of the dark sky outside. The floor had been done with gleaming marble tiles, glossy enough that the reflection of the grand gold and black chandelier above us could be seen in them.

Cirse noticed my gape and smiled, gently taking my arm in her's. "This is just the hallway. Wait till you see the drawing room one day."

I was too entranced in my surroundings to reply as she led me down the hallway. I hadn't paid attention to any of the lefts or rights we had made, and before I knew it we were standing outside a large double wooden door - one which was very similar to that of the bedroom I was in moments ago.

Cirse's grip on my arm tightened slightly as she pulled me closer towards her. Her voice was almost beyond a whisper as she maintained sharp eye-contact with her ocean eyes."If you are wise, you will keep your ears and eyes open but your mouth shut. And do not ask questions beyond the basics or those that challenge his authority - in the end it will only harm you."

With that she left my arm and fled down the hallway, leaving me standing alone outside this unfamiliar door. I was about to push my luck and turn to leave instead of requesting entry, but that was when I heard the door open with a low creak.

"Ah, Adeline," a deep voice with the same sultry and amused tone chimed, "How nice of you to join us."

...Us?

———————————————————

any guesses who uS is ? ;)

hope ur enjoying it so far!!! pls pls pls vote, comment and share if you do!!

lots of love to all of u for the support!!

- jen x

CHAPTER SIX

I turned back round to face the door hesitantly.

That same dickheadly gorgeous man was stood leaning against the large door - although the door now looked tiny due to his tall figure. My eyes couldn't stop roaming over his body. His finely woven black tunic embellished with threads of gold was hugging his biceps and waist nicely, showcasing his sculptured body. His plain black jeans matched his glossy black shoes.

Adeline, stop. You came here for answers, not for eye fucking a bastard - but jeans, angels wear jeans?

I chose to avoid eye contact to steer clear from his intense gold eyes, knowing that they were looking at me. Entering the dining room and passing him, I smelt his tangy cologne - strong and bitter in a pleasant way.

Not wasting any time, I looked around the enormous room. It was how I expected - simple yet elegant. Walls were beige and baby blue to almost provide a classy french country house vibe. In the middle of the room sat a huge wooden table with a golden border - large enough to seat two families.

I watched as the dickhead took a seat at the table, his motions elegant and regal. That was when I noticed an unfamiliar face also sat at the table looking as confused as I was. The pronoun 'us' began to make sense now.

The unfamiliar man shared a few similar things to his dark- haired friend with additional distinct features - ash blonde hair, bright hazel eyes with long lashes, pointed nose not as straight as his friend's, and sculpted cheekbones engraved into his tan skin. He was wearing a white tunic, also finely sown with what looked like expensive silver threading and I couldn't help but notice his tattoos seeking through it. My eyes darted to his long slender fingers, golden rings adorned on each of them.

Why is everyone here so good-looking? Even the maid.

Someone cleared their throat and snapped me back to reality - or whatever this was. The dark-haired man I had already met leaned back into his chair, a small smirk tugging at his lips, "Are you going to sit, or enjoy dinner standing?"

I rolled my eyes and started to head towards the furthest chair from them until he spoke up again. " Sit here," He jerked his chin towards the chair opposite him from the table, "It would be easier to talk to you."

You're flattering yourself if you think I want to talk to you, prick.

Either way, based on Cirse' warning I figured it wasn't a good idea to get on his nerves and so I reluctantly sat in front of him, huffing to let him know I didn't appreciate the instructions. The ash- haired stranger had offered me a charming smile to be polite but I decided not to return it. All that was streaming through my head was leaving this place and going back to my family.

The dark-haired man broke both the silence and the ice. "Julian, this is Adeline,"

Julian. The majestic name fit his striking features brilliantly.

"Adeline, this is Julian. You could say he is my closest acquaintance."

Best friend? Dicks had best friends too?

"I didn't come here to make friends, did I?" I spoke quietly with sharpness in my tone, staring at my plate to avoid both gazes, "Just tell me why the hell I am here."

Julian's eyes flickered wide as he glanced between his friend and I.

The dark-haired man had nothing but that irritating amusement on his face as he ignored my demand like nothing had happened. His fingers snapped and people, which I assume were maids, rushed in with trays of many different dishes. They remained silent with their gazes on the floor while putting the food on the table. People either feared him or they respected him, which was probably why Cirse had said what she said to me.

Julian thanked the servers with a soft smile, while his dark- haired friend leaned back into his chair and slid a wink at one of the female servers who passed.

Perhaps that's his way of saying thanks. Seducer.

I pushed my plate away from me. I found it funny of him to assume I'd actually eat his food - no matter how good it looked. My stomach was aching at the mere sight of it and so I eyed the dishes regardless. Steak with gravy on it and roasted potatoes with asparagus on the side. It looked like the food I would see the aristocrats eating in the expensive restaurants when I'd go to the city with Papa to sell his handmade rugs and scarves.

"Thank you for the food but if you think it'll take potatoes to seduce me into staying damn quiet then I hope you use that brain of yours - if it's there, and realise it was a dumb idea." I snapped at him. The silver-haired man choked on the water he was downing, covering his mouth as he coughed in an attempt to hide his smile.

The black-haired asshole slung an arm over the back of his chair with grace and raised an eyebrow at his friend, "Are you done?"

Julian let out a small laugh in between coughs and I had to bite my lip hard to suppress my smile myself, "Funny how you let her do you like that, Azriel."

Azriel. Finally the unfamiliar man had a name, and such a regal one.

"By the way, Adeline," Julian began, clearing his throat after his laughing fit, "You look a bit unique. Don't get me wrong, you're an attractive young lady but I have never seen someone like you."

"It's because-" before I could continue, someone kicked my leg lightly enough for me to notice under the table- definitely Azriel from opposite me. Out of annoyance I kicked him back hard enough to make him wince a bit. Looking up, I was surprised to see his eyes weren't fixated on me, but instead he had started eating. I frowned with confusion and looking down at my plate I noticed a white napkin beside it - which definitely wasn't there earlier, with something written on it. I eyed it from my seat.

'Pretend you're one of us and don't bring up anything humanly. I can't risk anyone knowing about you. Keep doing what I say and you'll get what you want'

I blinked. When did he write this? I could've sworn I hadn't seen his arm move from the back of the chair until now to pick up his utensils.

"To answer your question regarding why you're here," Azriel took a sip of his water, "I need you to fight for us in the upcoming war."

Had I been swallowing a morsel in that minute, I would've probably choked. A war?! I couldn't process his words.

"You want me to fight in a war?!" I repeated his words, not believing what was leaving my lips as I spoke, " You want me to fight in an angel war?!"

He stayed silent, chewing his food and seeming unbothered by my shock. I clicked my fingers to get him to look at me and he slowly obliged, boredom written across his features.

"You're being serious?" I asked again in disbelief, "You're really going to make me, a mor-"

"Yes," He interrupted me smoothly with sharp calmness, knowing what I was about to reveal, "Yes I am."

"Who do you think you are?!" I questioned his authority - Cirse's warning now the last thing on my mind, "How dare you kidnap me then expect me to pay you back by fighting for you in a goddamn war?! Do I look like a soldier to you?!"

"If you were sharp-witted, you would wait until I was finished," He chewed slowly, his voice carrying a tone of seriousness combined with a hint of amusement, "I am providing you with two options here: you can fight for me and I will ensure as a virtual certainty that you are returned back to your family without a scratch."

"And the second option?"

"I'll kill you."

I scoffed, "I'll die either way anyway, won't I prick?"

Azriel's jaw clenched and relaxed. He had stopped eating by now, and Julian had kept his eyes down towards his plate the entire time to avoid the uncomfortable situation. His chair groaned against the marble floor as he stood, giving myself and Azriel a small dismissive bow of his head, "I will leave you both to it."

With that he left the room.

After a couple moments of silence, Azriel spoke up again but now with a softer, more desperate approach. "Look, if you are to fight for me I will guarantee an end to the famine which has struck your...unfortunate village. I am being very considerate here - which is rare. I believe you're an intelligent and perceptive woman, Adeline, so think about it."

I was quiet for a minute, thinking everything through thoroughly. The Legend had stated that a woman, possessing both beauty and military skill was required to end the famine. Here, that is exactly what was being demanded of me - military skill in exchange for the abolishment of the famine. And I had been the sacrifice, so that meant -

"No way," I blurted my thoughts out loud, my eyes widening as I came to the brutal realisation, "You're the Legend. You're the one who began the famine knowing that my people would turn to a sacrifice - a girl with military skill. And that girl was me, so that's why you hold me here now... it was you."

Azriel looked satisfied with my decoding of the situation as he gave me a slight nod of his head in approval, "I knew you were an intelligent and perceptive woman."

I let out a breath I hadn't even realised I was holding in. This situation - me being here, the people of my village being so scared of the forest and saying it inhabited monsters - it all made sense now. I wasn't just a sacrifice in the eyes of Azriel and his people.

My eyes flickered back to him, his gold gaze already fixated on me as he awaited any form of reply. I swallowed before I hesitantly asked, "How long will I remain here?"

"I can't tell you the exact period of time, but if I was to be approximate - perhaps a year, maybe a year and a half. Who knows?"

A year.

"I'm a human. You're all supernatural creatures, or whatever you all are. How can you expect me to fight against them and make it out alive?"

"You will. I will train you - from start to end, and if need be I will hand you a portion of the powers I possess. Either way, you will leave this battle alive." Confidence danced through his voice.

I chewed my lip anxiously. No matter what the cause behind this war was, or the reason behind why I had been chosen specifically - the only question which seemed to repeat itself in my head was whether I could even trust his word.

"Yes, you can. Trust plays a big role here. If you do not want to do it then let us not waste anymore time"

My eyes widened in surprise as I was caught off-guard. Did he just...read my mind?

"No, I cannot read your mind - not that I wanted to either," He examined his nails on both hands, "I need answers now - every second is priceless. Will you fight or not?"

I sighed, reluctance clear on my face before I whispered, "I...fine."

"I can't hear you, say it loud and clearly."

"I will fight for you in the war." I rolled my eyes and increased my tone. If anyone had told me earlier that I would later agree to fighting in a fairy - or angel or whatever they are - war, I would've laughed in their face.

"Your training will start tomorrow morning within the garden at nine. Cirse will lead you there and ensure you are wearing your training suit." He spoke fluently, pouring himself some more of a deep purple drink. Without even looking at my untouched plate he continued, "And no, your food hasn't been poisoned or tampered with - so you can eat it. If anything, I'd rather you eat the food and gain the strength. There won't be much benefit training a skeleton for war."

I folded my arms and leaned back into my chair with my brows furrowed in annoyance, not knowing whether I should or shouldn't be offended by his comment. Thinking the reason for my presence at this dinner was completed, I was about to rise until he spoke up again.

"Aren't you forgetting a question you had?"

I frowned, trying to understand what that could be. And then it hit me.

"You say you're not the angel of death," I mused, mustering enough courage in me now to glare at him, "So what are you?"

I watched as he rested his chin on his hand, a swift motion, and those amber eyes flickered up to meet my gaze. A small smirk tugged at his lips, "Take a guess."

I blinked a few times, completely confused. Church sessions had really only taught me about the angels which served God, and those which served Satan. From his aura to his attire he didn't seem among the ones with God.

I swallowed, my voice catching in my throat, "Do you serve...Satan?"

I glared intensely as he first smiled, and then began to laugh - a low, gentle, husk sound. He leaned back into his chair again, crossing a long leg over the other, "No."

Starting to grow impatient, I frowned, "What are you then?"

"Are you sure you want to know?"

"Can you just-"

"Alright, goodness. I was kidding."

"Just speak."

He ran his slender fingers through his dark hair, a few of the strands lightly falling into his face, "I'm a fallen angel."

My eyes widened as I fell back in surprise into my chair. A fallen angel - a real one, sat a couple metres from me. It felt too surreal to be true. When he realised I hadn't comprehended what he'd said yet, he continued.

"We all are fallen angels here in Velastille. It is our division, our district - other angels remain in theirs."

"Which other angels?" I asked.

He slightly shrugged his shoulders, "All kinds. They all keep to their districts within Pandaemonium."

"Cirse said Velastille was the capital of Pandaemonium," I chewed the inside of my cheek, watching him. He was instead engrossed in examining his slim but large hand, flexing his fingers in and out perhaps in an attempt to give them a stretch, "Does that mean the fallen angels are the greatest angels?"

His eyes darted from his hands to my face and I could already feel my skin catching heat. He ran his tongue against the inside of his cheek as if in thought, and then smiled - a cunning smile.

"Arrive at training tomorrow, and we can discuss that."

And with that he rose from his chair, a swift and fluid motion, and slipped his hands into his pockets. As he turned to leave the room, I called out after him,

"Why me?"

He paused, looking over at his left shoulder so that I could see that side of his face. "Hm?"

"I said, why me? Why did I get picked to fight?"

He remained silent for a couple seconds before that signature smirk appeared again. Opening the door for himself, he replied with that same amusement laced in his tone,

"Come to training tomorrow and find out."

I rolled my eyes, slouching back into my chair as I heard him leave. The silence within the room left me with no choice but to inhale the strong aroma of the food laid out in front of me, my plate still untouched.

And no, your food hasn't been poisoned or tampered with - so you can eat it.

His words replayed in my head again and again and again. And so I ate, every last bit of it - my stomach feeling warm and full to capacity for the first time in as long as I could remember.

---

first impressions of julian ? jeez forget Azriel, let's take his homie.

any theories why Az chose her??

Do y'all like Adeline so far?

if you liked this chapter, please make sure to vote! very thankful for 200+ reads!

- jen x

CHAPTER SEVEN

Azriel hadn't been lying when he said training would begin at nine the next morning. Cirse, my kind maiden, had appeared at my door by half past eight - ready to have me dressed.

Her gentle knock had hurled me awake - not that I had slept much throughout the night at all. For a second, I had wondered why my bed had felt so much softer, why the air felt so light and the atmosphere so calm and quiet - and then it all poured back in.

After the second patient knock at the door, I slowly scrambled out of the bed in order to let her in. We awkwardly greeted each other, still strangers, and then she made her way to my wardrobe to select the relevant fighting suit while I freshened up in the en suite. When I exited, Cirse held the suit up to me. "Here you are. Slip this on and then I'll tend to your hair." I ran a brief hand through my brunette locks. It felt brittle, almost thin - nothing like how it once was but I had accepted it by now.

Slipping on the suit was a task and a half. The fabric was a combination of leather and another dense material - perhaps latex, which meant it sat tight on my skin and hugged what existed of my waist and thighs. Cirse had tied my hair into a low ponytail, leaving two strands out from the front -

a simple and practical hairstyle. She stayed silent while her fingers worked my scalp.

"Do you tend to everybody?" I asked in curiosity in an attempt to break the silence.

"Nope," She replied back, her voice gentle and hushed, "I was hired specifically to care for you."

My own maiden. Hired just for me? This was such luxury I hadn't ever been exposed to.

I leaned back against her touch slightly, "Do you live here?"

"I do. I have my own room in the servant quarters of the building."

"And what about your family?" I bit my lip, unsure as to whether she would even answer the question or not due to its personal nature. After a couple seconds, however, I was surprised to receive a reply.

"I have none. Not anymore, at least."

"What happened?"

"I was abandoned by my mother when I was a child.. I was left with no choice but to turn to the streets and remain there for almost half of my young years. That was until Master saw me one evening and I was fortunate enough that he pitied me, gave me some money, and said I would be the first to be offered a role in his estate when need be." She gave my ponytail a final gentle tug to secure it, "And so that is how I ended up here, caring for you."

She said she turned to the streets. Had that meant...prostitution? Although I couldn't even begin to imagine such a sweet soul like Cirse in that situation, I didn't dare ask her to clarify.

Following my silence, Cirse quickly stood up, "Anyway, I'm done. If you are ready, let me escort you to the gardens. There's only five minutes remaining until nine."

I stood after her and when our eyes met, I managed to pass her a warm smile. Out of everyone I had already met so far, I felt like she was the only one who I felt at ease with - the only one who I could truly trust and the only one who wasn't using me for selfish reasons.

We walked side by side to the gardens, passing through the majestic hallways once again with Cirse recommending key places I had to visit in the building. I couldn't even begin to comprehend how big the place must have been.

Finally arriving at glass doors leading to the garden, Cirse paused. "I hope you have a good session, miss. I will meet you after your session to bring your change of attire after your bath."

Before she could leave I gently grasped her hand and gave her a grateful nod. "Thank you, Cirse. And call me Adeline."I received a shy smile back before she departed, her shoes leaving rebounding echoes along the hallway.

With a sharp inhale to level my breathing, I pushed open the glass doors and set foot into the large garden - of course, a stunning sight yet again. That was when it occurred to me that it was still dark - pitch dark, with the moon and stars in the night sky exposed. I had sworn it was supposed to be morning time. The cold bite of the wind tinted my cheeks pink and caused me to pull my hands into fists to preserve warmth. Where was the daylight I was so used to?

Hesitantly, I walked along the finely paved path with my eyes attempting to adjust to the darkness. And that was when I noticed that there, with his back towards me, stood Azriel. Though he stared out at the sweeping view of the large, luminescent moon partially hidden behind the distant shadows of mountains, I knew he'd sensed my arrival from the second I had stepped into the garden.

When I took another step closer to him, he spoke - still facing the view, "You're four minutes late."

"Didn't know I was being timed," I approached him until there was a decent distance between us, "Are you sure I'm only four minutes late? Feels like I'm twelve hours late instead. It's night."

He chuckled, his hands buried into the pockets of his pants as usual. I realised he had his wings today too - the light of the moon dancing along the silver tips of his dark feathers. "It's winter in Velastille. This is how it is every winter season, with our nights lasting the entire twenty-four hour period. In the summer, however, we get our usual hours of daylight followed by nights similar to how it is in the mortal realm."

"Is it like this in all the angel districts?"

He shook his head, "The fallen angel district is the only district in Pandae-monium which experiences this. The rest of the districts adhere to the law of nature with all four seasons and differing hours of day and night - but if I were to be honest, I prefer how we have it much more."

"And why is that? Besides the fact you seem to like the dark and the colour black," I took another step closer, almost standing side-by-side with him now. His side profile was visible to me - his perfectly straight nose, his defined jaw and hollow cheekbone. It was as though he was art, crafted by the greatest of artists.

"I'm not sure," He spoke gently, his tone genuine for the first time, "The night gives me peace and puts me at ease. The sight of the moon and the stars twenty-four hours a day is like free therapy to me."

No matter how much I hated it, I agreed with him. Just this sight we were taking in of the dark sky, moon and mountains was enough to soothe my escalated heart rate.

"Are you ready for your first session?" He turned to face me for the first time so far. Those amber eyes were bright even in the dark and I tightened my hands into fists again as his gaze swept me from my head to toes and then back up again. The mischievous glint made an appearance in his eyes as he smirked.

I frowned, folding my arms to cover my chest after his stare left me feeling exposed, "What?"

"The suit is a little...tight, isn't it?"

Prick.

"Next time send a looser one then," I rolled my eyes, tearing away from the eye contact between us, "I'm not here to ask your opinion on my outfits. Start the session."

His smirk only widened as he pulled a hand out of one of his pockets, opening his palm, "Your wish is my command."

And with that, a large metal crossbow appeared in his grip. I blinked in shock a couple times in an attempt to make sure I wasn't seeing things,

"How did you do that?"

He shrugged, holding the crossbow out for me to take.

"Magic."

I stared at him with an ice-cold glare.

"What?" He frowned now, "I'm being serious."

"Magic." I repeated, my tone laced with skepticism.

"Yes?" He raised a brow, opening his hand out again so that his palm was exposed, "Watch this."

I observed as he slightly lifted the index finger of his hand, and it was shocking to watch the crossbow I was holding begin to float out of my grip. I tried to snatch it back but it swooped to the opposite side teasingly. After a couple failed attempts to retrieve it back into my possession I let out a groan of frustration, holding my hands up in surrender.

"Okay, okay," I rolled my eyes for the nth time in annoyance, "I get it. You can do magic. Can I have the damn crossbow now?"

"Wise choice giving up," he huffed a laugh as the crossbow slowly floated back into my vicinity so I could seize it, "It was like watching a cat try to catch a cotton thread."

"You're such a prick!"

"And you're such a killjoy," He teasingly pouted, slipping his hand back into his pocket again, "I was actually enjoying our little game."

"I'm not here for your cheap entertainment," I snapped, my tone sharp and blunt, "Tell me what I have to do."

With the click of his fingers an archery dart board appeared about ten metres away from us. He took a step back, his expression unreadable to me, "Let us assess your long-range aim."

I raised a brow at him. "What are arrows going to do to angels?"

"Shoot your shot and find out," He replied blandly, lightly jerking his chin in indication towards the dart board.

I sighed and obliged, turning my attention back to the crossbow in my hands. Wiping my now numb fingers over my eyes in an attempt to focus my sight in the dark, I took aim - my hands trembling from the cold as I double checked my form. Azriel stayed silent from beside me and observed patiently.

I pulled back the arrow, having my aim set on the centre of the dart board. To not hit a bullseye right now would be far too embarrassing for me to fathom.

Seeing the target in my aim now, I released. We both observed as the arrow glided through the air with smooth speed but then noticeably began to slow down mid-air as it approached the centre of the board. I frowned in confusion, watching closely as I noticed the tip of the arrow grow darker in colour - almost a charcoal black, and flames of orange and red started to erupt from it.

Fire.

The arrow once again picked up speed in its final moments and relentlessly pierced through the centre of the dart board before coming to a stop mid-air, and I continued to observe as the flames died down and the colour of the arrow returned to the original I had first shot - it looked brand new again.

Azriel took a step forward beside me, a look of sheer amusement prevalent on his face as he indicated towards the dartboard remains, "That is what arrows do to angels."

"What was that?" I asked him in surprise, "Fiery arrows kill angels?"

He pulled a hand out of his pocket and held it up, summoning the arrow back between his fingertips effortlessly. "This isn't fire like that of the mortal realm. It's Holy fire, extracted directly from the depths of Hell, and is one of the three things which can kill angels."

"And the other two things?"

"Angels can also be killed by the action of stabbing him or her with an Angelic Blade in a vital area of their body. And finally, powerful angels are able to overpower a weaker angel easily using nothing but their own power."

I pushed some strands of hair which had fallen loose from my ponytail behind my ear, now feeling overly hot rather than cold like how I did earlier, "Who are these powerful angels? Do they have names?"

Azriel straightened slightly, putting his hands behind his back. His posture was immensely upright and added to the graceful aura which surrounded him. He nodded in confirmation.

"They're called the Arch Angels and known to be the most powerful species of angel, consisting of four higher-born divinities governing the four differing districts in Pandaemonium."

"So they can't be killed?"

Immersed in the conversation, it was as though I had totally forgotten the reason as to why we both had met in the gardens in the first place. With everything I was being told all I wanted to do was know more and more. I couldn't even begin to imagine the complexity of this somewhat immortal realm which existed alongside the world I knew.

To my previous question, Azriel shook his head. "They can be killed but it is a very complex process. On rare occasions, the Angelic Blade can be used to kill an Arch Angel if the blade has been crafted by one of the four Arch Angels - but a very specific type of blade is required. Technically, it's easier to presume they're immortal."

I cocked my head to the side in curiosity, "You said there are four districts governed by the Arch Angels. What are they?"

Azriel grinned - a mischievously entertained grin. "This is the most you've ever willingly spoken to me."

I scoffed, snapping back into character, "And you ruined it. I won't be talking to you for the rest of the week now."

You've only known me a day anyway- if that.

He laughed in a way which showcased his pearled set of teeth and I noticed how his canines were slightly more sharp-edged compared to the rest, "It'll be far too difficult for you to resist."

Arrogant bastard.

"To answer your question though," His tone was now serious and sober as he played with the arrow between his fingers, "The four districts include Evangelica - where the evangelical angels created to serve God remain, Illysia - created for the angels of sustenance, then Zybern - where the angels of death reside and finally Velastille - which is here, home of the fallen angels."

Instead of replying I just stared at him in surprise, trying to register everything he had just told me. I was living amongst real angels - angels connected to God and death. Angels which, if they discovered I was a mortal, could kill me in one heartbeat - and I was being trained to fight against them. To me it didn't make sense.

"Anyway," Azriel's voice heaved me out of my thoughts, "Your little question and answer session has taken up our allocated training time. I have some errands to run now, so I believe it's best we continue on from this tomorrow. Perhaps we can try shooting further than ten-metres."

I nodded as he flicked a finger toward the remains of the destroyed dart board, causing it to disappear into thin air. He held the arrow out for me to take and I extended my hand to do so, giving him a doubtful look. "Are you sure you want me to keep hold of this?"

He slowly began to walk back toward the glass doors leading inside and I hated that I trailed behind him like a lost puppy. Waving his hand dismissively, he simply said, "It's yours from now."

"Wait, really?"

"If you're the archeress you claim to be, then entrusting you with a holy arrow isn't a big deal," He turned to look over his shoulder at me, smirking as he walked with playful glints in his vibrant eyes, "Just perhaps try not to kill anybody - I'm not in the mood to deal with a dead body."

"Sure thing!" I stuck my thumb out to him, sarcasm laced in my tone as he followed my reply up with a short laugh.

We entered the house again and I made sure I remained a couple steps behind him as we walked back down the hallway together in silence. From behind I eyed his elegant wings - they were most probably the most beautiful wings I had seen, not that I had seen any. I was too tempted to extend my hand and just stroke-

"Look, but don't touch," He said from in front of me and although I couldn't see his face, I could hear the lazy grin in his voice.

In shock, I quickly retracted my hand as my eyes widened, "You said you can't read my mind!"

"I can't. I could just sense your eyes on my wings - not that I wouldn't stare either if I were you."

Rolling my eyes at his arrogance, I was ready to snap back but the sound of quick, light footsteps cut my effort short. That was when she appeared, poking her head out of a doorway further down the hall to see who was approaching.

She most beautiful woman I had seen - beauty on the level of Azriel's female equivalent. She had the same shade of raven black hair - chest length, which flowed unswervingly straight down her back and shoulders. Her brows were long and shaped, framing her defined feminine features and highlighting the wolf grey shade of her eyes. From what I could see above her shoulders while she poked her head out the doorway, the sleek black of her suit - fashioned like my own, but tailored much more elegantly - off-set her sun-kissed skin, making her practically glow even with the dimmed lighting indoors.

Azriel slowed down his walk in front of me and instinctively I did the same. He looked towards the unknown female. "My morning would have been great if I hadn't seen your face so early."

She raised a perfectly shaped brow at him, glancing at him from head to toe with a challenging grin spread across her nude-painted lips, "Imagine how I feel having to see your face everyday."

He rolled his eyes and she watched in amusement before I felt her gaze fix onto me. My muscles seemed to contract - her stare alone made me feel humiliated and intimidated for some reason, perhaps due to how strikingly beautiful she was while I looked like nothing but a walking corpse.

Azriel followed her gaze and after giving my latex clad body another quick scan with his eyes, he smoothly said, "Adeline, it is unfortunate you have to meet my cousin, Celeste. Celeste, meet the greatly approachable, definitely wholesome Adeline."

I debated using the arrow from earlier to stab him, but Celeste strode out into the hallway. Now that she stood before me I realised how tall she was - not as tall as Azriel but still tall enough to tower over me. Her leather suit was tight in all vital areas, such as her slim, rounded hips and her defined, narrow shoulders. The zip across the neckline of her suit was undone to reveal the beginning of her cleavage, but she seemed unbothered about the provocative nature of her clothing.

"Ah, you didn't tell me there was a new arrival," she spoke at a leisurely pace, her accent clear and expensive-sounding like her cousin's. I awkwardly jutted out my hand to greet her but she ignored it, placing her hand on her hip instead.

Why the hell would you do that, Adeline? I wanted to stab myself with that arrow now.

I tried to swallow the lump growing in my throat, "It's - nice to meet you. You're...stunning."

Celeste smiled, an elegant smile - but it didn't reach her grey eyes which were framed by her curled, kohl covered lashes. "Thank you," She brushed her silky dark lengths off her shoulder and rested her weight on one long, slender leg, "You could say I am the better-looking cousin."

Azriel, ready to defend his looks, opened his mouth to speak but I happened to beat him to it, "You both look so alike."

Celeste's face twisted in disgust at my words while Azriel also scoffed in disgrace, "Woah, Adeline - do not align us like that."

"Honestly Adeline," Celeste agreed and slid an incredulous look towards her cousin, "You really complimented me and followed it up with such an insult."

I hid the smile aching to appear at my lips - it felt somewhat refreshing to see two grown adults act so childish like this. Typical cousin behaviour, and reminded me a lot of my relationship with Elena back home.

"It's unfortunate I have to acknowledge Celeste as my cousin," Azriel explained, "But she has remained with me since we were children. I have no other surviving family besides her."

I wasn't able to muster enough courage to question what had happened to the rest of his family and so I kept my lips sealed - presumably the wiser option.

"And seeing as she's the closest relative to remain of mine," he continued, "Celeste believes she's entitled to strut around my place like it's hers."

"What's yours is mine, darling," She waved a hand at him dismissively, a playful grin on her face. Once again, her cold orbs shifted to me as she folded her arms,

"Anyway, when am I going to find out why the fairy girl is here?"

---

omg celeste :') opinions on her?

let me know how you're finding the book so far! r the chap lengths okay?

plz remember to vote and comment!!!

ty!!- jen x

CHAPTER EIGHT

A ZRIEL

Celeste meeting Adeline made me glad that Adeline would have some company when I wasn't around. I could've guessed she'd prefer it over my company, and after all of this I wouldn't even blame her for it. My intimidating face and comments weren't making this easier for her.

When I, at five years old, had lost my mother - Celeste's family, in addition to my father stayed by my side. I was naive enough to believe that was the toughest experience I'd have to face as a young one, but I was wrong.

Never had I imagined I'd also watch my father being killed in front of my eyes.

Once my father had died and Celeste's family had abandoned her, we had stuck together from then onwards and vowed to be there for eachother whenever need be.

Celeste's voice snapped me back in to reality, "Can you stop daydreaming?" She waved a hand in front of my face.

"You're too talkative today," I mumbled, swatting her hand away. Messing with Celeste could be said to be one of my many hobbies.

"Cut the bullshit and go straight to the point - if you don't want to lose one of your legs, that is." Celeste warned, rolling her eyes at me with annoyance written all over her face.

Bloody hell. It wasn't even noon and I already had two sets of eyes rolling at me.

"Okay okay," I glanced towards Adeline, who surprisingly enough appeared to look quite awkward - perhaps intimidated by the situation even. I chose to brush it off, "I have chosen Adeline to fight for us in this upcoming war. Word came to me that she was a skilled archeress, and so I believe she is a useful piece to our military."

Celeste slowly turned to Adeline, an arched eyebrow raised high, "I'm surprised a fairy agreed to fight in an angel battle. What bargain did he make with you, Adeline?"

Adeline cleared her throat, her emerald eyes darting a quick glance towards me and I managed to pick up what looked like desperation or hesitancy in her gaze, "I..uh-"

"That doesn't matter, Celeste," I interjected, slightly stepping into the space between the two females in an attempt to separate them with my body, "What matters is that she will be fighting and requires the respective training for it, so she will remain in Velastille."

"You're telling me all this like I care," She knocked a sarcastic smile at me, but it didn't reach her eyes.

I didn't step down from glaring back at her with equal intensity, "I think you should. Especially since you will both be associates."

Celeste blinked a couple times in an attempt to register the information, then frowned - looking almost offended, "You're going to align me - a professional, who has been fighting since I was born, with a fairy girl who's amateur and probably hasn't even picked up a bow until last week? Are you being serious right now, Azriel?"

I waved a hand dismissively at her, turning my attention to my tunic. Picking at the dust particles which had collected on the suede material, I simply murmured, "If you knew better you wouldn't argue with my orders, Cel."

"Oh really?" She shot back, her tone laced with challenge, "What made you pick her, out of all of the scrawny fairy females dying to fight for us Velastillian fallen angels? Hm?"

I slipped my hands into my pockets and stood tall before her, "She has potential I don't see in anyone else. She can use her hands to her advantage and-"

"Is it?" She raised a skeptical eyebrow again and scowled at me with suspicious eyes, "To her advantage, you say?"

It was my turn to roll my eyes. "Before you say anything - no. Not in that way." Celeste knew better, I never mixed pleasure and work together. On top of it Adeline was a mortal - I already broke one of our rules by bringing her into our world, to touch her would be breaking another.

Celeste stayed silent for a couple of seconds, both of us continuing to send daggers towards each other in the form of stares.

Another fake smile appeared on her lips, and with an equally fake chirpy tone she beamed, "Sure thing, cousin." She cocked her head to the side so that she could see Adeline who I had unintentionally guarded behind me, "You're so lucky to have me here, especially since the lovely host Azriel tends to disappear for days at a time. I will be more than happy to show you around."

Classic Celeste.

With my heightened senses I felt Adeline stifle behind me, probably trying to debate whether Celeste was trustworthy enough or not. Slowly, I retreated with a step back from between the two women so that they were now face to face.

With no glance of reassurance towards me, Adeline replied, "Sure. The only places I've been to are the bathroom, bedroom, dinner hall and garden."

I raised a brow at her in a way to say 'are you serious right now?' but she cleverly ignored it.

Celeste chuckled. "No worries, darling. That is typical Azriel for you. Can't even be bothered to show a guest around." Her lips smiled but her eyes glowered at me in annoyance.

I stripped my gaze away from the intense eye-contact between us. "Anyway, you ladies continue doing... whatever it is you are doing, I have a meeting to attend and so I will not be eating breakfast with you."

"Like you ever do," Celeste scoffed.

Adeline now chimed in, "You say you're not coming to breakfast like it's a bad thing." Celeste bit her lip to suppress an entertained smile.

I let out a dry, sarcastic laugh much to the two female's approval and turned on my heel, waving a dismissive hand at them, "Females are the most abnormal creatures I swear."

I could've sworn I had heard the soft sound of Adeline's laughter from behind me.

****

My business meeting with the representative for the Arch Angel of Illysia had extended into a three day trip. That idiot had told me he would meet me at my base in Velastille but had sent me a letter soon after stating he couldn't make it and so I should come to him.

To my great luck, Illysia was also the farthest district from Velastille which made my trip even more daunting, but having the acquaintance of Julian by my side had prevented me from doing unintelligent things like punching the representative straight in the face.

The only thing which had kept me from cancelling this entire meeting was the deal we had conjured, where Lucanus - the Arch Angel of Illysia, had offered me a share of his sacred weapons such as Vorpal Swords in exchange for a few of my men. Since these weapons could provide more benefit to us than we thought, I had reluctantly agreed.

Midway through our return to Velastille, both Julian and I had decided to rest our wings for a few moments. As we landed onto the earthly ground the outskirts of Illysia inhabited, Julian accused me out of nowhere, "Why are you training her yourself? You've never trained a warrior on your own accord."

Where did that even come from?

In a weak attempt to change the topic I passed him a judgemental look, my lips curling into an amused smile, "Political matters aren't for children. Stick to your books and beloved fairytales."

"Leave my books alone for Heaven's sake!" He grumbled, folding his arms as my smile widened, "I've known you long enough to know how you think, Az, and your daft attempt to change the subject won't affect me. You could've just let Madoc or Drillan train her like you do with all new militia recruits but you insisted you would do this yourself."

He was right - I did insist. To be frank, I wasn't aware how to answer Julian when I couldn't even form the answer as to why I chose to train her myself.

Kicking the dirt on the ground beneath us with the heel of my boot to show boredom, I replied with a tinge of desperation in my tone, "Look, can we just talk about this afterwards?"

"Huh? Azriel sounding shy and desperate?" He made a playfully terrorised face, "Who are you and what have you done with my Az?"

I nudged his arm hard as he barked out a laugh.

"I just want her to learn fast, especially since time is not on our side," I tried to explain, keeping my gaze towards the ground beneath us to avoid eye contact, "And I have a feeling that Madoc will not be able to produce the results in her which I can."

"Well, we're all aware of that. You're the Arch Angel of the Fallen Kingdom, Azriel - you're the best of the best. But I don't think that is the reason you chose to train her."

"I don't care what you think."

"Of course you don't, you're an Arch Angel," He rolled his eyes, placing his hands on his slender hips, "She really is beautiful as hell though. Hats off to you for choosing the first fairy to fight alongside us. Do you think she finds me attractive? My abilities to style my hair have most definitely improved," He ran a hand through his birdnest of ash blonde hair, the wind from flying putting all of his styling efforts to waste.

"Your hair is ridiculous." I watched as he rolled his eyes at my comment, "And fairy or not - she isn't like one of the girls from your romance novels She'll snap you right back into your place with that mouth of hers."

"Oh, shut up," He shoved at my chest, beginning to walk away and with a laugh I followed him.

The remainder of the trip home we didn't talk about Adeline which I was somewhat thankful about. On arrival back to the house I had headed straight to the kitchen in order to find something to calm the sensation of pain which had erupted in my stomach due to hunger. Walking down the corridor at my own pace, sobbing sounds coming from one of the bedrooms down the hall forced me to stop. Upon inspection, it turned out to be Adeline's.

Why was she crying?

Instead of going to the kitchen, I figured I should detour and went to her room to see what was going on. Undoing the hinges, I pushed the door open very gently and peeked my head in. Adeline was perched on the windowsill; knees bent, arms hugging them and her face buried between her knees. It was like an entire recreation of our first proper conversation here in the home. I chewed on my lip when I noticed she clearly hadn't realised I was here.

This was so awkward. Not to my recollection had I comforted someone or knew what it was like to comfort anyone - especially a mortal girl. This entire situation just felt too foreign to me.

I cleared my throat.

She heard, and I knew because she raised her head from between her knees enough to see me. Quickly wiping her tears away, she pulled herself together as a result of my presence.

"Why the hell are you here? To mock me more? To make fun of how weak I am?" She spat in between sniffles. I noticed how the skin around her eyes was red from crying, bringing out the amethyst green of her eyes.

"Why are you crying?" I kept a decent distance away from her, "Missed me too much or did Celeste not show you around?" To my disappointment, I only received an eye roll and sigh of frustration in response. Clearly my jokes to lighten the situation here were not playing in my favour.

Like they ever do.

For fuck's sake.

"Can you just not?" She glared at me, before resting her head against the window pane, "Seriously Azriel, can you really just not?"

As hard as I tried to stop it, my face pulled into an expression of confusion. Can I just not? What the hell is that supposed to mean? There are thousands of things that I 'can not'.

Women are confusing creatures and this is exactly why I do not date.

Silence had consumed the room by now and I believed it probably was not making matters better between us, and so from a distance I murmured softly, "I know to you I might come as the devil in an angel form who took everything away from you, but remember the devil was once an angel too. I might seem like the type to be pleased by other people's suffering - and to be fair I am, if it's someone I dislike. But I have no reason to...kidnap a mortal girl from a mortal world without a valid cause, Adeline. And you'll understand why as time progresses."

She shifted her gaze from the window to my face, staring at me with intense green eyes in an attempt to find deception in my statement.

"How can I believe you after all of this? You think it's easy to leave my family after they already grieve the loss of my mother- and now yet another family member has abandoned them." She sniffled again, wiping the dampness of her under eyes with her sleeve, "You wouldn't know anything. You're just an emotionless, unattached prick."

I stared at her, feeling something along the lines of frustration beginning to course my blood. Trying to maintain my cool, I placed my hands behind my back - ensuring that there was still a relative distance between us. My voice left my mouth quiet in volume but stern in tone.

"You haven't abandoned anyone, Adeline. If I had the choice, I would have never taken you in the first place - but this Legend as your town and my district know it asks this of us and we must carry it out. The Legend also states once a woman has been taken to be used for the military - she mustn't leave the district, ever. I however, despite it being punishable, have bent the rules for you and have promised to take you home to your family as soon as your time with us is complete. Your family will be living in riches and sustenance when you return - all of which I will provide to end the famine once your role is complete here. There is just one thing I ask from you, Adeline, and that is co-operation."

The brunette mortal fell silent. It would be a joke to think I hadn't felt bad for her, and that was why I was trying to make her feel as comfortable as possible with new clothes everyday, nutritious food, warm water, a maid - and what had she done? Made me feel like the worst person in the entire world.

Not that it bothered me but I didn't intend to tarnish the flawless reputation of the fallen angels. When her seconds of silence began to turn into minutes I figured it was best if I left, and so I turned on my heel to head to the door.

"You said Celeste's been with you since your mother died," She called out behind me, her voice still hoarse from the crying. I paused in my step. "What happened to her?"

I debated just leaving and not having to relive the memory once again as I told it to her, but a friction in my body forced me to turn back round.

"She died of a disease that spread all over her body. It was a special form of disease - one unknown to the mortal realm."

"I thought angels couldn't be killed by that."

I shook my head. "She wasn't an angel. She was a Goddess."

I observed as her eyes widened in surprise, her thoughts trailing onto her tongue.

"No way - a Goddess? Really?"

"Yes. Goddess of war and beauty - polar opposites, I know."

"That's amazing," She breathed, her green eyes round with enticement and interest, "I'm sorry she passed. I had no idea-"

"Mhm," I interjected quickly. Sympathy was not something I could deal with and instead made me feel uneasy - it made me feel weak. "What about your mother?"

"Sort of similar to what happened to yours, really," She sniffled, rubbing a hand over her tired pale face, "She became ill with breast cancer shortly after my sister was born. We could have saved her if we had enough money - my Papa blamed himself for her death everyday. We all did. That explains why I began helping Papa bring income into the house when I got older - I felt guilty that all the income depended on him."

I took a small step closer to her, my tongue pressed against the inside of my cheek. "It's the broken souls who're always trying to help others to make themselves feel less guilty. It happens."

She didn't reply, resting her cheek against her knee.

"Shockingly at least we do have something in common."

She frowned, her eyes flickering towards me in confusion, "What?"

"Dead mothers."

"Has anybody ever told you that you have extremely dark humour?"

Multiple times but I didn't tell her that. Instead I let out a soft chuckle, ruffling a faint few fingers through my dark hair.

"Where were you for the last few days anyway?" She enquired with her gaze fixated on me.

"Why? Missed me?" When she rolled her eyes in response, I said, "I was supposed to meet for business with a representative from a different district, but since he couldn't make it I had to go there instead."

"Which district?"

"Ilyssia."

She sighed, her voice strained with tiredness, "Did it at least have sunlight?"

I smiled. "And still it was incomparable to Velastille in the night."

"What's so special about Velastille anyway - besides the night."

"You want me to show you?"

____

what do y'all think about Azriel's pov?what could he be showing her? Any guesses?Thank you for reading! Let me know how was it and make sure to vote!

-jen x

CHAPTER NINE

A DELINE

I woke the next morning to meet utter darkness again, excluding the bright luminous moon and stars which owned the night sky. Azriel had promised me a tour around Velastille - guided exclusively by him, which of course he said I should be honoured about, when he'd be free one evening.

A casual question tossed in Cirse's direction revealed that a nameless threat had broken out onto the lands today, and so Azriel and Celeste were called away to deal with it. I had further inquired Cirse to tell me what it was, but she herself had no knowledge of what was going on.

"What I can tell you-," Cirse said to me as we walked alongside the hall together to the dining room for breakfast, "-is that since Master isn't on the premises, maybe we can take a stroll around the exterior of the house. Take a look around?"

I huffed, "Honestly, I'd enjoy that. I feel like I'm on house arrest."

Cirse simply smiled in response and linked her arm into mine as we made our way outdoors, the cold air glazing my pale skin and breezing through my frail hair. Emerged in conversation, we both hadn't realised we had reached the outskirts of the property until we heard a voice from behind us.

"You ladies aren't making a run for it, right?"

Cirse and I both froze midstep, instinctively turning to look over our shoulders at the one who called out to us. There stood Azriel's beloved acquaintance - Julian, dressed in a rich chestnut leather jacket to protect against the cold. Around his waist hung a belt equipped with multiple hunting knives - from sharp tall blades to short blunt ones. His somewhat warm hazel eyes scanned us both, and I noticed how they briefly fixated on Cirse before looking away.

"We were just - just going on a walk before breakfast," I said, not understanding why my words were catching in my throat. Julian didn't appear as intimidating as his friend, but perhaps it was the height, or the variety of knives he had on him, or simply just the fact he was an angel which made my breath still hitch in his presence regardless.

Cirse gave my hand a quick gentle rub of reassurance and bowed in a small curtsey before Julian, turning to leave. I observed as he also lowered his head in return. His hazel eyes observed her as she retreated back to the house, leaving him and I alone.

"Morning, Adeline," He said smoothly and I tried to hide the stiffening in my shoulders, trying to smile a bit, "Sorry to have cut your walk short."

"It's not a problem, we were going back inside anyway," I simply replied.

I was just about to turn to leave, but from a short distance behind him I could have sworn I had heard the whinny of a horse combined with the stomp of a hoof on gravel.

A horse? On angel lands?

Julian must have picked up how intrigued I was from my expression alone and smiled, stepping back slightly so I could see the stables in the far end of the gardens. Three horses stood tall - chestnut, white and black, hoofs stomping against the gravel.

"I'm on patrol in the outskirts of the woods. If you like, you could join me for a ride and back?" He offered, hand indicating toward the stables. "Besides, I'm curious to hear some more about you and perhaps see some of your archery skills, I can't lie."

But my kind of hunting couldn't be done on horseback. I was able to hunt with plans consisting of stealth and careful stalking, but I had never shot an arrow on the back of a horse. However, I wasn't going to let him know that and so I shrugged, "I have nothing better to do I suppose."

"Perfect," Julian smiled as he motioned for one of the stableboys to prepare a horse. I observed as they moved with fluidity like everyone else did here, none of them daring to even make eye contact with myself or Julian.

Soon I was astride the chestnut mare, Julian alongside me on a white stallion. I kept a healthy distance from the ash blonde male on the broad path, silently praying he couldn't see me through the back of his head.

"You seemed surprised about the horses," His comment broke the silence I was starting to enjoy, "They don't have them back in your fairy kingdom?"

Shit.

I chewed my lip, blurting out a quick response from the top of my head, "Nope. We thought angels didn't either."

"We do, but they are a different breed of horse. They're Pegasuses."

Of course they are.

My eyes dropped down to the body of my horse which I rode upon, and in confusion I asked, "But they don't have wings?"

Julian chuckled gently - perhaps at how annoying I was or perhaps at my naiveness, I'd never know. "They're like angels. Their wings spawn whenever they require them."

I fell silent. To me that explained why the angels I had been around would possess mighty wings one day, and then none the next.

"Azriel hasn't told anyone enough about you," Julian pressed out of nowhere, "It's not usual for a fairy to suddenly join our militia and then be trained by Azriel himself."

I stroked the dark mane of the chestnut mare beneath me in an attempt to calm my own nerves. "Why is Azriel bringing me here and training me such a big deal?"

"Because Azriel is the Arch Angel of Velastille," He simply answered, "An Arch Angel never trains his own military, he has trusty commanders do it for him. To my knowledge, you're probably the first person I've seen this happen with"

I could've almost felt my breath hitch in my throat. Azriel - an Arch Angel? I would have presumed he had some authority around the house, but the fact he was one of four leaders of Pandaemonium - my mind was blown.

"I never-" I swallowed, making my surprise known to Julian, "He never told me he was an Arch Angel."

"Ah," He shook his head, "Typical Azriel. Loves being mysterious."

You can say that again.

"He said you were his acquaintance," I ventured, "So if he's an Arch Angel, what are you?"

Julian clicked his tongue, "I suppose you can say I am his second in command. I assist him with formal affairs such as meetings or act as his representative when dealing with the other Arch Angels. I also patrol here and there - it isn't one of my designated roles but it clears my head."

"And Celeste?"

"She's his commander in chief of his army. Azriel himself, although an Arch Angel, prefers to control his military. He's been brought up a warrior since he was a child, and so has Celeste. So whenever he is away, she takes control of the army for that period of time."

I hummed in response, peering around at the towering oak and silver birch trees which surrounded us. The wood was becoming deeper and darker and consequently the hairs on my arm started to rise - it was like reliving being thrown in here all over again and was causing my stomach to knot in anxiousness.

"You must be good at stealthing during a hunt," Julian remarked as my grip tightened around the reins in my palms, "You're very quiet."

"I just-" I swallowed hard and tried to keep my focus straight ahead, rather than at my sides into the dark depths of the wood around us, "I don't like where we are."

He shot me a sideway glance with his brown-green eyes and I caught a glimpse of concern in them. "Do you not like the dark or-"

"I don't like the dark or the woods." I answered far too quick.

Julian pulled on his reins, demanding his stallion to a complete stop while my mare herself did the same. He turned to look over his shoulder at me from his saddle, "We can go back right away. If you'd like you can sit with me if that would make you feel at ease?"

He extended a hand and I stared it down from astride my horse. I didn't trust him - like how I didn't trust anybody here, but at least his presence could make me feel less startled considering how deep we were into the woods now. Reluctantly I took his warm hand as he hoisted me from the back of my horse onto his saddle behind him. He took the now abandoned reins of my chestnut mare and tied it to the reins of his own horse, guiding her with us as we turned to go back the way we had come.

The utter darkness of the gravel path ahead combined with the deathly silence of the woods, excluding the clop of the horses hooves beneath us was making me wonder how he could possibly find this to be a relaxing ride without fearing for his life. Perhaps in hindsight I would regret it but I tightened my hands around his waist from behind and pressed my forehead against his back, clamping my eyes shut hard.

He chuckled softly and I felt the vibration through his back, "I take it you don't enjoy the views down here."

"How can you enjoy the view when you can't even see anything?" I retorted, my voice muffled against the thick leather material of his jacket.

"Fallen angels have night vision actually," He replied, "We can see everything normally, even in this darkness. I would have thought fairies did too."

"Uh no, they - we don't," I mumbled.

He answered with a simple hum, definitely sounding unconvinced but I ignored it. After yet another brief period of silence he suddenly asked, "Was that lady with you also a fairy here to train?" His voice was so quiet I had almost missed his question.

My eyes now opened, interested and intrigued. "No, she's an angel. She's been hired to care for me."

"Oh."

"Why'd you ask?" I pressed.

He shrugged lazily and I almost swore I could feel his pulse quicken through his back. "She looked unfamiliar and naturally I was just curious"

He's interested in her.

I bit my lip to suppress a smile and leaned my forehead off of his body, looking around to notice how we were finally approaching an opening in the woods which led back to the house. "If you say so, Julian."

He huffed, "Hey, what's that supposed to-"

The blonde male I sat with was cut short by the sound of a feminine voice from ahead of us. From over Julian's shoulder I peered up to see what I had prayed not to.

Celeste. And beside her stood Azriel.

Julian's shoulders tensed and I felt almost every body muscle in my body do the same.

"Oh, look Azriel," Celeste nudged her cousin in his rib, indicating towards us. A wide, smug smile was spread across her plump lips, "The fairy princess is with him too!"

Azriel's auburn eyes snapped towards me, his orbs noticeably darker than usual. His glare alone caused me to quickly take cover behind Julian's broad shoulder and my grip around his waist loosened.

Shit.

"Julian." Azriel's tone was stern as Julian brought our horse and my vacant mare to a halt in front of him.

"Azriel." Julian replied weakly as a stableboy rushed towards us, holding his hand out to assist me in demounting the stallion. I landed on the ground on my feet with a slight thud and my eyes reluctantly rose to meet Azriel's golden stare.

His glare didn't so much flinch away from me as he summoned the stable-boy, "Kalen. Take Adeline inside to the dining hall for breakfast."

I glowered at him, "I'm not hung-"

"Now."

The raw command in his voice - the voice of the Arch Angel of Velastille - had me acting on my instinct as Kalen, with his head hung low, began to guide me back to the house. Julian sat uncomfortably astride his horse and the smug smile on Celeste's lips had not ceased.

If only I could just smack it off her.

As I passed Azriel I made sure to meet his hard authoritative stare with my own, but the coldness I found in his eyes as he glared back at me forced me to look away. Following Kalen back into the house, I couldn't help but glance back behind at the other three. Julian was now on foot, his hands held up in the air in surrender while Azriel seemed to be confronting him about something.

I tried to make out what they were saying, but was pulled into the house before I could.

****

Before I knew it, I had found myself alone at the long wooden dining table on which most of the space had been filled. It was laden with food and wine - so much food, such a variety of fruit and custards and pastries that my mouth had already started watering.

"You must wait until His Lordship arrives at the table," A server had whispered to me while setting down utensils beside my plate and it had taken every ounce of effort not to roll my eyes or scoff in response.

Once all the food had been laid out completely, I was left alone in the large dining hall. I glanced over my shoulder towards the tall window and from it I managed to make out that the house gates were open. And then something struck me.

If I wanted to run, it had to be now.

But I didn't know where to go. I didn't even know where I was. All I knew was that the human realm couldn't have been far from the woods, there was no chance. All I had to do was run west once in the woods and eventually I'd reach the outskirts of the village. Now - I had to go now if I wanted to escape.

But then I paused.

I was weak and thin - only an idiot would run without strength. I wouldn't even make it past a mile before he'd find me and presumably tore me apart into pieces with whatever angel powers he had.

Looking back at the food, I took a long steadying breath. I'd eat. I'd gain strength. And then I would run - sounded like a solid plan.

The door to the dining hall swung open behind me and multiple footsteps echoed around the room. Julian passed from behind and took a seat on the chair diagonal to me. He was then followed by Celeste who, to my great luck, chose to sit directly in front of me. A couple moments later His Lordship entered and plopped into the seat at the head of the table, still managing to make his movements qlook graceful.

The silence was deafening and my stomach was yearning to feel the warmth of a full belly again, but I waited for one of the three angels around me to take a bite first. Just in case.

Julian leaned forward and took what looked like a crisp, french pastry onto his plate - his hazel eyes fixed on his food. My hands remained in my lap as I watched silently.

"So, Adeline," Celeste broke the silence and reached over to grab what appeared to look like a muffin, perhaps blueberry. My jaw clenched the second she spoke, "Did you enjoy your ride with Julian?"

I felt Julian glance at me from across the table, and before I could answer he responded for me sharply, "Why can't you just drop it Celeste?!"

"I was only just-"

"Enough." Azriel raised his hand from the head of the table and interjected swiftly. I mentally thanked him for doing so, I was in no mood to deal with Celeste's snarky comments today and I don't think he was either, "All I hear is yap from you two - you're like dogs in a shelter."

Celeste rolled her eyes while Julian just huffed, neither of them daring to snap a response back I noticed. After a couple minutes of no conversation and no external sound beside the clattering of utensils as we ate, Julian gathered enough courage to raise his head at me. I looked at him, his warm eyes apologetic for earlier, and then he asked, "How's training going for you?"

I pushed around the final few pieces of fruit remaining on my plate having already felt Celeste's silver eyes on me. "We've only had one session."

He raised a brow and looked to Azriel who leaned back into his chair, taking a long sip of his wine, "What? I've been busy - I'll be training her later today anyway."

Celeste, with her chin resting on her hand in an attempt to look bored now asked, "Have you told her information regarding the Velastillian war at least, Az?"

"Yeah I -"

"You haven't, have you?"

"I- "

"Have you?"

"No."

Celeste gave her cousin a long incredulous look, waving a dismissive hand at him, "I give up. You're probably the most stupid Arch Angel there has ever been."

"Shockingly I think I actually agree with Celeste," Julian shook his head in disappointment, dropping the last few bites of croissant from his hand into his plate. "How do you expect her to fight in a war she doesn't even know anything about?"

Azriel crossed his arms and shrugged, nothing evident on his face besides boredom, "I didn't think she'd care."

"I think it would be nice to know about the damn war I'm being expected to fight your side in," I countered and Celeste flicked her sharp eyebrows up in approval.

Azriel snorted, raising both his hands in a manner which meant surrender. The boredom had now been replaced with amusement across his defined features. "Alright, alright. Apologies - I made a mistake. I shall be more mindful of information you should know next time, Adeline darling."

I scoffed. What a prick.

Azriel clicked his fingers and a large piece of parchment paper appeared out of thin air, and from my seat I could see there were some drawings on it in black ink - like a map. He made space for it by pushing his plate aside, and spread it out onto the wooden table in a way all four of us could see.

His long, slender index finger rested on what looked like huge land on the map. "This, altogether, is Pandaemonium. This is where the majority of the angels reside, you know this."

I nodded, tilting my head to get a better view of the map in front of us.

"Now these," He pointed out the four divided areas on the large land, each area a different size. I noticed one area was significantly larger than the others, "These are the four districts, Zybern, Illysia, Evangelica and Velastille."

"Which of the four is that?" I indicated towards the largest area.

"That's Velastille, where we are right now." Julian answered and Azriel nodded, "It is the biggest of the four districts in Pandaemonium."

I studied the map from my seat carefully and happened to notice an isolated piece of land, almost like a different country on a human map. Curious, I pointed it out before Azriel could."What's this?"

His finger slowly moved to the isolated land I was enquiring about, and he tapped it a couple times on the paper as if he was thinking about what to say. "This...this whole 'island' is Blindcoast, known as Ancient Pandaemonium."

I leaned back into my chair, my eyebrows nudging closer together in confusion, "Why is it so isolated?"

"Because that's where Maximus, the King of Ancient Pandaemonium lives," Celeste spoke in for him, her voice with an undertone of disgust, "And that's the dickhead we've waged war against."

"He's a King?" I breathed, "I thought Arch Angels were Kings?"

Azriel pressed his tongue against the inside of his cheek and shook his head, "Not quite. You can see us as leaders of our respective districts, but there is a higher authority of us who overlooks all the districts combined. A higher authority whose power is above ours, no matter how powerful we may be as individual Arch Angels."

"And the reason why he's so powerful," Celeste continued, looking at me with her intense iced grey eyes from across the table, "Is because he holds the Blood Jewel in his crown - a jewel which makes him immortal, and not just partially immortal. It means he just cannot be killed, even if all the powers of the Arch Angels were to come together as one against him."

I blinked, the hairs on my nape and arms rising with each passing moment, "Then why bother against him if he can't be defeated?"

"We just require the Blood Jewel. Because if we don't claim it, not only will he strip all four Arch Angels of their power," Julian indicated towards his dark-haired friend, "But he won't stop until he conquers all which he possibly can, and that includes all other realms - like the fairy realm and the mortal realm."

The mortal realm. My world. His words clanged through me, freezing my veins and tightening my stomach and throat.

"But they're defenseless," I gasped out, "They're weak, they won't stand a chance-"

"We're not going to let him invade either realm - whether that be fairy or mortal." Azriel said too quietly.

Just the pure thought of my home - my world being claimed by such creatures was making me sick. I tried to take a deep breath, and was thankful for the open windows in the dining hall which allowed me to do so with somewhat ease. "Are the Velastillians going to fight him alone?"

"So far it seems it is just us and the Ilyssians," Azriel shook his head slowly, circling the two districts with his finger on the map, "The other two Arch Angels and their districts are scared - and I need to win them over before the time comes."

"But what's in it for you?" I asked, my voice barely a whisper, "Winning the Blood Jewel back and defeating the King of Ancient Pandaemonium?"

I observed as Julian and Celeste fell silent, both of them looking towards Azriel to answer. Each breath of mine was like swallowing glass as I waited for him to go on.

His jaw stiffened then unclenched, his eyes now multiple shades darker than the rich gold I was used to seeing,

"To avenge my father."

And with that he stood - a tall, fluid motion with the chair groaning against the floor as he did so, and left the room in silence.

---

is anyone making out the connection between maximus and azriel maybe?

i rlly hope u enjoyed this chapter!!! if so plllllease don't forget a vote and comment.

id really appreciate it. let me know how you're finding it so far and any feedback is welcome! X

- jen x

CHAPTER TEN

After Azriel had left, there was a brief period of silence until Celeste and Julian started talking among each other as normal.

I had zoned out. Was he mad at me for asking too many questions or was it about the King? I couldn't guess what the King may have done to his father, but it must have been bad enough if Azriel was willing to risk his life to take revenge.

Dinner after Azriel had left didn't last more than a quarter of an hour. Outside the dining hall was Cirse, waiting patiently for me to finish my meal and get me ready for training that same afternoon which I wasn't looking forward to, especially since I knew he wasn't in the best of moods.

"Cirse, do you happen to know anything about Azriel's father?" I had asked her casually as I watched her rummage through my wardrobes, trying not to sound inquisitive. Maybe I could get something out of her.

"Not much at all miss - I mean Adeline," She corrected herself quickly and I smiled at her, "Can I ask why?"

"I was just curious," I shrugged, "I'm sure you know about upcoming war. Azriel has waged an entire war against the King of Ancient Pandaemonium just so he can avenge his father. I was trying to make out the connection between them."

Her voice was quiet, on the verge of being a whisper and I could see the nervousness in her teal eyes, "All I know, Adeline, is that the King killed his own fraternal twin - Master's father, when Master was a juvenile. The reason why he did it is beyond my knowledge."

I felt my blood run cold and throat tighten - if Azriel's father and the King were brothers, that made him Azriel's uncle.

She glanced behind my shoulder toward the door.. "Master doesn't like discussion about his personal matters, so just don't tell anybody I told you."

I nodded, observing as Cirse placed my cleaned fighting suit on the bed besides me. She took a step back and bound her hands in front of her. "I will wait outside while you dress, and then I will escort you as usual."

"Can't you stay? I'll need someone to style my hair. As you know, I can't braid my hair for the life of me." I looked at her with hopeful eyes, my tone almost a plead. I didn't know why I wanted to be around her so much - perhaps it was the fact she reminded me ever so much of my sister Elena.

Her plump lips curved into a soft smile. "As you wish."

****

Three in the afternoon was our designated training time for today and I was already running late, as per usual. There was a change in venue for today - I had been called to the house's drawing room instead of the garden, which was a huge space finished with a glossy wooden floor and high walls. To my surprise, the man I was expecting to see wasn't there - even though I was over ten minutes late.

I waited. Almost half an hour passed with me lingering around the room as I awaited his presence. With each passing moment I was growing more frustrated - he was wasting my time. Annoyed, I decided to head to the door.

"Leaving already?"

I spun around on my heel. There he was, stood leaning against the wall back in the room - arms crossed and signature smug smile playing on his lips. He was observing my every move like a cat hunting down a mouse and I couldn't understand how a pair of eyes make someone feel so intimidated.

Perhaps because he's an Arch Angel.

I blinked, both surprised and confused, "I swear you - where did you come from?"

"Where were you leaving to?" He shot back instead, dismissing my question.

I frowned. "Somebody sent word to me that our session is at three, but after he didn't show up for about half an hour I decided to give up."

"You should have looked around for me."

"Couldn't you just make an entrance without it being hide and seek?"

"What's the fun in that?" His gold eyes sparkled, amused.

"Whatever."

I rolled my eyes. It felt like pissing me off was beginning to become one of his favourite hobbies.

My eyes fell to his outfit. The signature regal clothing - a long black tunic, black pants and dark leather boots. His long, slender fingers were adorned with a few gold rings, but most importantly I noticed how he carried no weapons.

"Why don't you carry anything?" Did he come here to mess about or for work?

"No weapons today because we are going to do something much more interesting."

"Am I going home?"

"You're so funny," He gave me a sarcastic smile, "Today, Adeline, I'm going to teach you the art of self defense so you can show others you aren't one of those who say but can't do."

"Who said I can't fight?" I took a challenging step toward him and rose my brow, "That's quite arrogant of you to assume females can't fight."

"Okay, but I didn't-"

"I can fight very well, thank you very much."

"If you're so sure about yourself-" I watched as a smirk laced with amusement appeared on his lips, "-then punch me."

"That won't be difficult," I scoffed, "Finally a chance to smack that smirk off your face."

He laughed, stepping away from the wall with his hands now behind his back, "Do it then."

And so I lunged at him, my arm in what I thought was a perfect fighting stance, ready to punch his face - but I gracefully missed and would have almost hit the wall hard if he hadn't grabbed my hand within a split second to stop it.

"If that is how you're going to fight, we're going to lose the war before it even begins."

How supportive of him.

He came close behind me to fix my position; straightening my back and re-positioning my arms - his touches sending shivers down my spine. He took my cold hands in his warm ones and spread my fingers out, tucking my thumb over my index finger to make a proper fist.

"Now punch me again."

This time it landed a bullseye on target - his face, and I could have done some beautiful damage to his stupidly perfect features if his hand hadn't grabbed my fist so smoothly before it came into contact with him. He looked as though he was proud of me, but at the same time looked at me like I hadn't done anything special.

This man is the epitome of confusion.

He taught me some other techniques I have never heard of, for example the elbow strike and roundhouse kick. He had explained that men could become touchy with the wrong intentions or how at any moment could I come into contact with certain creatures which lingered in immortal realms, especially in Velastille, and so it was useful I was aware of these defenses.

Time during train flew by extremely swiftly and I hadn't even realised how much he had covered with me in under a two hour session. That same late afternoon as I lingered behind him down the hall on my way back to my room had I realised.

Shockingly, training with Azriel wasn't as bad as I had imagined it to be.

———————————————————————

Dang the kings evilHow do you feel about the king and Azriels father? Any ideas whats going to happen next? Thank you for reading! Make sure to vote!-Jen xx

CHAPTER ELEVEN

A week went by.

I hadn't seen Azriel for most of it, or Julian and Celeste - not that I was concerned, but it felt strange being able to roam around the house without bumping into a six foot four cocky Arch Angel. The only people I had encountered were Cirse and a few of the other maids on the ground floor who served my meals, made my bed and would reluctantly ask how I was doing.

Seeing as I didn't have much to do today, I had decided to trudge along the second floor of the premises - a place which I had not yet explored despite it being perhaps my second or third week here already. It was majorly quiet and I hadn't seen any servants so far, which indicated they probably weren't allowed up here. As I continued to walk along the corridor, staring at the gold and white embellished walls, I had heard the soft humming of what was definitely a male.

I slowed down my walk to try and make my footsteps less audible as I approached the door of the room I believed it was coming from.

"You can come in, Adeline," A gentle voice beckoned me from inside suddenly and I jumped at the unexpected mention of my name.

Julian.

Remaining cautious, I peered into the room from the doorway and found Julian lounging on a dark purple sofa of velvet material, his head leaning on the arm rest and a book gripped between his two hands in front of him. He put down his book onto his chest and turned to look at me, giving me a smile.

"How did you know it was me?" I questioned, keeping a healthy distance away from him as I watched him from the doorway.

"I could sense you," He shrugged as though it was the most obvious answer, "I could sense you from the moment you started climbing the stairs."

I stared at him long enough to see if he was joking or not, but when he turned back to the book in his hand without another word I knew he wasn't. If Julian could sense me, that would have meant Azriel could too - and even Celeste.

I cringed at the thought.

"You want to sit down?" Julian pulled back his lounging long legs from the sofa to make room for me and hesitantly I obliged, leaning my back against the other arm rest so I was facing him. I observed his book from the other end of the sofa.

"Wuthering Heights?" I said my thoughts aloud, "You're reading that?"

He sat up slightly, folding the top of the page of his book as a bookmark and then closing it. His hazel eyes looked to me in delight, "Have you read it?"

"Of course I have," I nodded, "It was one of my favourite books when I was younger."

He smiled warmly, his tone enthusiastic, "Mine too, and it still is. I read it again here and there for the fun of it."

"For fun?" I now felt a small smile curl on my lips, "You read a twisted, dark romance story for fun?"

His finger ran along the edge of the copy of the book he held in his hands as if he was in thought, and then nodded, "It's because reading it reminds me of one of life's absolute truths: that love is pain - there can never be strong love without that little bit of pain."

I leaned back into the arm rest and released a sigh I hadn't even realised I was holding. His words generalising such a large subject like love so simply had me in awe. My voice due to hesitancy came out quiet as I asked, "Have you ever been in love?"

I almost heard his breath hitch from the opposite end of the sofa, as though he wasn't expecting me to ask such a question. I noticed he refrained from eye contact and ran a rough hand through his tousled ashy blonde hair.

I had regretted asking such a personal question immediately. "It's okay, you don't have to-"

"Yes."

"Hm?"

"I have been in love," His tone was hushed and fragile - he looked fragile in that moment, "She was of a different district - of Evangelica."

I didn't know whether it was a good idea, but I was so intrigued at this minute and so I whispered, "What happened to her?"

A flicker of hesitation crossed his features and I watched him swallow. His grip on his book became noticeably tighter.

"She was accused of witchcraft and put to death in front of me."

I couldn't control how my eyes had widened and my hand slowly came to my mouth in shock. To lose a loved one was tough, I knew that, but to have to watch them be killed for a crime they probably hadn't committed was another form of trauma in its entirety.

Without thinking, I reached out and placed my hand on his leg - my weak attempt at a comforting gesture. "I'm sorry, Julian."

He shook his head slow, "It was bound to happen. Whether she was practicing or not, she was still a threat to Azriel's power and district."

I froze, feeling a whisper of cold air tighten my muscles and run a chill down my back. My mouth was beginning to feel like it had been smothered in sand dust or something similar, and a gesture as easy as swallowing had become difficult.

"Azriel killed her?"

He bit his lip, reluctantly raising his gaze to meet my stare. It must have been too much pressure for him though because he almost immediately looked away again, "Hm."

I was longing to ask more - about why he had done it, how he had known for sure she was practicing witchcraft, how he had done it, why Julian had allowed it; but no words left my mouth.

Instead, something in me prompted me to lean forward and envelope Julian into a hug - and I did, in a tight embrace where I tried to give him the warmth and security he deserved. Where I tried to let him know everything was going to be okay without using words. I had felt him hesitate to return the hold, but it wasn't long until I felt the gentle touch of his hands snake around my waist in an attempt to feel some closure - some love, even if it wasn't romantic.

We remained in such position for what felt like a minute before Julian pulled away, an apologetic expression clad on his face as he scrambled to his feet, "There has been activity on the west border which I must attend to. I'm sorry, Adeline. I will see you afterwards."

And with that he disappeared into literal thin air, leaving behind his unblemished copy of Wuthering Heights on the velvet cushion beside me.

****

I had spent the remainder of my afternoon perched in the window seat of my room, my left temple leaned against the cold pane of the window as I rested some paper on my knee and chewed the end of my pencil in thought.

I had tried to imagine what Julian's lover had looked like. What her personality was like. I believed she was humorous and gentle, and was enough to give Julian butterflies. In my head she had long lengths of copper brown hair which reached her waist and eyes as brown as the ripe earth in the sunlight. My pencil stroked the paper as I lightly sketched the small tip of her nose, small and cute and round, and I was about to go onto how I had imagined her lips when the door to my room opened.

My eyes snapped to the doorway to see Azriel, stood tall in a signature dark tunic with slim back pants.

He raised an amused eyebrow at my sketchpad, "What's going on here?"

Instinctively I quickly turned my pad over so he couldn't see the rough sketch of the girl. I was worried as to what his reaction would be, and finding out new information about him everyday was making me fear what he was capable of more and more.

"I was trying to sketch but couldn't think of what to draw," I mumbled in response.

He gestured to himself and I mustered enough courage to pull a face at him, causing him to let out a chuckle.

"Anyway, put on your shoes. We're going for a training session."

I frowned, putting my sketchpad down beside me, "You didn't tell me beforehand. I'm not ready."

"You don't need to get dressed up to fight, Adeline," He rolled his eyes dismissively.

"Who said I was-"

"As much as I would love to see you in your fitted fighting suit, give it a miss today," He said, holding the door open with one hand, "Let's go."

I huffed, reluctantly getting up from my comfortable window position and trailing out the door and into the corridor. He led and as usual I remained a couple steps behind him out of caution.

My jaw had started to tighten when I noticed he had led us out of the premises and towards the forest, and due to the utter darkness of the outside making the woods look so daunting my heart had already started pounding in my chest.

What if he's taking me here to kill you and dispose of my body? What if he's-

"I'm not going to kill you," He casually said out of the blue, "If I wanted to do that I would have done it a long time ago."

I scoffed. "You lied when you said you couldn't read my thoughts!"

He barked out a laugh, tipping his head back in amusement, "I swear I can't. But I didn't figure you'd actually be thinking that."

I just rolled my eyes in response and trudged behind him, shortening the distance between us just a little as we neared the woods. Curious, I called from behind him, "Why are we going down here?"

Azriel came to a halt, turning back round to face me and I had to dig my heels into the ground to stop myself from banging straight into him due to his sudden stop.

"I know you're scared of this," He gestured towards the woods, "But the thing is - you can't be. Especially when we have many threats which come from these woods in Velastille, you have to be able to defend yourself."

I asked slowly, "What threats?"

"Creatures," He shrugged, "Weird, animalistic creatures with even weirder abilities. As a punishment upon the fallen angels, they only exist in Velastille and no other district. And since you're just a human, you can fall as an easy target for them."

My heart was pounding so hard by now I thought it would rip my chest open.

"But we won't let that happen," He reassured me, "Because I'm going to make you practice how to defend yourself against one, real-time."

I couldn't stop my jaw from falling as I blinked at him in disbelief, "You're going to make me fight some voodoo animal with no weapons?"

"It isn't so bad," Azriel mused, crossing his arms, "They can be killed with just physical combat, and from the results you have produced in our training you'll be fine."

"If you wanted to kill me it didn't have to be like this, prick."

He chuckled, studying the deep, dark mass of forest around us, "You're overreacting, Adeline."

"Me? Overreacting?! Why don't you try-" He raised a hand, hushing me immediately as his gold-eyed stare focused on something up ahead of us. I had remembered angels had night vision which meant he had more than definitely seen something worth a fight already.

"Ah," His voice was quieter now, but somewhat amused as his muscles relaxed, "Here's your first opposition."

And then he stepped to the side. I remained with my feet glued to the ground, my body frozen and unmoving. I knew I was being watched by something within the trees and Azriel knew it too, but I wasn't prepared to let him believe I was just some defenseless, frail human.

"Come out then!" I challenged out to whatever it was in the trees before me, even though I could hear my own fear in my voice and was pretty sure it could sense it too.

The bushes rustled ahead of me and I held my breath as I saw a paw step into the moonlight shining down on us. A large, dark paw with what looked like sturdy tainted yellow nails - perfectly sharpened at the tips. I retreated a step back and tried to stabilise my breathing as another paw came into my vision.

And then I saw it.

Crouched among the thorny brambles before me was what looked like a bear wolf hybrid - rounded black ears but terrifying beady eyes which were both all black with no trace of white. It's body wasn't too big, perhaps the size of an average wolf. It's snout was long and pointed, but what frightened me the most was its mouth. It's bared teeth were stained yellow and brown, dripping in saliva. It's mouth was curved into what looked like a devilish grin, like something out of a demonic horror tale, and I realised it was in a position which looked like it was about to pounce.

A predator had found its prey. And that was when it leaped.

I let out a shriek as my back slammed against the floor and the creature pinned itself on top of me. It attempted twice to slash my throat with its mouth, its breathed growls reeking of carrion. I struggled beneath it - the weight of its body was suffocating against mine.

"Azriel!" I called for him, not bothering to hide the desperation in my tone. I managed to catch a glance of him standing only a couple feet away, casually leaning his shoulder against a tree with his arms crossed as he observed, "Help?!"

"Pretend I'm not here," He casually replied, checking his nails, "Just believe you can do it."

I let out a loud scream in frustration as I used all my strength to hold the creature back from biting off my face. Being beneath it like this with it slashing at me gave me little to no advantage - I had to focus on getting it off me before I could even attempt to kill it.

And then - a white hot flame ran through me. Rage or terror or just wild-instinct, I didn't know and I most definitely didn't think. I managed to position my feet beneath its stomach as I squirmed from under it - and with all the power, anger, might and frustration I could muster I kicked both feet hard into its abdomen. The creature let out a whimper as its body slumped off my body and I tried to take in as much air as I could while I frantically stumbled to my feet again.

"Good," Azriel commented in the background. His face bored and tone even more so as he picked loose dark purple threads off his black tunic, "Now kill it."

"I don't need your goddamn approval, prick!" I managed to shoot out before the creature lunged for me yet again, but this time I dodged aside. It ran straight into the trunk of the oak tree behind me instead but shook it off almost instantly and turned back to face me.

Think, Adeline. You're not going to be able to beat it by hand - you must be mad. You'll die like this if you don't find something.

Third time. The creature pounced for me for a third time and although I was able to dodge again, it's knife-like fingernails caught in my shirt and tore the skin along my arms. I hissed in pain, feeling something along the lines of pure rage coursing through my veins as blood appeared at the surface of my skin.

As I took another stumbled step back from the creature, something crunched under my boot. When I glanced a quick look I saw a thick stick of branch with an edge that looked serrated. I grabbed for it, and as the creature sprung upon me for now the fourth time, I remained stood; holding the branch out like a knife.

When the beast was close enough mid-air, I slammed the sharpened branch into its fur-ridden neck - hard enough that I had felt it slice into the animal's skin and deep into its neck tissue. The creature's eyes flew wide as it paused mid-air, its weighty body falling flat onto my frail one again as I felt my back hit the floor beneath us with force.

I remained still, staring up at the tops of the towering trees and the night sky above us. Non Moving. Silent. The only sound now was my heavy breathing as I tried to gulp for air, the creature's lifeless body resting upon my own.

I had killed it. I had killed a mythical creature with no assistance and no weapon. It was dead, and I had done it. All alone.

Exhausted and panting, I weakly shoved the creature's corpse off of my body and staggered up slowly to my feet. The first thing I saw when I stood up was him.

"You," I hissed at Azriel, who's surprisingly concerned face instantly relaxed when he realised I was well.

I neared him, my teeth gritted tightly out of anger, rage and frustration as I grabbed his jacket roughly to pull him closer to me.

"Don't ever," I snarled into his face as I shoved his chest hard, "ever," I curled my hands into fists and pushed him again roughly, his hoarse laughing in response causing me to hit harder each time, "ever willingly put me in a position like that again."

He stopped laughing when he saw the clawed scabs on my arm after I raised my hands to push him a third time. My body pained me, my head spun, and before I knew it my knees gave out in defeat. I fell forward in exhaustion toward him and he grabbed me swiftly. Holding me close, he supported all my body weight as he crouched down onto the ground, resting my head against his chest while the rest of my body sprawled along the forest floor; my upper body supported by his arms.

I weakly observed as he took my arm in his hand but I didn't bother to fight against it - I was too tired for that. His thumb swiped against the clawed cuts I had received, my blood staining his skin as he did so - and I was shocked to watch as the wounds disappeared. They disappeared as though I had never received them.

"I know I was a prick for doing that," He murmured softly as his hands still held my arm in a gentle grip, his thumb now running small circles in the area where the claw marks had shortly once been, "But I would be more of a prick to leave you to defend yourself against any mythical threats when

I'm not around if you haven't even been taught. You know that. But, I'm sorry for the pain it's put you in."

My eyes flickered up to meet his stare, his auburn eyes ridden with an apology that only wanted the best for me. His auburn eyes which, among all other warriors in the human world, had chosen me; had trusted me enough to bring me here and nobody else. His fingers brushed the brunette strands of hair from my face, cold against my skin.

"You did very well today, you know?" He spoke in a hushed tone, as if he didn't want me to hear.

My eyes hadn't torn away from his gaze as of yet, but I could feel my eyelids becoming heavier. I could feel my body becoming colder and my head growing fainter. The sensation of Azriel's thumb circling my arm was becoming numb.

And then next thing I knew, I had become numb.

PLEASE don't forget to comment and vote!!!!

hope you're still enjoying the book!

- jen x

CHAPTER TWELVE

M y eyes flickered open, the sensation of a hard surface pressed against my back. My first sight was the ceiling which I believed looked like the dining room, although I wasn't too sure.

"She's awake." I heard a voice comment from elsewhere in the room. My vision of the ceiling was blocked when a few people gathered to peer down at my face - Cirse and a couple other maids I recognised from around the house.

"Miss," Cirse let out a gentle sigh of relief, quickly pushing some stray strands of her copper hair behind her ears, "We were worried you wouldn't wake up."

I weakly hoisted myself onto my elbows only to realise I had been laid down on the table in the dining hall. Scanning the room, I noticed there was no sign of whom I may have expected to be here, or his acquaintances.

Cirse quickly placed a hand behind my back to support me into a sitting position, my frail legs dangling off of the edge of the table, "What happened?"

My maiden signalled for the rest of the servants to exit the room, and once they had she said, "Master brought you in. He said you had an accident during your training session but was only unconscious. He gave instructions for us to stay here and monitor you, and help you once you are awake."

I huffed, my grip on the edge of the table tightening. Master brought me in - how? Had he carried me?

I cringed at the thought - but he could have at least dropped me in my bed.

"I'm fine," I said, even though the croak in my voice said otherwise. Regardless, when she handed me a glass of water I still took a sip, savouring the sweet taste of it which didn't exist in the human world.

Cirse touched my cheek with the back of her hand to check my temperature and for almost a second her soft touch reminded me of my mother. I smiled at her - half forced but half genuine, and took in her tender appearance. Her reddish brown hair spiralled down her back and brought out the depth of her blue eyes and the glimmer of her faint freckles. She was about to open her mouth to say something when the door to the dining hall flew open.

At the sudden movement, Cirse jumped and I would be lying if I said my heart hadn't leaped from my chest. Julian entered the room - tall and fluid like everyone else, his warm toned blonde hair pushed to the side and his slim body clad in fighting leathers.

He winced when the door hit the wall due to the force and cursed, apologising straight after, "Sorry - I didn't realise how much force that was." He laughed nervously.

Cirse's gaze dropped to the ground but I noticed as she smiled slightly, and seeing her shyness in that manner made me smile too.

"Anyway," Julian cleared his throat, "How are you feeling now Adeline? You didn't look so good when Azriel brought you in."

"I'm good - thanks to Cirse. She took good care of me." I indicated toward her on purpose and Julian's hazel eyes landed on her. Cirse didn't meet his gaze, keeping her eyes towards the ground.

"I'm sure she did," was Julian's reply, his eyes still fixed on the brunette angel beside me. He snapped out of it and his gaze returned to me, "I'll leave you both to it."

I nodded, thanking him as he left the room and made sure he shut the door gently this time. When I turned back to Cirse, her cheeks had become a deep flush of tender pink. Something childish sparked inside me as I nudged her, "I think you liked what you saw."

She swatted my arm away but immediately apologised, an embarrassed smile appearing on her lips, "Stop. It's nothing like that."

"I'd like to think so!"

"We all like to think things Adeline," She rolled her eyes, even that seeming like a gentle gesture, "Some of which are not true."

I flicked my eyebrows up in agreement and hoisted myself off of the table, dusting off my pants. I realised I was still in my fighting suit.

"I'm going to go and take a shower," I called to Cirse as I headed toward the door, "I will see you after it."

"Of course, Miss."

"It's Adeline!"

****

I sauntered down the spacious corridor back to my room alone, conversed in my sole thoughts. A door down the hall had opened but I didn't take much notice of it, continuing my stride. That was until a familiar female face stepped out from it and blocked my path.

Celeste.

Her long black hair was tied in a low ponytail as opposed to it running down her shoulders as usual. I noticed the dark liner gliding across her lashliner, accentuating her silver cat-shaped eyes and long lashes. Below she wore tight black pants to shape her slender legs, and was clad in a thick fleece jacket.

"Adeline," fake sweetness was injected in her tone, "You're up."

"You don't sound too happy about that, Celeste," I replied flatly, causing her to raise a dark brow in response.

"I heard there was an accident during training," She folded her arms and took a step closer to me, radiating her towering height over me, "What happened?"

I sighed. "Why does it matter?"

"I asked what happened." The sweetness had disappeared. Nothing but a cold and bitter bite in her words remained now as she stared at me with piercing eyes, the silver swirling like smoked glass.

I didn't know whether to tell the truth or to tell a lie. I wasn't sure why Celeste was so intrigued to know what had happened, but at the same time - she was Azriel's cousin, and if he hadn't provided her with the details then there must have been a reason.

"I slipped during combat training," I chose to lie, "Hit my head somewhere slightly and felt dizzy for the rest of the session. As we were about to leave

I collapsed. Now, if you'll excuse me-" I tried to go around her but she blocked me again, clearly a lot faster than I was.

"What's your problem?!" I snapped at her and she glared back at me with an equal amount of spite.

Slowly, she leaned in closer to me and I had to grit my teeth to stop myself from barking curses at her or swinging for her face.

"You know what my problem is, Adeline? My problem is that there is definitely something suspicious about you. You show up here randomly, you're not of angel land, and Azriel's accepted you into his army? And on top of that - he's made you my equal? It's a joke!"

"If this was about you being jealous, you should probably go and express your concerns to your cousin," I met her hard stare, "Believe me, I have much better things to do than to be training to fight for such ungrateful jerks."

When she failed to reply, I rolled my eyes and turned to leave. However, that effort was cut short when I felt her hand grab around my arm in a tight hold. I froze, being forced to look directly into her eyes which seemed to send daggers at me through the form of her hard glare.

Celeste's tone was resentful, her voice low as if to propose a threat to me as she said, "I know there's something to you, fairy girl, and allow me to remind you - when I feel someone is lying to me, I have never been wrong. I always - always find out everything in the end. And when I do, it's never pretty." With that she dropped my arm, nudged her way past me and strode down the opposite direction in the hall.

And that was when I let out a shaky breath I hadn't even realised I was holding while my heart drummed relentlessly in my chest.

Celeste was going to be a problem.

CHAPTER THIRTEEN

The following day I arose late into the morning - or what had felt like it, considering even the mornings here included a night sky with stars and a moon.

I stayed in bed. The tenderness of the silk sheets against my skin stopped me from leaving, but what sounded like sudden commotion from outside my window had pulled me straight out.

Rushing to my window seat, I peered outside and tried to make out whatever I could see in the darkness. It looked like a group of five, six or maybe seven people gathered outside, all looking down at something on the ground which I couldn't see.

Without thinking I grabbed my satin dressing gown hanging off the foot of my bed and hurried into the corridor and out the door leading to the front courtyard of the house. I pushed past a couple of the people, realising they were house servants, and eventually made my way to the front of the crowd. What I saw next made icey chills summon down my back.

A head.

The head of an actual dead person - or angel, lying there on the cobbled ground of the courtyard. There were murmurs of horror and shock coming from the small crowd gathered around it, and I swear I felt bile coming up in my throat just at the look of it.

"Alright, there's nothing left to see here," called a male voice with a tone laced with dominance and authority. Azriel appeared from among the crowd and the servants instantly bowed their heads and quietened at his presence, Julian stood at his side. "Everybody please return back to your roles in the house."

Reluctantly the servants started to turn away a few by a few, leaving until it was just myself, Azriel and Julian stood with the dead head on the ground.

"What is it?!" I instantly asked Azriel, shuddering at the sight of it. Azriel placed his hands behind his back, looking more disgusted than I was as he prodded the body part with the tip of his boot.

"Biological warfare," He answered with deathly calm, "From Ancient Pandaemonium."

"They're known to be the most gruesome district in existence," Julian added, his face lethargically pale.

I took a step back from the head, noticing the murder blade was still in the forehead of the angel. His eyes were wide in perhaps a combination of pain and shock, his whole area beneath his neck severed. Poor soul.

"Why did they do this?" I whispered, looking to the faces of the two males besides me for answers.

Azriel shrugged, his eyes still fixated on the severed head by his feet, "It's a war tactic. It's used to dampen morale - make the opposition, meaning us, think twice about attacking."

"Well, are you thinking twice ?"

"Not at all," He replied sharply, "In fact, I won't stop until it's the King's head which is severed at my feet."

I chose not to reply, but grimaced at the thought.

"Julian," Azriel turned to his male counterpart, "Inform Raymond that we require him to come and dispose of this."

Julian nodded and instantly turned to leave and oblige to his master's orders. I on the other hand, as lethargic as I felt, couldn't stop staring at the head on the ground. What confused me was how although there was a hole in the skin where the blade had gone through, there was no wounding or bleeding of any sort which I found extremely strange.

"Angels don't bleed," Azriel spoke up, his hands in his pockets as he wiped the tip of his boot which had touched the head into the gravel perhaps to wipe any germs off, "That's one of the few things which differentiates us and humans. We also don't throw up, or receive wounds."

I frowned at him and my eyes formed into narrowing slits as I confronted him, "You lied! You can definitely read my-"

"And so that's why, when you got that wound by the creature in the woods a day or two ago-" He continued, completely ignoring me. As he did so, however, I noticed one corner of his lips curl in amusement, "- I had to dissolve the cut and bleeding altogether. Angels recognise human blood or other bodily fluids like vomit, so you have to be careful. Any cut or wound can land you and I in infinite difficulties."

"What would I do if I got a cut or started bleeding?"

"Then don't get a cut or start bleeding."

I rolled my eyes and let out a sigh, responding flatly, "Just answer."

"You come straight to me. Whatever the time, whenever it is - you come to me. And you hide the cut or blood as you do so," He explained sternly, "If you vomit, you try to mask the sound out as well as you can. Don't vomit if you know angels are in the surrounding area."

I clenched and loosened my fingers, not noticing that with every word he continued a pit of nervousness was developing in my stomach. I was a human - in immortal lands, and was stepping on nothing but eggshells trying to survive here. Azriel took one last glance at the severed head on the ground before turning away to go back to the house, and I had to speed-walk in order to quickly catch up with his large strides. The silence between us was deafening, both of us not in a mood to discuss what he had just saw any further.

"So are we going to act like you didn't almost have me killed two days ago?" I asked to break the quiet, significantly out of breath as I tried to keep up with him.

He bit his bottom lip to hold back what must have been his signature cocky smile as he simply replied, "How could I forget? It happened to be one of the most entertaining days of my life."

I groaned in frustration, nudging his arm from the side harshly as he huffed a laugh. Again I looked to him as we walked side-by-side, "Did you not at least feel bad?!"

"I did. But it would hurt my ego too much to admit it."

"At least you admitted that you have an ego," I muttered, earning a smirk from the dark-haired male beside me as we re-entered the house.

****

Many days following the discovery of the severed head which had been sent as a warning by the King, security in Velastille had been a lot tighter. Before

I had rarely seen troops, but now they were almost everywhere all the time - in groups of two's and three's. Julian had said that Azriel had hated the fact the King's men had been able to get onto his territory, and this was his way of ensuring it never happened again.

I wasn't allowed out of the regions of the house - not that I had been allowed before, but Azriel had been very strict about this now. He believed it put him and I at risk if I was voluntarily exposing myself as a human, and it made me an easy target. In basic terms, he had more important things to deal with than worrying over a human girl all the time - understandable.

I had risen that morning ravenous and ready to eat, and so Cirse had escorted me to the dining hall by nine forty-five. The table had just started to be set up - multiple dishes from the finest brioche to the silkiest fruit laid out. To my great luck, Celeste was already sitting at the dinner table when I had arrived.

"You may want to skip the low-fat yoghurt," She commented from across the table, shooting me a side-way glance. "We don't need a corpse dancing around on the battlefield."

I didn't bother glaring at her, picking up a slice of toasted brioche with the tongs provided, "You don't suit giving weight gain tips, Celeste."

She leaned back into her chair and her arms crossed over her chest - a challenging gesture, "And why is that?"

"I don't know," I shrugged casually, pushing around the sliced strawberries and kiwi on my plate in order to make room for the brioche, "I was much rather expecting you to recommend some laxatives that have helped you stay skinny."

Her smokey orbs blazed at me in a deathly stare and her jaw clenched in offence, "You little-"

The door flew open behind us and both of us spun in our seats to get a look. Azriel stormed in, his face aflame with what looked like anger or frustration. A man followed beside him - he looked considerably slightly older than Az, dressed in heavy fighting leathers and thick boots.

"I don't understand how it happened, my lord," said the unfamiliar man in a desperate tone which sounded almost like a plea.

"How could you not have understood, Harland?!" Azriel snapped back with a voice thick of dominance and authority - the Arch Angel's authority. This may have been the first time I had ever seen him so truly agitated. "I assigned you as the Commander of Security for a reason! And what do you go and do? Allow the second district of Zybern to steal from us from right under our noses!"

I stifled in my seat and tried hard not to make any excessive noise which could potentially further trigger the dark-haired angel in front of me. I was confused, to say the least, but equally as curious to know what exactly had been stolen.

Celeste had paused eating ever since Azriel had come in. Her smouldering grey eyes were fixated on her cousin, concern flickering over her defined feminine features while she remained in her seat.

"I know, my lord," the unfamiliar man - Harland replied. He sounded noticeably worried having earned the wrath of the Fallen Arch Angel, "But you know what these Zybernians are like! We were all guarding in motion that evening yet they still managed to get through us. With their portal creation abilities and telekinesis, it makes our job so much more difficult."

"They may be Angels of Death," Azriel growled back, "But we are Fallen Angels. We have the power of soul manipulation - which they don't have. You could have easily guarded against them if you were aware that they were there."

Soul manipulation. I shuddered at the sound of it alone.

Harland fell silent, shifting nervously on his feet with his head low in front of Azriel. Celeste rose from her seat with an inquisitive look on her face, "What's been stolen, Az?"

"The swords," He began to pace back and forth and it appeared that a dark dust of the night and stars followed him as he walked, "Every single one has been stolen by those goddamn Zyberians."

Celeste froze, her slender hands curling into fists as she demanded, "Which swords? The Amethyst blades or the-"

"Yes, all of them," Azriel ran a frustrated hand through his midnight black hair, "Along with my mother and father's Swords of Michael."

Celeste slammed down her palm onto the wooden table, the sound of the hard collision causing me to jump, "The Michaelian Swords too?! Did you go blind and deaf when they were stealing, Harland?!"

Harland again remained silent, his hands fumbling nervously in front of him. A part of me felt somewhat bad for him - everyone makes mistakes, but at the same time it seemed this was a mistake he couldn't recover from judging by the anger of the two cousins.

Azriel slowly sunk down into his usual chair at the dining table and massaged his temple with his fingers, waving a dismissive hand at Harland , "Just go." The chief guard obliged, bowing his head at his master before quickly stumbling out of the room to avoid any more anger directed towards him.

I didn't know in the moment if it was a good idea, but I straightened in my seat and swallowed the lump of anxiety forming in my throat before asking, "What's so important about these swords?"

Azriel didn't so much flicker the smallest glance at me, his deep gold eyes directed elsewhere while he continued to massage his temple. Celeste, however, looked at me as though I had to be the stupidest person in existence, "You must be thick. How do you not know-"

"The blade was wielded many centuries ago by an ancestor of ours - the Arch Angel Michael," Azriel explained, cutting off Celeste which I had mentally thanked him for in my head, "He used it to defeat Lucifer and only four replicas of it were created - two of which got passed down to my parents. They're extremely important not only to my family lineage, but also to the Velastillian weaponry collection we have."

I leaned back into my chair, registering everything I had just been told. The politics of this place alone were far too complicated for someone as admittedly simple minded as myself to grasp.

"So what's going to happen now?" Celeste ran a frustrated hand through the silky long lengths of her dark hair, "It's going to look like a joke if we just sit back, Az! We're meant to be the strongest district!"

"We aren't going to sit back," Azriel confirmed with a deadly calm in his voice. He sat up straight in his chair and his tongue swiped pressed against his cheek as if in thought, "We're going to get those weapons back."

Intrigued, I tilted my head. "How would you do that?"

He turned towards us, his aflame amber eyes flickering back and forth between me and Celeste. He hesitated noticeably, but then said, "You two are going to bring them back."

"Hah!" Celeste scoffed, throwing her hands into the air in frustration, "Please tell me you're joking."

"No seriously, please tell us you're joking," I hissed in agreement - much to Celeste's surprise. I had agreed to fight within the upcoming war and

I acknowledged that, but my contract didn't include being sent out on missions which could potentially leave me dead. He must have been insane if he thought I stood a chance against angels of other districts with no weapons.

"Do you want those weapons back or not?" Azriel glowered in annoyance, leaning back in his stance to stare us both down in an intimidating glare at once.

I returned back the glare with equal hardness, "Why can't you just go?!"

"He can't," Celeste sighed, sinking back into her chair in what seemed like defeat, "Arch Angels can sense when another Arch Angel of a different district enters their territory. Azriel going into Zybern with us is nothing but a suicide request."

Azriel flickered his dark brows up in agreement and pointed his palms towards his cousin - a graceful gesture which seemed to mean 'exactly what she said'.

When I remained silent with my arms folded in order to provide myself with some comfort, Azriel placed his palms flat on the table, slightly leaned toward me and for a second it almost seemed like a whisper of black smoke with iridescent glitter replicating the sky curled over his slender fingers. "So, will you go?"

I didn't dare look at him and replied bluntly, "I'm not going for you."

"And why, Adeline, will you not go?" I almost felt the dark calm which settled over him.

I placed a hand down with force onto the wooden table and met his lightning stare, my voice laced with agitation, "I'm not here to act as a weapon for your kingdom! You say I am for your assistance in this war but it seems more like you want to make me a military pawn to use for your benefit!"

Celeste, to my shock, remained silent. I could feel her wolf eyes piercing into me from my peripheral vision.

"I want your help, not to manipulate you," He snapped in response.

His flare of temper made me lower my tone slightly, but I didn't back away from the intense eye-contact we both held, "What's so special about my help? You have troops lined up everywhere! Or is it that you want the satisfaction of watching me fail?"

Dark shadows danced around his broad shoulders.

"I'll be honest, Adeline, I'm to be blamed for the trust issues you have with me," He breathed, "But sending troops would be far too obvious. They're trained to fight in open battles - not secret missions or whatever the hell this is. Secondly, I trust my troops with my life - but there is still that one percent chance that they could betray me and leak this plan to the other district if they wanted, and I can't risk that."

With my palms flat on the table beneath me, I leaned slightly closer to him and without retreating from his hard stare I slowly asked, "And what if I betrayed you?"

Brown smoke rose like flames in his gold eyes, "You wouldn't."

Celeste stood up again, and the sound of her chair screeching against the floorboards below was enough to pull me away from the intense eye-con-tact between myself and the dark-haired angel in front of me. Azriel re-moved his hands from the table and took a step back from me, both he and Celeste somewhat making me feel inferior due to their towering heights when stood. I remained in my seat regardless.

"Look, Adeline, I don't have the entire twenty-four hours to sit here making plans over breakfast," Celeste twirled a strand of her dark hair around her finger, a hand supported on her hip, "Are you doing it or are you not?"

The winter winds seeping through the open dining hall window seemed to howl an answer in my ear, seemed to beg me to agree. Despite how long I had slept, I was so tired - tired in my bones and in my crumpled heart. My mind pounded with conflicted thoughts, and then all went silent.

"Fine."

"Fine?" Both cousins repeated back to me simultaneously with tones laced with surprise.

"Just - just do what you have to," I said reluctantly through gritted teeth, "But if I get killed I swear I will return in ghost form to haunt you both for the rest of your sad lives."

Azriel studied my face for a split second, and finally gave me a soft half-smile,

"And you have my full permission to do so, Adeline."

____pls vote and comment!!

i'm so sorry for this late update. i have been super unwell and only got the chance to write now.

let me know how u found it!

-j x

CHAPTER FOURTEEN

I hadn't even realised the stars had risen to signify the start of the next morning. That was, until I felt two solid hands shaking my shoulders in an attempt to awaken me.

Slowly, an eye of mine flickered open. Followed by another. And I was met with the face of the Velastillian Arch Angel, hovering over me while I lay.

"Good God, I thought you were dead," Azriel muttered, retreating away from me as soon as he realised I was awake. I shuffled into a seated position on my bed - still in a sleepy haze of confusion.

"What's your problem?" I rubbed an eye tiredly and that was when I acknowledged his outfit. He was dressed in steel fighting leathers, his dark hair tousled. "What time is it?"

Azriel made his way over to my closet with heavy footsteps and opened it up, beginning to rummage through. He replied casually, "Four in the morning."

"What the hell do you want at four in the morning?!"

"We need to set off early if we want any chance of getting those swords back," Without a glance towards me he threw my fighting suit onto the bed I was still sitting upon, "Put this on as fast as you can so we can leave."

I snatched the fighting suit from in front of me. "Get out so I can change then."

An amused smirk played on his lips. "I was hoping you'd let me stay instead."

"You're such a prick," I snapped, kicking the silk sheets off my body as I rose to my feet. The contact of my bare heels with the cold marble floor sent a shudder through my body. "Go annoy Celeste or something."

"I already have by sending her with you," He chuckled, heading to the door.

I rolled my eyes. "It's not like I'm over the moon either, believe me."

His sniggers continued as he left the room, and although he had gone I knew he was waiting for me to finish dressing outside the door.

Within minutes I had slipped into the dark suit but I had wasted more moments by staring at myself in the mirror - at my still dull face and unruly hair. With the palm of my hand I attempted to smooth out the frizz on my head, quickly pulling my brunette hair into a rough plait with my shaking fingers. I was ready - ready to deal with whatever I was going to face today, and I would do it without fear. Before I left, I grabbed my bow and arrow which lay in the corner of my room. I didn't know if it would be of use, but something in my heart beckoned me to take it along - and so I did.

Celeste had met us in the courtyard and I had to hide the envy I felt when seeing her look so effortlessly put together at such an absurd time. We exchanged basic greetings, and without wasting any time Azriel had clicked his fingers and a black cloud of smoke had gathered around us, restricting my vision and lifting my feet off the ground.

I didn't even get a chance to scream before I felt my feet touch solid ground again, and as the black smoke which cocooned us disappeared - what I saw next shocked me.

The sun - just a small glimpse of the sun rising from behind rocky mountains which stood tall before us. I noticed the sky, a mix of baby blues, yellows and oranges as it prepared for the rise of the sun. It looked exactly like what I had grown up seeing in the human world and the sight alone pulled a nostalgic string in my heart.

"Where are we?" I breathed.

Azriel dusted off his dark pants in an elegant motion without a single glance sideways towards me, "Zybern. District of the Angels of Death."

"Watch your back," Celeste warned, her tone stern as her grey eyes gave my suit a distasteful glance, "You can't trust anything here. Nothing is what it seems, okay? So stay close, fairy girl, and don't grow a mind of your own."

As much as I wanted to reply with a sarcastic comment, I bit my tongue to maintain some form of acquaintanceship between us. Azriel must've noticed, because he gave me a smug smile and flick of an eyebrow which I simply ignored.

"I can't go any further, so I'm going to remain on this border." Azriel said, flexing the large black wings behind him, "If you need me, I'll be here."

Celeste waved a dismissive hand at him, her accent clear and classy, "Don't get ahead of yourself, darling. I have it covered." Her cousin simply replied with an eye roll, his arms crossed over his chest.

And so Celeste and I set off. The grainy sand on the ground crunched beneath our dark boots with every step we took closer to the mountainous cavern ahead.

"How do you know where these weapons are?" I trudged besides her, having to stand a metre distance away from her to give her dark wings their space.

"It's not hard to miss," She replied bluntly and pointed to the cavern we were approaching, "Their weapons are kept in there."

We continued straight and I failed to see any entrance to the rocky dugout before us. That was, until I was suddenly pushed into a crouched behind a large rock with full force by Celeste. Her finger pressed against her lips, indicating to me to remain silent. I pulled my bow and arrow tight to my chest and tried to quieten my heavy breathing as much as I could manage

Slowly, Celeste peered from the edge of the rock we hid behind. I couldn't see what she could but from the multiple footsteps I could hear along the sand nearby I knew we weren't alone here.

"Guards." Celeste confirmed my suspicions, her voice barely a whisper, "Goddamn it."

"Can't we distract them?"

"How? Show them our tits and hope they give us a pass in?" She snapped and I couldn't help rolling my eyes.

"I wouldn't expect you to have any better ideas!"

We both fell silent again, Celeste keeping an eye on the guards from the side of the large rock while I remained crouched - my mind wandering relentlessly.

You can't distract them, Adeline. Exposing yourself to them would run the risk of them discovering you're human. But you can't fight them either - you'd lose instantly. Goddamn it, Adeline think. You're supposed to be a skilled fighter. You're meant to-

I gripped Celeste's shoulder to get her attention. Her head snapped towards me, her face clearly annoyed. "What?!"

"I have my bow and multiple arrows in my backpack," I breathed, "You can do magic, right? Can't you summon a bottle of tranquilliser liquid or something?"

"I don't need to summon that," She muttered, dropping her large dark duffle back enough to carry the weapons we were about to steal off her shoulder as quietly as she could and quickly zipped it open. She reached a hand in, and a couple seconds later a small bottle of blue liquid was in her hand.

I took it from her. "I'm impressed."

"Don't be," She scoffed, "I"m Celeste. I'm always prepared.

Of course you are - flipping heck.

I pulled an arrow from the sheath stripped to my back and unscrewed the lid on the bottle, dipping the arrowhead into the liquid. Celeste watched intensely, her eyes focused on my actions.

"What are you doing?"

"Making a tranquilliser dart." I explained, drying the excess liquid against the neck of the small bottle, "Angels don't die from basic arrows right? These arrows will pierce their skin, but it'll work as a tranquilliser to make them unconscious instead of killing them."

"How long will they be out cold?"

"I'd say twenty minutes - if your liquid is good." I positioned an arrow in the bow I held, "Now move over so I have a better place to aim from."

Reluctantly Celeste agreed and we both swapped positions, remaining crouched to avoid being seen. Holding the bow and arrow tight in my grip, I peered past the rock and caught sight of the three guards standing - each of them three metres or so away from the other. To my luck they were all facing away from one another too, which made my job easier.

I made the closest my first target and closed an eye in order to maintain focus. My aim was directed towards his neck - the liquid would travel faster into his body that way.

Focus, Adeline. This is your thing.

And so I shot the arrow. Less than a minute later I heard the thump of the sand as his body lost consciousness and fell to the ground.

"Good one," Celeste approved from behind me and I couldn't help but smirk to myself at her comment. When Celeste compliments you - you take it.

Thankfully the other two guards hadn't still recognised what was going on, or what had happened to their co-worker. I placed my attention on the second one now who faced my direction. This made things slightly trickier and I knew that.

I pulled out another arrow from behind me and dipped it into the liquid again. I then positioned it along the bow. I was going so fast I hadn't even realised my fingers were shaking - not so much from fear, but rather adrenaline that coursed my veins in the moment.

I took aim at the second guard's neck and shot, and seconds later the satisfying thump reached our ears. Before we knew it, down went the final guard and we both made a run for the entrance as soon as it became accessible to us, time draining as we did so.

Once inside the cavern, my skin tingled and the small hairs on my arm stood underneath the warm leathers I wore. Celeste and I surveyed the rocky tunnel we walked alongside in but didn't dare risk a light due to the open doorway. Thankfully, however, the cracks in the stone overhead provided enough sunlight for illumination.

"If I knew there would be so much sand I wouldn't have worn such expensive boots," Celeste muttered, her dark shoes crunching against the grit beneath us.

"Can you just focus on finding the weapons so we can leave?" Time wasn't our friend here, and I knew that. I couldn't even begin to imagine the consequences our actions would have if the guards swapped shifts and discovered us.

As we entered deeper into the cavern, we went only slow enough for Celeste to detect any sort of trap - but there was none. Then again, who would come down here to such a place like this?

Fools - desperate fools, that's who.

The long rocky hall led up to a large steel door. There was nowhere else to go, and so I pointed in its direction "The weapons are in there."

"Obviously."

I scowled at her, both of us shivering. The cold here, even with the sun, was far much more deeper than that in Velastille and I began to wonder if I would even be able to survive another ten minutes down here without freezing to my death.

Celeste laid her palm flat on the steel door and I noticed how it had no knobs, keypads or anything that signified entry. A click and a groan and the steel door slowly rolled open - to Celeste's surprise too, judging by her expression.

"Watch your back," She murmured as she took a step into the room ahead of me, "That was far too easy."

What I saw when I followed after her almost made me fall to my knees in astonishment. A magnitude of weapons, from polished swords the size of wingspans to lustrous bows and arrows arranged neatly against the wall. On another wall was a glass cabinet full to the brim with tiny bottles of liquid in varying colours, arranged neatly in what looked like a specific order.

"Right. Let's be quick about this," Celeste said from beside me and I didn't disagree.

She approached the swords tied to the wall on the right, some with majestic amethyst jewels encrusted to the handle and two blades enrobed in all gold - enclosed in glimmering sheaths. From what they looked like, they must have been the Michaelian Swords stolen from Velastille.

"How are we going to do this?" I spoke my thoughts aloud, watching as Celeste surveyed the swords against the wall but didn't yet touch them.

She took another step closer to the wall of weapons, "We've checked for any mechanisms or triggers - weirdly there's none."

"Does that mean we can just take them?"

"I guess so. Maybe if I just-" Celeste, looking unsure, gently wrapped her fingers around one of the handles of the gold swords and pulled it off the wall - with strange ease. We both froze, waiting for the guards to burst through or the cavern to blow up or something - but nothing, except silence.

"Holy shit," I breathed out a chuckle, my eyes wide, "Let me try."

I approached the second gold sword and with two hands lifted it off of the wall, my knees almost giving out due to the sheer weight of the sword alone. Again, nothing stopped us.

Celeste dropped the large bag she carried off of her shoulder and onto the floor, the sand flaking up from the ground at the heavy contact. She unzipped it quickly, spread it open and very carefully placed the first sword into it. "This is going to be easier than I damn thought."

I hummed in agreement. Helping her out, I also unloaded the sword I held into the same bag. It wasn't long before one quarter of the wall was now bare - void of the Velastillian weaponry they had stolen. As we were about to zip up the bag again and prepare to leave, Celeste's attention fell on the glass cabinet to our left.

"What is it?" I pushed, raising an eyebrow at her.

Her grey eyes glinted in interest while she rolled back her slender shoulders in an attempt to stretch them, her dark wings hanging back behind her. "While we're at it, why don't we just grab a few potion bottles too? You never know - they may be handy."

"If you're just going to steal back - we're missing the point. Those potions aren't Velastillian property so it would just lead to back and forth stealing."

"Sorry, Angel Gabriel," She rolled her eyes at me and I mimicked her in response, "All I'm going to do is take two tiny-"

Above us, the stones began to shake - dust from the rocks descending into our hair, landing on our skin and in the area around us. Panic writhed in my gut and coursed through my veins, but I pushed it away and steeled myself. Nonetheless, my hazel eyes shot towards Celeste.

"What the hell is going on?" I demanded.

Her wings had stilled and her mouth ajar as her eyes surveyed the stones above us in what looked like pure fear and rage. Quickly slinging the duffel bag over her shoulder, she looked to me in an icy stare. "We need to get out, Adeline, and we need to do it now."

And that was when we noticed the metal barrier beginning to slowly drop down from above to seal the steel door we had entered through and lock us in.

"NO!" Celeste screamed at the door in an instant, and within seconds was already running towards it. My body felt glacial - chilled, in a way none of my muscles would move due to the pure and utter shock of the situation. But when I saw Celeste sprint with such urgency towards the steel door, something in my body urged me to do the same.

The barrier was halfway down the door when we made it - the dark-haired angel alongside me slamming it open with the force of a kick as we ran through. Behind us, the barrier sealed the weaponry room. And it didn't end there.

Looking back down the long rocky cavern we had walked through, we noticed how another metal barrier was being lowered - this time at the entrance of the stony underground chamber. My eyes widened in realisation. "Celeste! They're sealing off the exit!"

"No shit!" she clamoured in response. The rumbling of the rocks above us grew increasingly more violent with every passing minute, "RUN!"

And so I ran. Ran towards the exit faster than I have ever done, ignoring the buckling pain in my weak knees and the strain of my calf muscles against the sandy ground while my heart hammered away in my chest at the sight of the lowering metal barrier up ahead. Celeste did the same, a couple steps behind me; her body sinking under the weight of the duffel bag she carried with all her might. I gripped her free arm to assist her, my urgent hold hard enough to probably leave a bruise.

The metal barrier had sealed more than half the exit now and heat was beginning to emerge upon my forehead and my neck - sheer panic. Sand and dust falling from the violent rumbling of the rocks above us left harsh debris in our eyes and a foul, bitter, drying taste upon our tongues.

Behind me, Celeste demanded, "Take the bag!". She tossed it to me with all of the remaining strength in her body and as I took it into my possession I felt like my body was about to give out any second from the intense mass. The mass of the bag loaded with Velastillian weaponry under my weak bones felt crushing and suffocating, and the only thing which kept me running was how close we were to the descending metal barrier - and how fast it was descending.

Screaming in pressure against the pain, I threw the duffel bag harshly through the remaining gap between the barrier and the ground and then dropped to the floor - sliding through the sand and out onto the land outside the cavern. Under a second later Celeste did the same behind me, and I was about to release the tight breath I hadn't even realised I was holding when I heard her piercing shriek of agony.

Her body thankfully had passed the metal barrier, but the dark feathers of one of her wings had caught in the gate. The barrier was just seconds worth of space away from touching the ground which gave me nothing but seconds - seconds to release her wing before it would be crushed under the force of the heavy metal.

I reached her, shoving my body into the gate in a pitiful attempt to delay it as I tugged on her wing - her feathers soft and silken against my fingers.

"Just go!" She gritted out, her neck craned and her face twisted in pain as I ignored her, continuing to hold my body against the barrier as I pulled forcefully on her wing. My lungs were on fire, my lungs were seizing - where the hell was Azriel?

Two seconds left. The cavern behind us shook with full force, the ground even outside rumbling beneath us as the gate just about lowered to the ground.

And then I screamed. And clutched. And tugged.

A tear, and her wing was free. Celeste jerked forward to save herself as the metal barrier dropped down heavily against the earth, sealing the underground dugout completely. And the running didn't cease here - we scattered to our feet and continued, her holding one side of the bag in her grasp while I the other. And we continued running till we crossed the Zybernian border - till the glowering sun above us faded into the moon and the stars and utter darkness - we continued running.

And we both reached a quiet, moonlit cove on Velastillian territory, we collapsed in exhaustion.

****

My eyes flickered open when I felt the tip of a boot nudging my calf.

"What," said Azriel, peering over me and still in battle-black, "are you two doing?"

I was too exhausted to look over, but I felt the movement beside me as Celeste hoisted herself up onto her elbows.

"Where the hell were you?!" She seethed at him, her tone layered with agony and ice. My throat was ravaged and sand tickled my cheeks - I couldn't even muster enough energy to join the conversation and so my eyes clamped shut once again.

"You knew I couldn't cross the border," He shot back in his defence, "You told me you had it under control. I never knew you meant triggering all the metal barricades by that."

Celeste paused, before she asked slowly, "How do you know we did that?"

Upon hearing that my eyes fell open again in curiosity. She was right - he was a good five kilometres away from us at the time. How had he known what was going on without being there?

I observed the noticeable hesitation on Azriel's face as he crossed his arms over his chest, staring straight back at Celeste. "I-I presumed. Anyway, did you get them?" Not at all concerned that we had almost been sealed in and very nearly been dead.

I nudged the loaded dark bag beside me - the sound of metal clattering within it.

"Good," was all he replied before everything fell into silence again. Celeste sighed deeply and fell back onto the ground again beside me, both of our scalps scaled with sand and grime. I was surprised she hadn't complained about it as of yet.

We remained on the floor with Azriel towering above us, his arms folded as he watched our surroundings, probably providing us with some time to regain our breath and strength.

And that was when Celeste quietly started laughing, her body shaking.

"What?" I demanded, my throat burning due to the grit and my newly pointed ears ringing.

"Imagine I'd been crushed by that gate. You'd have to write on my tombstone 'death by metal barrier'. It's so-" She laughed again, wiping some sand from her jaw with the back of her hand as she lay beside me, "I don't know who you are, girl, but teach me your ways of sliding in sand so my fat ass doesn't get smashed by a gate like that again. That was the most action I've gotten all year."

I knew Azriel was watching, but I felt a chuckle whisper out of me which was followed by a laugh, as rasping and raw as my lungs - but a real laugh.

We looked at each other and laughed even more.

"Ladies," Azriel mumbled. A silent order. We managed to bring our laughter to a halt. "Let's move. Staying so close to the border after what just happened now isn't safe."

I groaned in exhaustion as I rose to my feet, sand and dust falling off of me, and offered a hand to Celeste to rise. Her grip was firm, but her quicksilver eyes surprisingly tender as she squeezed it as I hoisted her up.

And while her and I trailed behind Azriel as he led us back to the house, we both couldn't help but burst back out into ribbons of laughter all over again.

---

idk about y'all but Celeste and Adeline bonding makes me so happy i can't even lie LMFAO.

please please remember to vote and comment and let me know how u found it!!

-jen xx

CHAPTER FIFTEEN

J ULIAN

Waking up in your parent's house was so different to your own.

Julian's childhood room, his mother's cooking and the unique scent of his home gave him nothing but pure nostalgia. Don't get him wrong - he loved living with Azriel and was so grateful to him for providing him his own room and personal service in his huge estate, but visiting his parent's home remained superior.

Seeing as he was staying at his childhood home for the weekend, he had attempted that morning to wake up early so he could have breakfast with both of his parents. Emphasize the word tried - his brain decided to begin functioning at ten, which had made him miss breakfast altogether. What could he say? He believed God knew how powerful he would be by being an early riser and so He made him a night owl.

He dined alone at breakfast that morning - a filling breakfast of eggs, meat and toasted sourdough made by his mother's hands, even though they had chefs at their service. His mother was nowhere to be seen when he had entered the dining hall, and he believed father had already most likely left for work in the city. As a talented and reputable sword-fighter, he trained young boys in the Velastillian youth training camps.

Julian hadn't properly spoken to Azriel in a few days - he wasn't aware how to approach him since he was so angered about the robbery. Others were hoping he didn't end up killing Raphael - the Arch Angel of Zybern - for it.

To Julian, Azriel wasn't the cold hearted bastard everyone believed he was. Yes, he came across as rude, cocky and having anger issues but he also had his reasons. His past wasn't as bright and fortunate as many thought it was, and anyone who believed they knew him only really knew him at a surface level. Even Julian believed he wasn't aware of the real Azriel despite knowing him since they were both but youngsters.

When Julian had entered the estate he also called his second home, he realised it was far quieter than normal. A couple maids here and there, but no sign of any familiar faces.

Perhaps Azriel was training Adeline but where could Celeste be? She was the one who would spend her entire morning ordering the servants around like a maniac with all thanks to the OCD she shared with Azriel.

To Julian, these cousins were going to be the death of him.

Entering the kitchen, Julian came across Briella - the first familiar face so far. As one of the head chefs in the estate for as long as he could remember, she had become like a second mother to him. He leaned a sturdy arm across the counter while her back faced towards him, and he noticed how she was kneading what looked like chocolate dough in a bowl with her hands.

"What are you baking?"

"Heavens!" Briella jumped, knocking the rolling pin she had placed beside her on the counter to the ground. When she turned to face him, her blue eyes were wide in shock. "Julian! You still haven't rid yourself of your habit of sneaking up on me!"

The silver-haired male threw his head back and laughed. "You have a very limited awareness of your surroundings, Briella. That isn't my fault."

She swatted his arm with a tea towel and rolled her eyes in denial. "Oh, stop it. Look at this - I'm making a chocolate torte with homemade ice cream on the side. And before you ask me, I made you your usual double espresso with no sugar. It's there." Her doughy fingers pointed at the mug at the end of the counter.

"You know me so well." He winked at her.

"I wonder why! It is almost as though I have been catering for you for more than a decade."

"You're funny," He rolled his eyes and brought the hot mug to his lips, taking a sip and feeling the warmth of the liquid course down his throat. "You haven't seen either of the three avengers by any chance, have you?"

"The three avengers?"

He sighed. "Azriel, Celeste and Adeline?"

"He didn't tell you?" Briella frowned and blinked hard in confusion, pausing her dough-kneading.

"Would I be asking you if he had told me?" People here sometimes made Julian want to murder someone, and he swore he wasn't the violent type.

"I heard Master, Celeste, and I believe her name is Adeline have gone to another district. I'm not sure which and why since we aren't informed of such affairs."

So many questions ran through Julian's head in that moment - the first one questioning why Azriel believed it was a good idea to take Adeline, who didn't seem to be fully militarily trained yet or familiar with angel lands, to the district of the Angels of Death. But, he had his reasons for everything and so he left it.

With the coffee in his hands, he headed to the door. "Thanks, Briella."

Having supposedly nothing to do that morning left the young warrior sprawled on his bed with his mug in one hand and a heart-wrenching book in the other, the unusual silence in the house alone adding to the emotions of the book. He felt like he could actually think - he hadn't felt this way in far too long, but eventually the words on the pages and the feel of the rough paper beneath his fingers weren't enough for him. They weren't enough to ease his mind or calm his chest, but he recognised exactly what was.

Placing his mug onto the wooden bed-side table on his left, he dropped his upper body over the edge of his bed and extended a lengthy arm underneath it. His hands patted the soft carpet blindly in an attempt to find what he sought, and when he felt something come into his grip he pulled it out in a swift motion.

A picture frame - still facing downwards.

He could already feel how his fingers began to shake, how his body shuddered and heart raced. Hesitantly and without haste he turned over the frame and his breath caught in his throat as he did so.

There she was - painted in the finest of oils, her hair in strokes of honey blonde and her eyes blue, with the smallest tint of rose to enlighten her cheeks.

Ophelia.

The weight in his chest felt suffocating as his hazel eyes stared into her sapphire orbs, then flickered down to her silken plump lips which had been painted into an innocent smile. He reminisced - remembered how he had kissed those lips and how they had whispered over his skin during intimate times of love-making. He remembered how they'd curve when they'd say his name, or how they'd pull into a beautiful grin when he'd make her laugh.

He remembered her far too vividly. His lover. His life. His heart. And she was gone.

The painting in his hand shook under the grip of his trembling hands and the air he was inhaling felt too hot - far too hot for him to breathe in. He had to get out of here. He had to get out now.

With whatever strength he could muster, he slipped the painting back under his bed and stumbled out the door. He didn't even understand where he was headed but he was in need of the cold Velastillian air to fill his lungs and calm his drumming heart.

Julian aimed for the rooftop, roughly climbing the stairs which led up to it only to find it already occupied. His senses had not warned him.

It was too late to turn back, for Cirse had already seen him from her seat, her ocean eyes glimmering wide in the moonlight with both surprise and confusion. She quickly rose to her feet and noticeably gripped the mug in her hand tighter, her gaze towards the ground in respect. "I'm sorry. I didn't think anyone would be up here at this-"

"It's fine. I thought I forgot something up here." The lie was smooth and cool, as was the expression on his face. The young maid smiled and tucked a piece of her reddish brown hair behind an ear, still remaining standing. The moonlight radiating onto her milky skin, vivid eyes and light hair made her look ever so angelical and ethereal.

Silence fell between them, until the young warrior cleared his throat.

"Aren't you cold?" Julian's breathing clouded into wisps of cold smoke in front of him due to the freezing temperatures. He noticed she wore nothing but a thin silk robe, with bare feet.

She shook her head - a gentle motion, and lifted her mug, "I-I have hot cocoa in here. A cup of this is enough to warm me up."

"I'll have to try some one day."

"Of course. Enjoy the rest of your morning," She replied in a way which sounded more like a dismissal than a blessing.

Julian's head cocked to the side, "You could've at least tried to hide the fact you wanted me to go."

"No, no," Cirse's blue orbs flashed in alarm, "You may stay here as long as you would like - this is your home. I-I just presumed you'd like to be alone, especially if you came up here."

"I forgot something," He reminded her.

"At six in the morning?"

The faint freckles on her nose creased as she gave him a small smile which glittered with amusement. No matter how much he had tried to ignore it, he couldn't help but notice how beautifully she executed that expression on her face.

"I thought I left one of my rings up here last night," He pretended to scan the rooftop with his eyes, then shrugged his shoulders, "Looks like it isn't here."

Cirse's smile widened and he feared he was transparent enough for her to realise he was making everything up. Nonetheless, she remained silent, bringing the mug of cocoa up to her lips to take a sip.

After a couple moments of quiet and breathing in the crisp air, when he felt like his heartbeat had returned to a normal pattern and his mind was not clouded any longer, Julian asked, "Why are you up here?"

Cirse blinked a couple of times, as though his question had taken her by surprise. "I-I come here during the early mornings when Miss Adeline is asleep and have my morning drink, though she is out with Master today and so I have a l-little extra time to myself."

"Why the rooftop in particular?"

She angled her head as though she was carefully thinking about her answer, her lightly curled hair shining in the moonlight. Her eyes glimmered as she stared out towards the dark mountains in the distance and the towering forest of pine trees which surrounded them.

"The rooftop is the only place where there is actual silence. Actual s-serenity," Cirse replied, her voice just above a whisper. She refrained from eye contact, "It's where I can go and be alone with my own thoughts before I'm running around with Miss Adeline the rest of the day."

Julian offered her a small yet gentle grin, "I do the same sometimes. Being Azriel's right hand man has its disadvantages."

She did nothing but smile in response, her gaze flickering from him to the contents in her mug, and then to the ground. Silence fell around the two angels and Julian almost started to see this as an indication to leave.

"Do you paint?"

He froze. It wasn't every day he was asked that, especially since he hid this talent of his. "Why do you ask?"

"F-Forgive me, but when I was assisting Helen in cleaning your room I came across some oil paints in a bag in the cupboard. I-I left them there, though, I s-swear."

Julian narrowed his hazel eyes, studying her, "I see."

"Do you, though?" She pressed, "P-Paint?"

Julian couldn't help his soft chuckle, "Yes, I do."

She opened her mouth to ask more, but he didn't feel like explaining or demonstrating - since that was surely what she would ask him to do next. So instead Julian jerked his chin towards her, "Do you have any hobbies?"

Cirse pulled her satin robe tighter around her frail body. "Besides making good cocoa, not really."

Julian laughed, his palm rubbing the nape of his neck which ached for a reason he didn't understand, "This cocoa must be damn good then - I have high expectations."

"Of course!" She smiled broadly, her ocean eyes glimmering in excitement. Julian felt something restless settle in him, his heart calm and his mind content enough to lounge.

But he needed to attend to his duties - that was what he was here for.

"It was nice talking to you," Julian turned towards the steps leading back into the house, "Don't stay out much longer, you'll freeze and even your cocoa won't be able to save you."

Cirse let out a soft giggle and nodded her farewell, and Julian descended into the warmth of the stairwell.

He could have sworn all he wanted following that moment was hot cocoa.

****

ADELINE

"Ouch!"

"I'm so sorry, Miss, I'm trying my hardest not to-"

"Ow!"

I winced as Cirse pulled the strands in the centre of my head into a plait, attempting to be gentle but noticeably struggling. I sat on the polished wooden floor while she sat behind me upon a chair, both of us enjoying the warm gusts of air from the fireplace.

It had been over a week since we had returned from bringing back the stolen weapons from Zybern, and since then I hadn't seen Azriel, Celeste or even Julian around much. Today was the first time in a couple days where Azriel had arranged a training session.

"Braids are so much harder than I remember them to be," Cirse sighed, her voice muffled due to the few hair pins between her teeth.

"Do we need braids? It's only training."

She pulled another piece of my brunette hair between her slender fingers, "They're the most practical. Braids will keep the hair out of your face and you'll love them when I'm done."

"I hope so," I mumbled and closed my eyes to try and ignore the pain, "This reminds me of when my sister would do my hair."

"Really?" Cirse fell silent for a couple moments, clearly hesitating, before asking, "What was her name?"

"Elena."

"That's a beautiful name," Cirse breathed and I could hear the smile in her voice.

"Yeah," I picked at the loose threads on the fabric of my training leggings, "My mother picked it. I miss her so much sometimes."

Cirse arrived at the final ends of my braids, her hands warm against my scalp, "You should go and visit her some day."

"I wish. I'm here until the war is over - at least that's what my agreement with Azriel is."

"Hm," Cirse hummed, taking a hair tie to secure my hair, "Which district is your community from?"

I frowned. "My community?"

"Yes - your fairy community. Which district do they live in?"

My hands rose to run a finger over my still pointed ears.

Shit. I had no idea what she was talking about, and not even enough knowledge about fairies to bluff either.

"I-I..Uh..I-"

A knock at the door, and I let out a tight sight of relief. Saved - for now.

"Come in!" I called, standing up from the ground and Cirse followed after me, rising from her chair.

The bedroom door creaked open and Julian peeked his head into the room, his luminous hazel eyes freezing on Cirse first but then instantly after flickering to me.

"Azriel just told me to grab you a little earlier for your training session since he has somewhere to be in forty minutes." He spoke gently, his tone warm.

Sighing, I nodded. "Not like I have anything better to do."

Julian held the door for me with one hand as I approached, and I noticed how his gaze was fixated on the copper-haired maid behind me. When he realised I was staring at him he snapped out of it, quickly looking away into the corridor instead.

I had to bite my lip in order to hide my smile.

As Julian directed me to where my ever-so-amazing training partner was waiting, he looked at me while we walked side by side in the hallway. His black wings remained flared behind him. "So. You think you ready to beat some angel ass yet?"

I scoffed. "Not even close."

"Uh huh," Julian smiled, showcasing his pearly white teeth. "Celeste told me about how you saved her life in Zybern last week."

I fell silent. Celeste sounding grateful was alien to me - but the fact she'd had enough decency to still mention it, even if it wasn't to me, made me feel quite pleased with myself.

"She might not say it," Julian interrupted my thoughts, slowing down as we approached a room. I did the same. "But Cel really does appreciate things like this. She'll remember it forever and pay you back whenever she'll get the chance."

I raised my eyebrows. "I'll believe it when I see it."

Julian simply laughed in response, pushing the door open for me.

"I'll see you around later, Adeline."

"You too."

I walked into the room - a foreign room I had never been in. It appeared to me like a spare sitting room, a theme of silver and white prominent through the walls and furniture.

"You're never that nice to me." A deep voice laced with elegance spoke, and my eyes darted over to the source. Standing by the window and facing away from me was Azriel.

Raising an eyebrow, I folded my arms. "You honestly tell me if you're worth being that nice to."

He turned round to face me slowly, his hands deep in his pockets and a smug expression on his face. "Honestly speaking, I think I'm nice enough to deserve a hello and a goodbye. Maybe a little kiss on the cheek too."

"Such a funny joke."

"What can I say?" He huffed some dark strands of hair out of his face and with slow strides walked over to where I was stood near the door. "I'm a funny guy."

"Quit turning yourself on."

A smirk from him, laced with amusement, as he pressed his tongue against the inside of his cheek. "Have to do it myself seeing as there's nobody to do it for me."

I rolled my eyes and let out an exasperated sigh while he laughed a short laugh at my reaction.

"Anyway," His hand snaked down to the leather belt he wore around his waist. Sliding a pocket knife out of the belt, he gave it a clean, skilled flip into the air before holding it out to me. "Following on from hand-to-hand combat, we are going to learn the art of the dagger today."

I carefully took the dagger from his grasp, wrapping my hands around the handle as tight as possible. He was brave to hand me such a sharp blade so easily - if he got on my nerves enough today maybe I would just stab him.

"You can't stab me. I'm almost immortal." He rolled his eyes and I blinked wide.

Azriel can definitely read my thoughts. There's no chance he can't - the bastard.

"No, for the hundredth time I can't read your thoughts. Your face alone speaks volumes to me."

I instantly looked away from him, turning my attention elsewhere. I could still see that sheepish smirk from the corner of my eye regardless.

"Right, darling Adeline. Shall we begin?"

CHAPTER SIXTEEN

- -

A DELINE

Beneath the thick leather of my fighting suit, even with the freezing temperatures my skin was slick with sweat. We had been practicing different stab techniques with the dagger for almost half an hour, and my arms trembled so badly that every time I wrapped my hands around the handle of the dagger my pinkie would shake uncontrollably.

Azriel closed the gap between us, gripped my hand and said, "This is because you're holding onto the handle too hard. You're wasting all your strength here." He tapped my knuckles with his index and middle fingers, "hence why your fingers are shaking."

I may have been skilled at hunting, at archery and quick-thinking, but this session had made me realise how I really lacked at using my left side. Moving fast with my left leg and slicing with the dagger in my left hand at the same time I found so difficult. The right side, however - that was easy.

"So," Azriel had murmured from behind me as I practiced slashing the dagger into the areas of a sheet which he had pinned against the wall and marked targets on, "In this human... world of yours, you were the breadwinner of your family?"

My grip around the dagger handle grew tighter, my focus remaining on the targets in front of me, "Mhm. My father was getting old and sick."

"What would you do, to be specific?"

"I hunted," I wiped the slicken sweat from my forehead with the back of my hand, "Sometimes deer, sometimes fox and sometimes rabbit - depending how lucky I was. If the animal was large enough, we'd cut a portion to last us a couple days and the rest would go with my father into the city to be sold in exchange for some coins."

Azriel fell silent behind me for a couple moments while I continued my slashes into the white cloth sheet, majority of the time either digging the blade right into the centre of the target or being off by just centimetres.

"And your father," He began from behind me again suddenly, "Was he the only male figure in your life?"

I froze, the dagger in my grip mid-air doing the same. My back remained facing towards him but I could still feel his persistent, aflame stare burning into me from behind.

"That's none of your business." I managed to quickly choke out, blinking myself out of the suffocating memories beginning to arise in my mind again.

Pull yourself together Adeline. For goodness sake, stop.

The rest of the session continued in silence. Azriel must have realised the consequences of asking his question, because I didn't make even a comment towards him for the remaining twenty minutes and he did the same. Occasionally he would step forward to correct my form - but that was it.

As I gulped down some water at the end of our session and watched him as he clicked his fingers to make the torn sheet disappear from the wall, a kernel of emotion - either regret or sympathy - coursed through my veins.

I gnawed on my bottom lip, weighing whether to do so or not, before reluctantly speaking up. "I've never heard your name before. What does it mean?"

He turned to face me slowly, an eyebrow raised in definite confusion over my sudden will to talk. Thankfully he didn't question it and slid his hands into his pockets, his shoulders noticeably relaxing. "It means God is my helper - in the Hebrew language."

"Oh," was all I replied.

"What about yours?"

"It means nobility, in French I think."

"You're anything but noble."

I rolled my eyes, but was inwardly somewhat grateful his cockiness had returned and the awkward silence between us had diminished.

"And you definitely don't look like you need God's help - your ego is way too big."

He flicked his eyebrows up in agreement and said, "Fair enough," before huffing a laugh, both a graceful motion and sound. "Another thing - your name is too long and I simply do not have the energy. I need something shorter."

"I have no nickname."

He rubbed his chin with his slender fingers which were adorned in silver rings as if in thought, and a mischievous smile appeared upon his lips. "What about Addy?"

"No."

"Why not?"

"No way."

"I like it."

"I don't care what you like!"

"The feeling is mutual, so I'm still going to call you Addy."

"Addy is revolting," I gripped the handle of the dagger that was still in my hands tighter, "Stop calling me that, dickhead."

His smirk widened and that same amused glint returned in his auburn eyes. "What's wrong with that nickname, Addy?"

"I'm going to kill you!" I swiped the dagger at him in frustration, but within a blink he disappeared and left me stumbling. Dark smoke spiralled around where he was under a second ago. I frowned.

"Told you that you can't kill me." His voice, thick with a regal accent mused. I spun around to find him now standing behind me, arms crossed over his chest and the same sheepish smirk playing on his lips. "You're more than welcome to try though, Addy."

I took another lunge towards him with the dagger, and once again the blade sliced straight through thin air and the dark smoke which lingered about after him. Again, he had vanished.

Remaining still, my hand holding the dagger remained ready and my free hand curled into a fist. The only sound in the room in that minute was my jagged breathing, but I waited for him. Waited until I felt the warmth of his chest pressed against my back, the unique coldness of his breath teasing my neck, and the soft tips of his fingers tracing my waist. Waited until I heard his enticing, sweet voice whisper into my ear, "Try again, Addy."

And then I seized the hand he had on my waist tightly, locking him into my grip. Using all my strength I had remaining I pulled him in front of me, before shoving him roughly against the wall. I raised the dagger in my hand to his neck, pinning him there with my face just mere inches away from his. His eyes were wide - clearly taken aback in surprise as his body tensed.

"I said," My teeth grit as I spoke, the blade just only hovering over the skin on his neck, "don't call me that."

And then his body relaxed, the small amused smirk slowly returning as he held my sapphire stare with his own auburn orbs. I didn't back down from my position, continuing to hold the sharp blade in a horizontal position along his neck without applying any pressure.

My breathing was heavy, my heart racing as I watched how he broke the stare we held; his eyes lazily flickering down to my lips for a couple moments before returning back up. It was as though he set aflame every place his gaze roamed on my face, my cheeks growing warm with heat and my lips running dry.

Azriel's voice was a raspy, sweet mess when he murmured, "I need to go, Adeline," and I almost didn't hear him - entranced in the brown flecks which spiralled in the gold iris of his eyes.

It was when his shoulders moved slightly against me that I snapped back into reality and pulled away the blade from his neck, taking a good few steps back from him as he stepped away from the wall.

He scanned my flushed face before his gaze dropped to the dagger I still held in my right hand, and with a swipe of his tongue against the inside of his cheek to hide the smirk aching to appear he said, "Keep the dagger. I think it'll be of more use to you than to me."

I instantly looked away - whether that was from embarrassment, regret or intimidation - I wasn't sure.

"I'll see you at dinner tonight, Addy. Perhaps you can feed it to me off of the dagger, too."

Before I could hurl an insult at him in response, he had already disappeared into thin air; leaving behind the dark spiralling shadows and smoke which lingered in his wake.

And as I replayed back what he had said to me in my mind while I walked back to my bedroom, I couldn't help the chuckle which rasped out of me.

CHAPTER SEVENTEEN

AZRIEL

"You seriously told him that?"

"Of course I did."

Julian tipped his head back and laughed as I let out a small chuckle myself. "You're a dick, Az."

"You have to do what you have to do."

Julian and I were sat in the sitting room together, talking over a bottle of white wine with the fireplace raging beside us. It felt like forever since we had an opportunity to sit like this. To talk - not like adults, but rather like friends.

Julian sprawled out his long legs, crossing his ankles over, and let out a deep sigh. The quietness of the Velastillian winter night was enough to put our aching heads at ease. "Do you ever feel like we missed out on a normal childhood?"

I took a lengthy sip of my wine and placed the tall glass back down onto the coffee table in front of me, amused. "Define a normal childhood, please."

"I don't know," Julian merely shrugged his shoulders. "A childhood where you weren't learning how to stab people with blades at four years old."

I breathed a small laugh, running my tongue along my teeth in thought as I slouched back into the sofa. "The truth is, Julian, we did miss out on a normal childhood - for specific reasons. Think about it. I was the son of one of the future Arch Angels and the Prince of Velastille, and you are the son of Velastille's longest serving commander of the army. We aren't normal."

"That doesn't mean we didn't deserve a normal childhood." The ash-blonde angel sat opposite me traced the rim of his wine glass with his finger, his voice low. In all honesty, he was right. We had our joyous childhood activities stripped away from us and replaced with training and learning etiquette. There was no normality in the past life we had lived, and we had been forced to mature a lot sooner than other children our age. With all that taken into account, we both acknowledged we had roles and responsibilities to carry out - we were in these positions for a reason.

"Even the way we met wasn't normal," a smile came to my lips as I reminisced, remembering that day I had come across the ash-haired boy. Julian finished off the remainder of his wine and mimicked my smile, shaking his head as though he could remember everything as vividly as I could. "We were practicing archery that day, if I recall well."

"I had asked you if I was allowed to even stand next to you because I was that shit-scared of being near the Arch Angel's son," Julian folded his arms, "I thought your father would come and sever my neck off."

"Being the Arch Angel's son made me so anti-social. I was probably just as scared to talk to you as you were to me."

"You didn't seem so scared when you pulled that boy's fighting pants down when you saw I was in the process of being attacked," Julian chuckled and I couldn't help do the same as the memory replayed in my mind. "God forbid, I will never steal anyone's food again in my life."

"I was planning on walking away but I'm just such a good person and so naturally, I had to intervene. I wish I hadn't though, because in the dead of the same night your prick-self woke me up and asked if you could stay in my tent so that you didn't get attacked by those boys-"

Julian cut me off swiftly, "Firstly, Az, your tent had a constant burning fire to keep you warm. Secondly, you had guards stood outside your tent day upon night and lastly - you had rugs hand woven to sleep on whilst I slept on grass in my piss-poor tent. Of course I was going to come and hijack whatever the hell you were sleeping in!"

"So our friendship was materialistic?" I grinned in teasing amusement.

"It would be a lie to say it was not materialistic that night." Julian rolled his eyes in defeat as I let out a soft laugh at his response, "But you know I would take a wound to the heart for you. I even put up with Celeste in her hormonal bleeding phase just because she was your cousin."

My smile faltered slightly as I glanced to the hallway from my seat. "Where is Celeste, anyway?"

"I haven't seen her since early this morning."

Frowning, but attempting to hide the concern I slowly rose, "I'm going to go and check on her." I received nothing but the rise of his empty glass from Julian to indicate his approval as I stepped out into the corridor. Majority of the candles which were only lit in the night had been smothered seeing as it was approaching perhaps three or four in the morning, and the night was nothing but dead and quiet.

When I passed by Celeste's room I left a brief knock at the door, but upon receiving no reply I continued down the corridor. This wasn't like her - she would either be in her room or sat with us by the fire at this time.

That was when something caught my eye from outside the glass paned walls of the hallway - our childhood treehouse. It had remained in the estate gardens since we had been small and naturally, I didn't want to destroy it and so it remained there.

My curiosity caught the better of me, and before I knew it I was outside and climbing up the trunk to reach the treehouse. Shoving the door open with difficulty due to the years of neglect, there was Celeste - wrapped in a blanket, alone.

Her widened eyes eased and she let out what sounded like a shaky sigh of relief, shaking her head when she realised it was me. "Goddamn it, Azriel, you scared me. Why are you here?"

"I couldn't fall asleep," I took a step into the treehouse, having to duck due to my towering height. The wooden floor beneath us groaned with every reluctant step I took. "I could ask you the same thing though. Why are you here?"

She chose to ignore my question and instead shifted in order to make space for me beside her. There was this deafening silence between us which I didn't understand the nature of; she was so distant recently.

I decided to break the quiet. "What's wrong?"

"Like you ever cared," She rolled her eyes. Her attitude was coursing cold frustration through my veins as I turned to look at her.

"Good God, Celeste! If I didn't care I wouldn't be asking you about your wellbeing, would I?"

"Seems you're concerned a lot more regarding another someone's wellbeing recently."

I knew in the start I would struggle getting them to like each other's presence and granted, it was funny to watch their first few clashes - but it was starting to become annoying. "What has Adeline got to do with this?"

"Since that fairy girl came here you've forgotten us! What happened to our so-called trio, Az?"

"Oh, come on," I scoffed, "That isn't true. You're being completely cynical right now, Celeste."

"Is that so?" Her grey eyes narrowed, almost like a feline preparing to attack. "For these past four months all you've done is train her. Do you even remember the last time we spent a moment together? Right - it was we went to get the weapons back. It's always business, business, business!"

"Celeste-" I tried to cut in lazily but was overpowered almost instantly.

"Can you shut up and listen to me for once? "

I nodded in defeat, motioning her to continue.

"Do you remember when we used to sneak out here and play games all night? Before the sun rose we would run back to our rooms and after doing this every night we developed eye-bags" Celeste lightly chuckled to herself, pulling her knees to her chest.

"Yes, and your eye-bags still exist." I commented teasingly as she nudged my arm with the full force of her elbow.

"Ouch, okay! Okay - I'm joking !"

"You better be."

She rested her head on my shoulder as the silence consumed the atmosphere again. I didn't understand why she felt like this when she was like a sister to me - one which I never had - seeing as we practically grew up alongside each other and Julian.

"Why fairy girl?" Her question shook me back into reality, and I had to hide how desperately I wanted to roll my eyes.

Good lord, Adeline, your existence here has brought along so many issues with it - all of which better be worth it.

"What?"

"You know what I said."

And I knew she suspected something - you had to be stupid not to.

"I told you already. She has the skills I require."

"Do you like her?"

"What kind of a question is that? She is only for business and nothing more."

"Hm," was all she managed to reply, giving me a brief tight smile.

"Celeste smiling? Let me go and fetch somebody to witness this salient moment."

"Sure," She rolled her eyes and nudged me again; a lot lighter this time, but her smile widened alongside it. "Anyway, it's getting pretty late. I'm going to go back in."

"I'm right behind you." And once she had left, I didn't follow right behind her. Instead I remained sitting as my thoughts consumed me. Celeste had picked up a scent on Adeline, and it wasn't long until she discovered who she truly was.

Not unless I took action - now.

****

JULIAN

Once Azriel had left to search for Celeste, Julian recognised the fact he should have gone to sleep due to being committed to an early morning training session the very next day; but instead he remained by the fire, opening yet another bottle of wine. The whole atmosphere of the fireplace, the wine and the warmth of the room had made him too lazy to leave.

Taking small sips as he lounged on the sofa and studied the flames which danced for him so dead in the night, the sound of footsteps incoming down the hall shifted his attention to the entrance of the room. He presumed it would be Azriel, back after failing to fall asleep due to the insomniac he was. Perhaps it was Celeste coming for a glass after returning from wherever the hell she had been , or maybe one of the servants trying to make their way to their fellow colleague's room without being caught. But when he saw the tinge of copper which caught his eye enter the room, it could only be one person.

Cirse.

With all his effort he pushed himself up from his slouch in an attempt to make himself appear half-decent, while she jumped in fright after clearly not expecting him to be there.

He chuckled to himself at her reaction. Her fragility and vulnerability alone made him feel somewhat protective over her.

"I-I'm sorry," She retreated a step towards the door, ready to leave. "I didn't know you would be in here."

"It's just me." Julian reassured her softly and nudged an empty glass towards her on the coffee table. "You want a drink?"

She declined politely. "Thank you, but I don't drink."

"What's the fun in that?" Julian bit his lip to suppress his smirk. At this point he couldn't differentiate between whether it was him speaking or the alcohol.

"Well," She began, clutching what looked like a novel to her chest. "I would much rather have fun and remember it also, rather than being hungover the following day."

Julian flicked his eyebrows up in agreement, taking another sip from his glass. "I can't argue with you there even if I tried."

She let out a soft giggle, still standing by the door with the book to her chest. He had just only now properly managed to steal a look at her tonight. How pretty and pure she appeared with her reddish-brown hair tousled down her shoulders, her fluid ocean eyes lowered to the ground in shyness and the silken night gown which hugged her petite body.

"God, you're gorgeous."

The words left his mouth before his mind could even process them, and the second he realised what he said his eyes flew wide open. The maiden standing in front of him had the same reaction, looking almost surprised as though this was the first time someone had said such a thing to her - but then a warm, comforting smile splayed on her lips.

"I believe you are drunk," She said with such softness that her voice felt like silk and cotton to his ears, "So I won't question anything you say."

Julian gnawed at his lip, putting his empty glass down quickly. "I-I'm not drunk, I-"

"Why are you here at this hour with two bottles of wine then?" Her ocean eyes sparkled in amusement as she awaited a reply, and Julian let out a long sigh - the sound of complete and utter defeat.

"What about you? If you're not getting wine-drunk, then what are you doing?"

Her frail knuckles tapped the book placed against her chest as if to indicate towards it. "Miss Adeline recommended a book to me and I had only just finished it, so I was coming to return it." She nodded towards the bookshelf in the far corner of the sitting room.

"You know, I have a much larger selection of novels in my bedroom upstairs." He paused, replayed what he had just said in his head, then quickly clarified, "I am not inviting you to anything sexual - I do actually have a much better bookshelf upstairs."

Cirse laughed - a satiny, velvety smooth sound, and Julian couldn't hold back his smile either - still embarrassed. Her copper-brown hair glowed red and gold in the firelight. "I know what you meant."

"I'm glad, believe me."

"I think I would be far more interested in seeing your painting collection though."

"You would?"

"Yes."

"I shall show you then, as soon as I get the chance."

Cirse bowed her head gratefully and then smiled, her striking eyes meeting his lazy hazel stare - and he swore he felt something burn in the pit of his stomach at the distant contact alone. Something inside him was childish; wanted to grab her hand and run down the estate corridors together, or invite her to sit with him in front of the fire while he read her a novel from one of the classics - but he came to the conclusion it was the drink talking, and not him.

Immersed in his thoughts, Julian hadn't realised Cirse had already returned the book onto the shelf and was heading towards leaving. He watched her with stillness, scared he would say something that would intimidate her or do something that would dishearten her due to the alcohol coursing through his veins.

The copper-haired maiden turned in her step to face him as she approached the door, and with a small, shy wave in his direction she left - the only sound audible to his ears being her retreating footsteps.

And Julian didn't move that night. Not when he had a new bottle of wine, the warmth of the fireplace and her to think about.

---

pls remember to vote and comment! every single one benefits the book and myself as an author so pls! thank u so much!

- jen x

CHAPTER EIGHTEEN

A DELINE

Today had marked three months since I had been brought to Pandaemonium. Three whole months away from my father, my sister, my home - which didn't seem much like a home to me any longer.

I had spent most of the evening in my bedroom listening to the crackling fire and the utter silence of the outdoors of Velastille - so different from the chirping birds and evergreen melodies I was used to back in the human world.

With a gentle knock, Cirse had entered my bedroom; her reddish-brown hair secured in a loose braid and her hands carrying a tray upon which was a mug. I met her gaze and she noticed my confusion at her sudden appearance.

"Hot cocoa," She clarified, her voice as sweet and gentle as her features, "Since you didn't come to dinner, I thought a warm drink in this cold would do you good."

I smiled with gratitude as she placed the drink on the bedside table and then hesitantly perched herself on the edge of my bed, near my waist. The smile splayed on my lips remained in order to let her know I approved.

"Master was asking about you," She spoke up, and I instantly felt my face tighten and smile falter. "He kept asking me why you didn't come down for dinner."

"And what did you say?" I pushed.

"That you wanted to rest as you were tired."

I leaned over to grip the mug from the tray besides me. "I'm surprised he didn't argue with that. A month or so ago he would have come to my room himself to drag me down to eat."

"Well, people become more understanding of each other as time passes." She simply replied, watching me as I took a sip of the drink and sighed at the sensation of the warm liquid coursing down my throat. After a few more seconds she rose from my bed and moved to shut the curtains, sealing the room in darkness. My heart stumbled at the act, and I blurted out, "Leave them open - please."

Cirse nodded and left the curtains open, wishing me goodnight and telling me to send word if I needed anything after she had departed. Within the next thirty minutes I had fallen into a swift and deep sleep.

The following morning when I had awakened I was confused, but not surprised to find Azriel stood outside my bedroom.

"Are you decent?" His voice, deep and laced with rich regal accent asked me from the other side of the door.

Still sat in my bed I quickly gathered the duvet at my shoulders and chest in an attempt to hide the sheerness of my sleeveless nightdress. "What's so important at this time?!"

Azriel took that as an indication to enter, and after making sure the door was shut tight behind him he looked towards me. His dark eyebrow lifted. "I've seen women look better in the mornings."

"You're such a prick!" I seethed, throwing a pillow from my bed straight at him. Of course he dodged it, but a smirk appeared on his lips at my reaction regardless.

"Adeline, I've been thinking." He pressed his back against the bedroom door, as if obstructing entry for anyone else. His tone of voice was also significantly lower. "I think we need to tell Julian."

"Tell him what?"

"Tell him that you're a human and not what he thinks you are."

My eyes narrowed in confusion. "And what's with this sudden change of plan? You were so content on hiding me from everyone-"

"And I am hiding you from everyone - nothing is changing," He interrupted sternly, "But it's starting to become obvious that you're someone else. Julian, bless him, probably doesn't put much thought into it. But Celeste has picked up a scent and I'm not running any risks here. By telling Julian at least we can have another person to protect you."

I sighed, gripping tighter onto the duvet covering me. "Okay. So what are we going to do?"

"We aren't going to do anything. I'm going to talk to Julian tonight so we can put this matter behind us, and then we continue going about like how we do."

I nodded - the least I could do. When he continued to stand there I arched a brow. "Aren't you going to leave now?"

"Why?"

"So I can get changed."

"Why would I leave for that? That's something I'd love to watch."

"Idiot!" Another pillow found itself in my grip, and then flew straight for his head. He dodged it again and let out a raspy laugh, turning to open the door quickly before I could hurl any more abuse or pillows at him. "I'll see you afterwards, Addy."

****

Majority of the day passed with me not doing much besides helping Cirse with some basic chores or practicing my aim with my bow and arrow alone in my room. I hadn't seen Azriel and Julian, or even Celeste and so it became clear to me they must have had errands on their plates to deal with.

In all honesty, some days I would wish I could go along with them - although I had almost run my lungs raw when I had set out with Celeste. However that is where I felt most belonging; where I could use my mind and body to solve complex situations and actually achieve something.

Another thing that had constantly been on my mind since the morning was Julian's reaction when Azriel would tell him. I guess I was worried whether his temperament or attitude would change towards me now after discovering I was human. Would he even accept me? Like Azriel had said, hatred for humans was embedded in fallen angels - and I still didn't know why.

In fact I still didn't know a lot of things.

Albeit, I was pulled out of my thoughts by what sounded like awfully loud commotion in the hallway and after dropping my bow onto my bed I quickly rushed to the door to see what was happening.

A couple of servants were gathered by the glass wall in the corridor, and after my eyes searched for Cirse but failed to find her among them, I called out. "What's going on?"

One of the maids - a young lady who was stunning to be in such a position - said with a lit up smile, "It's snowing, ma'am!"

Snow? Here?

I hurried over to the window in my bedroom and my eyes widened at the scenic view beneath me. The gnarly forest trees which surrounded the estate had been dusted in fine white snow - whiter and brighter than any I had seen. My usual view from the window of the cobbled ground and green lawn in the garden had been transformed into what appeared like a winter wonderland, and I observed the flecks of icy flakes dance down from the sky.

Although it was dark -as Velastille apparently always was in the winter - it was truly an idyllic moment.

"It's beautiful, isn't it?"

My eyes reluctantly tore away from the scenery outside the window to meet the hazel gaze of Julian, who stood by my door with his hands in his pockets. The light curls of his ash-blonde hair had flecks of the snow trapped in them , signifying he had most definitely just arrived from outside although his wings were no where to be seen.

My breath hitched. Had Azriel told him yet?

"I-It is," I agreed, finding the urge to swallow to keep my throat moist. "I didn't think it snowed here."

He moved over to the window besides me, now also looking out at the snow-dusted garden and forest. His expression still remained unreadable.

"Snow is rare here."

"I see."

"It isn't guaranteed every winter as it may be in the human realm."

There it was. My breath caught in my throat.

Slowly, yet hesitantly I looked up towards his face which remained unreadable. The green of his eyes burned in the light of the glimmering snowflakes gently waltzing past the window.

"J-Julian, I-"

"I understand why you wouldn't tell me, Adeline." He shifted his gaze to meet mine, "And after hearing the entirety of the story - I can't bring myself to dislike you, even if it is ingrained into our minds. Besides, Azriel is whom I have plead my allegiance to. If that means protecting the identity of a human in our lands, so be it."

I swallowed hard. "So you don't hate me?"

A gentle smile spread across his lips, his serious expression now softening. "Far from it. I could tell there was something special about you from the moment we met."

I chose not to reply, but the returning thankful grin I gave him acted as just that. With my heart at ease, I shifted my attention back to the snow outside. Memories - so many memories came flooding into my mind, from back in my village. How we would glow when it would snow, or how we would watch the ladies sew the woollen gloves and thick coats for us in preparation for winter.

Julian's voice pulled me back into my reality.

"You're thinking of something."

"I'm remembering."

"Would you share?"

I pressed my forehead against the window, the pane cold against my warm forehead while my breath kissed the glass with fog. "When I was younger, my sister and I would spend every summer anticipating the winter. Snow-fall would happen probably every year and we would hours crafting sleighs from abandoned wood so we could use them in the snow," A sigh escaped my lips as I reminisced. "This snow, although beautiful, is not the same without Elena."

The fallen angel male besides me remained silent for a couple moments, perhaps thinking of the most appropriate thing to say.

"Elena - your sister...do you miss her?"

"Of course I do."

"Well, would you like to go and see her?"

I froze.

___

hiya!i'm so sorry this update has taken such a while. i have been so busy but i am so glad ot finally have more time to write. your comments and votes are what keep me going - thank u!

pls dont forget to comment and vote!

-j x

CHAPTER NINETEEN

I t had turned out Julian had been sent by Azriel to ask me that very question - if I wanted to go back to the mortal lands to see my sister and father.

I guess it must have struck him how much I had seemed to think about them recently, especially with the Christmas months drawing in. It was a time I cherished with them both every year- although this year was about to be very different.

The following morning after myself and Julian's talk, I found myself in front of my dressing wardrobe rummaging for something to wear that wasn't black, tight or revealing in line with true Velastillian fashion. I was compelled by Azriel to give Cirse the morning off in order to keep our plans about visiting the human realms quiet.

Julian sat at my window seat, his back slouched against the wall with his long legs sprawled as he watched me.

"So, what does one wear in the human lands?" He said.

I continued to rifle through the endless dark clothes in my wardrobe, growing frustrated due to how every time I'd think I had found something suitable to wear - it would end up having a plunging neckline or be cropped at the stomach.

"Layers," I answered without sparing a glance in his direction. "Just wrap up - its never warm in my area of the human world."

"And which area, to be exact, is yours?"

"A village. A small village who believe many things about your kind." I paused on a black dress, but after seeing the length I tossed it onto the pile of rejected clothes I had accumulated. "They probably believe I've been murdered already either by a monster or a pack of wolves. I was their sacrifice."

"And a very good one," Julian raised his brows as I continued to toss clothes into a pile on the ground, "I don't think anybody would have reacted this well in your position, Adeline. I think that is why Azriel's found it within himself to risk everything just to let you visit your family."

I sighed, pushing the brunette hair out of my face. "I just hope it's worth it."

He slowly rose from his seat, tall and overpowering thanks to the steel and leather armour he wore on his body, and begun to head to the door. "I'll be waiting for you downstairs alongside Azriel. Try to make your journey downstairs discreet if you can." He took a step outside the door, and before it shut he popped his head back in. "Oh, and that black blouse would look killer on you."

I chuckled to myself as the door shut behind him and pulled off the satin black blouse from the hanger. No cuts, no plunges, and not too dramatic. Perhaps he was right.

Standing in front of the mirror, I tugged the blouse over my head and buttoned the cuffs before adjusting the fitted sleeves into place. For below,

I pulled on some simple black pants and stared at the complete outfit in the mirror - although the outfit wasn't what I noticed first. My eyes instead darted to my ears, still pointed. I hadn't looked at my reflection in the mirror for so long that I had almost forgotten my identity - and my ears, my fairy ears. I also noticed my physique and how I didn't look so starved, so sullen any longer - a positive.

When I finally made my way down to the reception room by the entrance, I found Azriel and Julian waiting for me. Azriel was dressed similar to Julian- with steel and fighting leathers. Their wings were out too - dark and broad.

"Relax," I let out a small laugh inwardly, "No need to armour up so much, it's only the human realm."

Azriel raised a brow. "They were able to throw a girl into the forest on the basis of salvation. Gives me a good enough reason to believe they're radical, no?"

Prick.

I rolled my eyes and started to walk towards the main door, but still managed to catch sight of the smirks Julian and Azriel had exchanged between one another before following behind me.

"A couple of things to take note of, though," I heard Azriel call out behind me as I descended down the front marble steps of the house and into the courtyard with the two males not far. He waited for me to pause in my step and turn to face him before continuing, and I noticed how his voice was a lot lower - more secretive almost. "First thing I'd like to make clear, wherever you go either Julian or I will have an eye on you. Don't try anything stupid, or try to run because a fallen angel will outrun you. Secondly, you mustn't give your family any information on Velastille, the war or what you've seen here. And lastly - we return back to Velastille at the end of the visit. This is non negotiable. Don't make me regret taking you, Adeline."

"Were you planning this pre-adventure speech in your room last night or something?" I arched a brow at him, and Julian chuckled a low laugh while Azriel snorted dismissively. "Anyway, how are we going to get there? Do you guys even know the way? We can't possibly go on foot can-"

The last thing I saw and heard was Azriel click his fingers before my vision instantly faded into nothing but stars and blackness. My legs felt liquid - and I could no longer feel the support of the ground beneath my feet. Sharp winds blew thick between my hair, then blinding sunlight towards my eyes - so blinding I succumbed to squinting, then shutting my eyes completely.

And then the winds retreated, and my feet finally felt stable ground. Land. Human land. My home.

Hesitantly, my eyes flickered open to meet the blazing sunlight above us and I quickly shifted my gaze away from it and towards my surroundings again. We were standing at the clearing of what appeared to be a deep forest, and when our whereabouts finally registered in my head I froze.

We were in the west wood. The same wood I had been mercilessly thrown into as a sacrifice by my village.

My eyes frantically scanned our surroundings, and through the thorny brambles of the bushes where the three of us stood hidden away was when a house caught my eye.

My house.

My family's once decaying, crumbling home had been transformed into something now so warm and beautiful. The once chipping paint had now been replaced with fresh, glossy coats of white - and same with the porch and front door. Bits of evergreen and holly adorned the outline of the house's windows, and also the village's street lampposts. Houses on the same street as mine appeared to be in the same condition, glossy and refurbished, adorned with wreaths for Christmas. A smell lingered in the air - the strong scent of slow roasting turkey, or perhaps a stew. Something thick and stodgy but flavoursome.

The sacrifice had worked in their favour.

"I told you," Azriel's murmur from behind me snapped me into reality again. "If you agreed to fight, this is what I'd do for your village and your family. Not a trace of a famine in sight."

My teeth grit. "It's not as though this village deserved it. They were all evil, evil people."

"Well, I proposed the promise and you agreed. So here we are."

Deep down I knew I was grateful to Azriel for this - because I knew my family had also benefitted from this wealth, and so I didn't argue with him. With my hood up and fingers tucked into my fur-lined pockets, I made my way to the front door of my house. I made it my priority to keep my head down - avoiding eye contact from the butcher up ahead or the newsboy on his bicycle racing past to deliver a few Christmas cards.

My heart drummed in my chest as I left a sturdy few knocks on the main door. Further behind, hidden between the darkness of the tall trees in the wood, my two companions waited and watched unseen. I told them it was best if I met my father and sister alone at first.

A few moments passed with no reply at the door. I shivered, wrapping my wool coat tighter around my body. The cold temperature in Velastille seemed to be nothing compared to the negative temperatures of the north of the human world. Either that, or I had grown far too used to the Velastillian winter.

Still waiting, I spared a quick glance towards where Azriel and Julian remained hidden in the shadows. From the outline I could just about make out, I saw Julian jumping up and down on the spot in perhaps an attempt to generate heat in his body, while Azriel just stared in confusement at his friend's daft efforts. A small smile subconsciously appeared on my lips as I watched them.

And that was when the door opened.

CHAPTER TWENTY

The door opened, and a youthful- faced girl now squinted at me.

"May I help..." Her words trailed off as she noticed my face hidden beneath my hood.

"Elena," I managed to choke out, and her earthy-brown eyes slowly widened with what looked like both shock and euphoria.

"A-Adeline?"

Something in my chest broke at her voice - her sweet, youthful, humanly voice, untouched by what raged above in Pandaemonium. I wanted to back up. I couldn't do this. I didn't want to bring this upon her - upon Papa, I couldn't. Their belief in my death would have been better than this.

The next thing I knew, I had been engulfed into a tight embrace. Warmth like I hadn't felt in months coursed my veins as I returned the squeeze, feeling Elena nuzzle her nose into my neck as her soft cries muffled against the fabric of my hood. "I missed you s-so much! I thought you had d-died!"

I didn't answer, but gripped her tighter.

I believed Elena could feel my body shiver from the cold against hers, and so she quickly took a step back from the embrace and instead took my hand into hers. "You m-must come inside, it's too cold out here."

Inside, the home was beautiful. The exact same layout to what I had remembered from when we were younger, but fully refurbished - although I noticed there was something untouched and new about it in comparison to the worn love and unity in Azriel's estate back in Velastille.

Elena quickly poured me a cup of hot tea, her slender hands evidently shaking as she did so and her cheeks still wet with tears. She looked the same - but older, more mature. Her once unruly brown-blonde hair was now silken and long, and her boyish way of carrying herself had now changed into something more adult and feminine. Her skin, due to the harsh nature of the winter months, remained a doll-like porcelain colour with a glassy pink rush to her cheeks.

"I-I can't believe you're here," She said hoarsely, as she handed me a teacup and saucer. "It's been so long, Adeline - h-how did you survive this long?! Where were you?!"

I clutched onto the handle of my teacup slightly tighter. "How long has it been since I was gone?"

Elena's eyes darted away from the tea she was pouring and instead towards me, and I could see the confusion evident in her earthy orbs.

"It's been t-two years, Adeline. Two whole years."

My mouth ran dry.

Two years? How was that possible? I had kept full track of my time in Velastille - it was impossible that I had spent more than a mere seven months there, but Elena's confusion said otherwise. My mind was aching, and then I froze.

"Where's Papa?"

It felt like the only safe thing to say. When Elena didn't respond, I asked again with an increased demand and desperation in my voice. "Elena, where is Papa?"

Elena set her shivering tea cup on the low-lying desk between us and I noticed how she avoided eye contact, her bottom lip quivering. I could already feel cool tears pricking behind my eyes and her refusal to answer my question made me almost want to throw my cup of tea against the wall.

"Elena - where is-"

"Dead!" She quickly interjected me, her tone a mix of soft cry and strain. Her eyes were squeezed shut. "He had a h-heart attack a couple months after you been thrown into the woods. W-We tried to save h-him, Adeline, I-I swear - but there was n-nothing we could do!"

I was wide-eyed, my chest aching with such an ache that I felt I may collapse right there and then. In that moment I didn't care about anything - nothing, not even the two fallen angels awaiting my presence outside.

The next thing I knew, I was on my knees wailing in pain while my sister caressed my shoulder.

****

It had taken me perhaps almost an hour to calm down, to finally breathe again without tearing up. My father's death was just failing to register with me. He was old - I knew, but the fact he only suffered a couple months post my disappearance had made my mind attack itself with blame.

Elena's words of relief and love had helped me. I hadn't been comforted like this in too long of a time. It felt as though all my trapped in anxieties and suffering had wanted to spill out today - and in a sense I was glad they had.

To my surprise, Azriel and Julian were still nowhere to be seen, although in the back of my mind I knew Azriel must have been aware of every small detail that was occurring within this house. I was now sat by the crackling fire with a new, fresh cup of tea in my hands - my coat still wrapped tightly around me with my hood refusing to be pulled back.

Elena sat besides me, and lifted her hand to caress my shoulder. "Whatever the reason you're back, Adeline, I'm so happy to see you. I thought you were-"

Hesitantly, I pulled my hood back before she could go on. Elena's teacup rattled in her hands as she noticed my ears - long and slender, and undeniably inhumane.

"I was dead," I spoke slow, "I was dying until he saved me."

Elena quickly put her teacup down onto the wooden ground beneath us, the dark, rich amber liquid pooling in the saucepan as she did so. Her tone shook with suspense as she asked, "Who's he?"

I held her gaze as I said, "I need you to listen."

And wide-eyed, she did. I told her in as much detail as I could mention where I had been. I told her about Velastille, Pandaemonium and how I had got my ears. I explained the deal I had made with Azriel, and how he had promised my village riches if I were to fight for him in the war. When I finished, my sister's eyes remained just as wide as they were before - a mixture of shock, excitement and even fear present in her orbs.

"When the m-money came in, I would have never thought it was connected to you," Elena sat back, eyebrows raised as though everything that had happened in our village in the last year or so was finally making sense to her, "Papa had said the stock market had boomed. The British pound had i-increased in value, and as a result money was pouring into the village and into the council. I-I don't think anybody believed it was t-the doings of God, or even a-an angel from the legend this village sacrificed you for. They thought it was luck - we thought you had just died at the hands of a wolf. I-I can't believe it."

I held her shaking hands in my own, cold grip as I remained silent. Her chocolate eyes flickered up to meet my own.

"But what is this about a war?" She held my stare intensely, demanding answers. "You c-can't be expected to fight in an angel war, A-Adeline! You're a human, n-not a super-being! You can't do this. There is no way I'm letting you go back"

"Elena, please." I breathed, "If I don't go back, the deal will most likely be revoked and you'll go back to poverty. What will you do?! E-Especially without Papa. And I'm being trained - day and night on how to fight."

"Are they even looking after you?! They're training you but are they feed-ing you?!"

"Yes, I-I have my own room and a maid to tend for me. I g-get three meals a day, new clothes to wear, a warm bath - I share what you have here. They care for me - they were the ones who offered to let me meet you today!"

Elena brows furrowed, her expression skeptical as she slowly asked, "Who's 'they'?"

I didn't know if I would regret this, but my mouth moved before my mind could process anything. "Would you like to meet them?"

i'm so sorry for the delayed updated. i have been so busy as xmas is approaching and work is becoming busier.

i do hope u all keep coming back to this book! i promise the updates will become a bit more regular now.

thanks so much for the support. pls vote and comment!

-j x

CHAPTER TWENTY ONE

O utside in the human world, the light had already started to fade and the sky was thick with shades of navy and black and grey as I opened the front door of the house to find the two fallen angels sat on our porch - playing what looked like an oh-so-serious game of cards. From where the cards came from, I had no idea.

"What are you guys doing?" I hissed in a whisper at them, causing them to both turn to look at me from their seats. "If someone sees you two-"

"Relax, lady," Azriel raised a hand to silence me, shifting his attention back to his cards. "They can't see us. Now, are you ready to leave?"

"I think Az is ready to go. He's sick of the defeat," Julian smirked as he threw a card onto the wooden porch between them. An ace. Azriel's head threw back in frustration as he let out a groan, his counterpart gathering his winning cards with a gleeful grin.

It was just way too hard for me to believe these idiots ran a whole district.

With the mere bite of my cheek, I took a deep breath as I said, "I want you guys to meet my sister." Both the angels paused, and again turned to look at me as though I had announced I wanted to run through the streets naked. I frowned at their reactions. "What? "

"And why would we meet your sister?" Azriel asked with a skeptical brow raised.

"Just - I want her to feel at ease that I'm not living with some pyscho monsters. I don't even think she believes what I've told her so far. Just ten minutes, please." I pleaded, not enjoying even a second of it. "Just ten minutes and then we can leave."

Julian remained silent and looked towards Azriel, who was still looking at me with a skeptical expression. After a couple moments of me staring back with hopeful eyes, he sighed and rose to stand. "Fine."

After seeing them both stood by the door, ready to enter, I must have forgotten how tall they both were - and adding the length of their wings they were huge. I pulled the door open as wide as I could to let them in, and then shut it quickly against the bitter cold.

Julian let out a low whistle as he surveyed the entrance hall - not grand, but appeared regal and beautiful when adorned with all the Christmas decorations. "I thought your human village was in poverty. This doesn't seem like the poverty I was imagining."

I acknowledged his remark with a nod, but didn't comment. Nor did Azriel, although inwardly I was ever-so-grateful to him for what he had done. He had taken such good care of my family, and I was content that my father had passed in riches - rather than the rags we were once used to.

"What's these for?" Julian reached his hand out to touch a wreath which had been pinned to the wall, but Azriel smacked his hand back like a father teaching his son not to touch. I held back a smile at the sight.

"They're holly wreaths. In the human world, there's an event called Christmas where we celebrate the birth of Jesus Christ. The wreaths represent the wreath Christ wore when he was sacrificed on the cross." I explained to Julian. Azriel studied me from the side, and I could see him watching me from my peripheral vision - as though he could see the weight that had pressed into my chest since arriving here.

When I finished explaining, he stepped forward and motioned at me to lead the way. "Alright, you babblers. Let's meet your sister so we can leave."

****

Elena had been waiting in the front room - the largest room of the house, coaxing a new fire as the previous one had died down. I entered, the two Velastillian males a step behind me and it was not towards me that my sister looked when she turned around - but at them.

The two angel males - both unnervingly tall and slender and dressed in rich fighting leathers, belts strapped at the waist with varying serrated knives. Both their wings had disappeared, something I hadn't even noticed - and stood alongside them in the room in that moment - it made them look a lot more human.

Elena's eyes were wide, her mouth agape and speechless as she stared back and forth between the two devastatingly beautiful angels - and to her credit, she didn't faint.

I remained near the door with Azriel and Julian behind me, maintaining a large gap between us and Elena to give her breathing room in a space that suddenly felt deprived of air. "This is my sister - Elena."

The fallen angels bowed their heads simultaneously in respect, both their hands tucked behind their backs but Elena did not return with a curtsy. In fact she hadn't moved from her star -struck position since we had walked in.

I inclined my head to the left, "This is Julian. And his prince-" I now turned to the right, "Azriel, the Arch Angel of Velastille."

Julian passed on a warm smile to Elena, while Azriel attempted to do the same but failed. Smiling wasn't his strong point - especially in awkward situations such as this, and so I let him off.

Elena finally rasped, "D-Did you say...Arch Angel?"

I nodded.

And then she started. "Holy - am I seeing things? Am I drunk? But I haven't drank since yesterday - I can't be d-drunk, but there's n-no way I'm seeing what I'm seeing right now. H-How are t-they so tall?! So big?! I swear if this is a prank, Adeline, it isn't funny-"

"Elena," Julian interjected, hushing her. I could see how hard he was trying to hold back a laugh, "We are real. You aren't drunk."

I heard Azriel shift behind me, before muttering under his breath, "Silly humans."

I jabbed him in his ribs at his remark, and Elena quickly straightened herself out - as though she was trying to come to terms with her reality. "You guys are lucky - I was just about to serve dinner. Please do join me."

My gaze naturally flickered towards Azriel who had his eyebrows raised in hesitation, and before he could open his mouth to speak Julian chimed in, "Of course! I don't know about these two - but I'm famished."

Elena's fearful expression broke into a soft, grateful wide smile as she started guiding us down towards the dining area. I don't know why I was inwardly surprised when I had seen that the once rickety, tarnished wooden table we had grown up eating our suppers on had been replaced with one of marble stone - modern and glossy. She wasn't joking when she had said dinner was ready - there were two dishes laid out on the table already, covered with a lid to preserve warmth.

I did the two males a favour by taking the seat on Elena's left, while Azriel slid into the chair across me with Julian to his right opposite my sister - who clutched her fork so tight when he did so that I was becoming fearful she might stab him with it.

Then again, I wouldn't blame her. She reflected the exact state I was in when I had first met the angels.

Elena lifted the lids from the two dishes, one of them revealing what looked like slow-roasted chicken - large and juicy, while the other contained a variety of seasonal vegetables from potatoes to peppers tossed in what looked like a dill sauce.

In my head I thanked Julian for his eagerness to eat, because by looking at the food I had started to notice how hungry I really was too.

As I began to scoop food onto my plate with my companions doing the same, Azriel looked up towards Elena. "Thank you for this."

Elena, who appeared to be sweating due to the light glisten on her forehead, replied, "You can thank me later! I'm not a good cook - you'd rather eat up now and then decide whether you want to thank me or not. I wasn't expecting guests so I apologise for how small the meal is. I would have made you something to take home but I don't really know what angel food is! Hah! I don't even know if angels eat!"

She laughed nervously and I noticed how her hands shook around the grip of her knife and fork as she tried to slice into her chicken. I bit the inside of my cheek to stop myself from laughing at the sight, and then placed a hand on hers. "You've done fine, Elena. It was our fault for showing up uninvited."

"No, no!" She dropped her utensils in her place, the loud clanking causing both Azriel and Julian's eyes to dart towards her. Elena grimaced,
"Whoops, sorry. I think I'm getting a bit overexcited!"

Azriel raised a dark eyebrow, the corner of his mouth lifting in amusement.
"A bit?". Julian choked a small laugh at his companion's comment but
masked it with a sip of water.

After a couple moments of silence as we all ate, savouring the taste of the
nourishing food which oddly tasted no different to that in Velastille, Elena
looked to Julian across from her. "Can you truly fly?"

He paused the bite he was about to take from his fork and blinked, clearly
surprised by the sudden question but open to answering it. "Yes, we fly
most of the time but we also use horseback as a mode of transport too."

"Is it not scary though? To fly, I mean. At such a height?"

"Not really," He lightly shook his head, setting his fork down now. "We
were trained to use our wings before we even knew how to run. We have
centuries of practice, and so for us flying is how walking is to you.

"Centuries?" Elena blinked. "How old are you?"

Julian swiped his bottom lip with his tongue, and from his expression
I could've almost called him self-conscious. In an attempt to hide it, a
mischievous grin appeared on his lips. "Take a guess."

"Oh, no no. My guesses are always far too off and can be offensive-"

"I don't think any of your guesses will be offensive, believe me." Azriel
interjected, amusement clear on his face and Julian nodded in agreement -
both eagerly waiting to hear her estimate.

Elena took another long glance at Julian, as though she was using her
chestnut-coloured eyes to scan his face for age.

"Twenty one."

Julian frowned slightly. "What?"

"I think you're twenty one."

Silence in the dining room. Silence to the extent even I was grinding my teeth into my lip and pressing my nails into my palm as I glanced between the two angels who both wore stunned expressions, waiting for one of them to say something. Was she right, or wrong?

And then the next thing we knew, Azriel and Julian were howling in laughter. Julian had his hands in his face as he did so, while his Arch Angel slumped back into his chair in hysterics. I sat awkwardly, unaware to what the joke was, and when I glanced sideways at Elena she was in the exact same position as me - although she was nervously laughing along with them.

I clicked my fingers to catch the attention of the two jokers, a frown indented on my face now. "At least tell her if she's correct or not."

Azriel ran a hand through his dark hair, using the finger of his other hand to wipe away a tear threatening to fall from all the laughter. "You weren't joking when you said you're always way off, Elena."

I rolled my eyes, and when Azriel saw my unmoving, unamused face his laughter began to falter. He jerked Julian with his elbow to provoke him to do the same.

"Well, how old are you then?" Elena stared at them both intensely, her fingers tapping on the stone of the table as we anticipated their reply.

"For starters," Julian tried to control his re-emerging smile, "I'm over four-hundred years old, and Azriel here is in his five-hundreds."

My jaw fell agape the exact same time Elena's did, and we both didn't make an effort to hide it. In the human world they could have passed as between twenty to twenty six judging by their exterior looks - but hundreds?

"We've existed long before you two were born, although some of us like to act as though it is the other way round," Azriel smirked slyly as his gaze fell to me, and I sensed what felt like the tip of a shoe nudging against my calf. I retracted my leg sharply, shooting him a glare with as much hate as I could muster in that moment only causing his smirk to grow wider.

"That's crazy!" Elena slumped back into her chair, her eyes wide with disbelief. "In that many years you could have travelled the entire earth, eaten so many cuisines and had so many girlfriends! Wait - do angels have girlfriends? Do you even experience emotions?"

Julian's gaze dropped to his empty plate and I watched him as he avoided eye-contact, clearly a cue to signal Azriel to answer instead. And so he did - although he didn't look half as comfortable answering the question either. "We do. We experience every form of emotion and desire that humans do - sometimes to a more intense level."

Julian nodded in agreement with his Arch Angel, then added, "And this 'girlfriend' culture that the human realm has - we do not. We don't think of lovers as something barely significant - in fact, we believe every being in Pandaemonium has a respective partner who has been written for them in the stars. We call this a starmate."

I found myself listening just as attentively to their words as Elena, both of us consumed into wanting to know more about such powerful beings. Through this interest, I found myself asking a question too.

"How does one know they have met their starmate?"

From my peripheral vision, I felt Azriel's auburn eyes flicker towards me. When I looked to return his gaze, he shifted his attention to Julian.

"It isn't a simple process. The two mates have to have created a strong bond between each other - without knowing they are mates. When both mates reciprocate the same feelings for each other, both of them should expect to see a shooting star one night in the sky. This signifies that they have found their written starmate who their soul has been entwined with."

While Julian explained, I hadn't even realised how fast my heart was beating in my chest and how clammy my palms had become. I was unsure as to what the cause was - but simply just hearing all of this, I wanted it to be my reality. I wanted to have a starmate written in the stars for me - a guarantee that I would find loyal love in my lifetime at one point, but my hopes turned to ashes as soon as that desire appeared in my heart.

I was a human, not an angel. If I had a partner written for me - he would be of this land, and that seemed to be enough motivation for me to want to return to the human realm as soon as I could.

"That is a beautiful way of finding love," Elena breathed and Julian nodded to signal his agreement. Azriel, oddly, had been awfully silent since this topic had started - avoiding eye contact and twisting the rings which adorned his slender fingers.

"You don't have a lover?" Julian flicked an eyebrow up at Elena, who gulped down a healthy amount of water from her glass before shaking her head quickly.

"Nope."

"I find that strange for a beautiful lady like yourself."

Both my eyebrows raised at the comment as I looked from Julian to Elena - who's cheeks had already started to flush. It was true though, Elena was beautiful; some would say the more beautiful one of us both. Her rich silky blonde hair, honey skin, chocolate eyes and plump rose lips were surely a dream.

"I've never had a boyfriend for that matter. I'm only eighteen, but at my age Adeline already had many admirers. One was a boy named Nate who-"

"Thanks for such a lovely dinner, Elena. You've become such a good cook," I sharply interjected and quickly rose from my seat, the chair groaning against the wooden floor, "But I think it's time to leave."

Azriel's eyes tore towards me, intense and glaring - glaring so bitter and deep that it was almost as though I could feel his gaze set aflame the skin on my face. I didn't dare look at him although I very much knew he was looking at me.

Elena and Julian both shared puzzled expressions at my sudden outburst, but in the moment I possibly couldn't have cared less. Pulling down my coat which hung on the dining room door, I glowered at the two angels who, to my surprise, were still sat.

"It's not safe for us to fly back in this weather, Adeline." Azriel murmured, his voice sharp and impassive as he kept his eyes towards his half- empty plate. "I think we should rest here for tonight."

He cannot be for real.

CHAPTER TWENTY TWO

A DELINE

To my great dismay, Elena had reminded me that there was only one spare bedroom within the house with just one double bed. Julian had insisted on taking the couch, although I knew it would be too small for his over six foot build, but he had reassured us that he would be comfortable. That left Azriel and I to the bedroom.

I sighed at the one double bed in the centre of the room as Azriel shut the door behind us. Slightly annoyed, I quickly turned to face him. "There's no way I'm-"

Azriel lazily lifted his index finger and out of nowhere a single bed appeared in the corner of the room. He plopped down onto it and lifted a leg over onto his other thigh, starting to remove his dark boots, "Your sister is a delight, Adeline."

I didn't even acknowledge his words but instead stared at the mystical bed which he had summoned from thin air in disbelief.

"Y-You just...how did you-"

"It actually shocks me you both are sisters," He continued casually, kicking off his remaining boot and then leisurely sprawling himself onto the magical bed, "You're nothing like her."

"I guess not," I shrugged, perching myself onto the double bed I had now claimed for myself. "We grew up polar opposites. I was always known as the fiery one, and her the poise and sweet daughter."

Azriel clicked his tongue, resting an arm behind his head but gave no response. In the midst of all the conversation I had realised I had brought no night clothes, and that the warm fleeces I had clad myself in would be far too hot to sleep in.

Great.

And with that, a snap of Azriel's fingers and my nightclothes - the same black satin pyjamas I wore on my nights back in Velastille appeared on the bed beside me. I also instantly happened to notice a pair of dark coloured lace placed besides them.

"Lingerie? Seriously?" I held the flimsy underthings on my finger and wafted them in the air, unamused.

Azriel barked a laugh at my reaction. "It was a hard choice but I thought this was the one you'd look best in."

"You're so annoying," I rolled my eyes, snatching the pyjamas from the bed as I head into the adjoining bathroom to get changed.

Once I emerged, the room which was once cold and desolate now felt toasty and warm. Azriel was led in the bed he had summoned from wherever, his back toward me, and a few candles were lit around the room. I didn't even bother asking where they had come from, and instead slipped between the sheets.

A couple moments of silence passed between us and I was beginning to think the dark-haired angel had fallen asleep, until I heard him suddenly say, "I feel like everyone failed to protect you growing up."

My body paused where I lay and with confusion from where this had come from, I replied.

"And what makes you think that?"

"You were the family breadwinner from such a young age. A vulnerable, young girl forced to venture out into dangerous areas of her village to hunt food to eat."

"That's just how it is when your village is struck by poverty," I said quietly. "Not like you'd really know much about that."

"You had been going into the West Wood to hunt food alone since you were only seven years old, Adeline."

And then I froze.

"I have never told you that."

"You have."

"Azriel, I have never told you that I begun hunting at seven. How did you know that?" I demanded. Any warmth in my voice had leeched away.

There was a couple seconds of pause before he simply replied, "I just guessed."

As much as I didn't believe him, I didn't bother arguing. He must've guessed - there was no other logical explanation for him to know that, and so my restless mind convinced me it was just merely a coincidence.

"Anyway," I murmured, returning back to the conversation prior. "I may have not been protected, but if I hadn't been thrown into those woods that one night then my father would have died bound in the clasps of poverty and famine. He got to feel a full belly and a warm house before he died. Besides, if you hadn't found me then I wouldn't have a highly-skilled, undoubtedly professional archeress to fight for you in this war. You'd probably be sat in the estate bored out of your mind too without me - I bring humour to that place. It has the atmosphere of a cardboard box."

He let out a soft chuckle, "Perhaps so. You humans are so stupid it becomes funny."

"Excuse-"

"I wouldn't have it any other way, though," He filled in before I could grumble at him, "It's nice to have someone who challenges me from time to time."

"I'm sure you love it, cocky bastard."

Another soft laugh into the night.

"Perhaps I do, Adeline."

I wasn't given enough time to reply before the golden flames of the candles which ignited the room were suddenly extinguished, plunging the room into pure darkness.

------

ahhhhhhh guess who's backkkkkk

finally got a chapter in lmao but i'm so glad to be back with this book. id recommend refreshing ur memory of the book considering it's been so long.

thank u so much for following along! please comment and vote if you enjoyed!

- j :) x

CHAPTER TWENTY THREE

A DELINE

The next morning we arose to the sweet songs of sparrows, a melodious tune I had forgotten about during my time in Velastille. The three of us had breakfast with Elena - a breakfast of various fruits and pastries. What would've once been juicy and delicious, now ash in my mouth.

As midday in the human realm fast approached, Azriel had made it clear that we needed to leave. He and Julian agreed to wait outside while I said my final goodbyes to my sister.

"When will I see you again?" She asked nervously, her chocolate eyes welling up with tears. She gripped my hand anxiously as if she was scared to let go.

"I'm not sure, Elena. I'm really not." And that was the truth. I wasn't sure how long it would take to convince Azriel to bring me back to the mortal lands.

I wasn't even sure if I would make it out alive.

"But," I continued, using my thumb to wipe a couple tears which had escaped her eyes while I choked back my own, "What I do know is that your life is going to be beautiful. You have a beautiful house, you will find a loving husband and have a wonderful family here. And best of all - you have Papa and Mother's memories."

"I won't have a sister," She rasped, "I thought you were dead for so long Adeline, but now knowing your alive, living with...with angels? How can I go about my life like this?"

"You have to. You have to live this life for me, Elena. For the life I couldn't have."

My younger sister remained silent, her eyes to the ground as she sniffled. I engulfed her into a warm hug in an attempt to provide comfort, feeling nothing but intense pity for her. Something in me wanted to stay here forever - to hide away in the house and not return to the immortal lands, but I knew that wasn't an option.

I gave Elena a final squeeze before I head for the door, tears prickling behind my eyes. Outside, Azriel and Julian waited for me. I had expected them to be doing something empty-headed like playing cards or arguing about who had the best style in tunics yet instead they stood silently as if they knew this whole situation was difficult for me. Within a couple minutes of dark smoke, we had returned to the immortal lands of Velastille.

Back at the estate, I retired to my room immediately and did not come down for dinner that evening.

****

A few days had passed since the last time I had seen Azriel. As for Julian, I had seen him earlier in the morning through my bedroom window at the stables; chatting with the stableboy. Celeste however, I hadn't seen since we had taken back the Velastillian weaponry from the cavern in Zybern, along with a few precious potions and tonics which she had indefinitely stolen while we were there.

It was only late in the afternoon but the moon had already made an appearance, glowing yellowy-white and loomed large in the blue-black sky. A couple million stars sprinkled behind it, a few large ones but mostly a multitude of little white pin pricks. It looked so lovely that I took a book from the shelf provided in my room, and head down the corridor towards the back garden of the estate.

Passing by one of the drawing rooms of the house, a voice rich with regal British accent called to me from within.

"Adeline."

And when I peered in, of course - of course - Azriel was lounging on one of the tufted chairs in front of a large window which had been accented with grand taupe-coloured jersey drapes. He had an arm slung over the back of the chair while his other hand idly gripped a glass of what looked like Rosé, a glass bottle full of it set on the table before him. His dark wings were draped behind him onto the polished marble floor beneath us.

I cleared my throat. "You called?"

He lazily gestured towards the empty seat across from him with his free hand - not a fruitful, glowing invitation but I still walked over and sat down anyway.

Besides the glass bottle of Rosé was a white envelope, the seal of which had already been broken. I could have sworn I smelt the ashes and the smoke and the soil which was Zybern. "What is that?"

"Open it and see."

Gingerly, I pulled a letter from the envelope. Black watery ink had been used on a sheet of parchment paper, and the Arch Angel spoke before I had the chance to begin reading.

"In the district of Zybern, when a crime has been committed by residents of the district or non-residents, the perpetrator receives a letter to their home - an official declaration that they are being hunted. It arrived a little under two hours ago."

I could have sworn I felt my blood run cold. "We rightfully stole back what was ours - I don't see the issue here? Besides, it's been over three weeks since we set foot in Zybern."

"You made a mistake." He said, massaging his temple. I opened my mouth but he went on. "You knocked the guards out, using the bow and arrows stamped with Velastillian weaponry. It took the Arch Angel of Zybern, Raphael, not long to understand the attack was from us. Yes, we took back what was ours, but Celeste also stole tonics precious to them."

"He would have noticed the tonics and potions were missing soon enough."

"Perhaps we could deny we stole them and leave it to coincidence," He took a drawl from his glass. "I should have put the guards to sleep from where I waited at the border, wiped their minds and manipulated their souls so that you didn't have to shoot the arrow. I made a mistake."

I lounged back into my chair, unsure of what to say or do. Silence engulfed the room until Azriel looked to me,

"You have been told you are an enemy of Zybern and you are relaxed about it?"

"I am not. But it was not your fault and not mine - and perhaps Celeste can't be blamed either."

He loosened a breath, staring out to the bright Velastillian city lights which glowed beneath us in an array of whites and icy blues.

"Perhaps you could replicate the tonics and return those instead of the original, and apologise?" I suggested.

Azriel snorted, swishing the bubbling drink in his glass. "No. He isn't stupid and it'll only anger him more."

"Then just return the original tonics?"

"No." He chewed the inside of his cheek, "It was a good steal - could be helpful to us in the coming months."

"So, let me get this straight. You want to be on good terms but you don't want to just return what we stole?" Amusement laced my tone.

He gave me a half smile. "Feuds we just started could last centuries - even millennia. I guess if returning the tonics is the cost I must pay to keep our alliance with Zybern in the war, then so be it."

"How noble of you."

He gave me no reply, and so it became apparent to me he was in a tensed, distressed state of mind.

Watch it, Adeline. I cleared my throat, "Do the others know - about the letter?"

"Celeste brought the letter to me. I'm debating how I'll tell Julian - if I tell him."

I rubbed my palms together to generate heat, noticing that he had not lit the fireplace which consumed majority of one of the walls in the room. "I am sure you, being the Arch Angel of Velastille, can sort at least something out with the Angel of Zybern? Just give it a chance, perhaps you can visit him. Ask for forgiveness - or at least try to - and we'll move on with preparing for the war, preparing the troops and stopping the King from attacking and enslaving other angel districts and the mortal lands."

"You speak as if you plan on staying here a while."

I scoffed, "I have no choice."

Come on. Wink at me, laugh at me, smirk at me - just stop that stern expression.

All I got from him was a lean over from where he was sat in order to pour himself some more alcohol, and then swiftly stood up in one fluid regal movement. "I'll think about what to do. In the meantime, enjoy your book in the yard."

And with that he left me in the chilled room with nothing but confusion splayed on my mind as to how he knew where I was going.

****

"Try not to hesitate so much with your dagger," Julian said to me three days later, as we spent the expectedly cool afternoon in the garden. I believed Azriel was busy and so I had Julian train me for almost majority of the week. I took another strike towards the target he held, off by a couple centimetres again. "Honest opinion, do you think I'd survive on the battlefield right now?"

"Honest opinion - probably not." Julian tried to hold back a smile and I rolled my eyes jokingly in response.

"Isn't that brilliant."

"There's no chance you'd survive anywhere if you have Julian training you."

Celeste stepped into the garden with us, a casual poker face written on her sharp features. I couldn't help but stare at how she radiated grace, dressed in a tight cropped black tee which cut just above her navel along with a pair of dark cargos and boots.

"Carry on like that Celeste, and I'll drag you here and see how much training you've been doing." Julian scoffed at her.

Celeste held up her midnight blue coloured nails, checking them - an act she shared with her male cousin, "Touch me, Julian, and I'll chop your micro-penis off with no effort."

He let out a low chuckle. Standing between them, a dagger gripped between both my palms which were clammy with sweat, I considered using this child-like feud between the two as an opportunity to slip out and return to my chambers. Five days of this - of training physical combat with Julian and yet I still felt I made more progress with Azriel, wherever he was.

I had not heard of any updates regarding the situation with the letter from Zybern, and I wasn't quite sure if that was a good thing or not. What I was sure about, however, was that Azriel would deduce something from the situation and devise a suitable plan - he always did no matter what, and so I had let the matter go to rest in my mind.

"Hey, where'd you go the other night?" Julian stood back into his stance as he stared down Celeste, his tone more accusatory than curious.

Celeste's eyes narrowed. "What night?"

"The night Az and I took Adeline to the mortal realm. I was told by the stableboy that he saw you leaving the estate a couple moments after we had left."

Celeste held the stare with Julian, her wolfish eyes reflecting a piercing glare in his direction. For a quick second her attention flickered towards me - as though she was checking what sort of reaction I was having, making sure I was not seeing her as the weaker, vulnerable one in this situation. "The last time I checked, Julian, I don't answer to you. Or report to you. So where I went is none of your concern."

"You didn't tell Azriel either."

"Well-"

A dark, unearthly feeling of presence cut her off. Azriel strolled into the garden, approaching us, and I failed to decide whether I was relieved or disappointed that Julian versus Celeste had been put to a halt. He was in his casual attire, fine clothes woven with the highest quality of silk. His strenuous dark wings which normally trailed behind him were no where in sight today.

Azriel looked between them both and then towards me, and the daggers I held in my hands, and then said, "I feel I interrupted when things were getting interesting."

"Fortunately for Julian's cock, you arrived at the perfect time." Celeste seethed, brushing her dark hair from her shoulder in one fluid, regal movement.

Julian snarled at her while I stood in between awkwardly - as I had been doing for the past however long.

Azriel playfully rolled his eyes and while tucking his hands into his pockets he asked nobody in particular, "Ready to go on a little trip?"

Celeste raised a perfectly shaped eyebrow. "Where?"

"Zybern."

"They invited you?" Julian asked in confusion.

"Wrong, I invited myself. Celeste, Adeline and I are going tomorrow."

"We are?" Celeste and I chimed in unison.Clearly Azriel still hadn't told Julian about the letter from Zybern and I guessed it was because he simply couldn't be bothered to explain it to him.

"Zybern is full of arrogant assholes," Julian warned, "I should come with you."

"I agree. You'd fit right in!" Celeste crooned sarcastically.

Julian snapped back almost instantly. "There's a reason he's chosen to take you over me, my love."

Celeste stuck up her middle finger at him, scoffing in disgust at the remark. Azriel massaged his temple, his tone hesitant. "Julian, considering what happened last time you came along with us to visit Raphael-"

"Oh please. I've explained myself a-gazillion times - I thought he said throw the steak, not stow the steak!"

"So you decided to throw the steak from your plate right at his face?" Celeste asked unamused.

Julian shrugged while I had to gnaw eat my lip to stop a laugh from emerging, "I thought he wanted to have a food fight. You can't blame me-"

"Either way," And Azriel cut him off, "Considering the fact Celeste knows how to deal with the Zybernians better than we do, I think she would be a better choice."

"Celeste knows how to deal with any male better than we do." Julian muttered under his breath. "Whore."

Celeste's eyes flew open with rage. "You little fucker!"

This just got interesting.

And that was when I felt an elbow to my rib. Azriel was staring at me, and mumbled quietly enough that the two fighting adults wouldn't hear as they cussed one another out. "The fact you're enjoying this. You're a little sadist, Addy."

I frowned, my tone sharp but quiet. "Firstly, don't call me that. And secondly, no I'm not. Speak for yourself, prick."

He smirked, and then turned back to his two accomplices - probably realising that he should intervene before his counterparts fought till the death.

"Children, children," Azriel stepped between the pair, raising his hand. "Let us not forget our humanity."

"Humanity? You say that as if she knows what that means." Julian huffed, much to Celeste's dismay. Shaking her head, she stuck a slender middle finger up at the Arch Angel's left-hand man before storming back towards the estate. Julian, also clearly bored, bothered and annoyed, flounced after her.

Alone, Azriel and I watched them retreat - him smirking in amusement while I blinked in an attempt to register what just happened.

"They get like that sometimes," He shrugged, turning to face me.

"I was waiting for one of them to turn the other one to dust or something."

A low chuckle into the night, to which I saw an opportunity to comment. "You're in a better mood - it seems you took my advice to visit Zybern and apologise."

He scoffed jokingly, "Don't place so much importance on yourself. It was the only reasonable option I had."

"Of course you'd never give me the credit. Typical you."

"Typical me?" He repeated, his voice now low and drawly. "You say that as if you know me, Adeline."

"It's not hard to understand how you are. Cocky, arrogant and a bit of a dick when you're stressed." I now held eye contact with him - those gold eyes piercing right back into my own. His stare was almost blinding, and it took plenty of effort to refrain from looking away.

A corner of his mouth lifted. A smirk.

"I was a little rude to you back in the drawing room when I informed you about the letter, wasn't I?" He purred, amusement lacing his tone. "Perhaps I should make it up to you.'

My mouth went dry. But fighting with him was fun, perhaps I could learn to entertain his flirtatiousness - give him back something he would never expect.

And so I closed the distance between us, smoothly stepping past him so close that our bodies brushed against one another, and I could have sworn I had almost heard his breath hitch. "Maybe you should. And whatever you choose to do, I'll be waiting for it."

With that I began to walk away back towards the Manor House - and no matter how badly I wanted to turn back round just to catch a glimpse of his reaction, I didn't.

"You're a wild one, Addy." I heard his low, rich voice teasingly call out to me. "Perhaps it's time I treat you that way too."

My cheeks were flustered and burning with heat before I had even got back into the house.

---

ahhhh an update!

I know its been so so long, but every time I come on the app and see how well Azriel is doing - it gives me so much motivation. I want to thank you all so much for the support you're giving my book, I LOVE you all so so much!

im so sorry for the delayed updates. im at uni and stress and work can really build up but I really am going to aim to update as frequently as I can (and not months at a time) so please don't give up on the book!

if you enjoyed the chapter please please drop a quick vote. thank u so much for the support.

- j xxx

CHAPTER TWENTY FOUR

A DELINE

In the end, only Celeste and I joined Azriel in his journey to Zybern with Julian remaining behind to guard Velastille.

Azriel and Celeste were dressed in their typically regal attire - both wearing black accentuated with threads of silver and white. Nothing but the best for the Arch Angel of Velastille and his cousin. For my own clothing, I had opted for something with a little more colour; a baby blue flowy dress which ended at mid-thigh, accompanied by sheer dark tights.

For my hair, Cirse had crafted it into a simple loose braid cascading down my back. It had swished as I had descended the final two stairs and hopped into the foyer to join the dark male. He had simply cast his gold eyes in a swift glance from my silver-slippered feet to my hair, and with a subtle nod said, "Good, let's go."

My mouth popped open, but Celeste explained with a swift eye roll, "Don't mention it, fairy-girl. He's always pissy."

I watched as Azriel held out his hand to me in an invitation to come closer. He lifted his free hand, and a concoction of sleek black smoke with chimes of sparkles began to appear from his palm - exactly like how it had once done when he had taken Celeste and I to the border of Zybern the first time when we had been tasked with stealing back our weaponry. My eyes squeezed shut tightly, somewhat nervous somewhat panicking as the black smoke began to consume the surroundings - engulfing us tightly before I felt my feet lift from the ground beneath me.

Within seconds I had been placed on solid base again, and when I mustered enough courage to open my eyes I was shocked at our surroundings - the same bone-chilling, cavernous, dusty land Celeste and I had found ourselves upon when stealing back the weaponry - Zybern, the land of the Angels of Death.

We seemed to be upon a gravel path, standing tall in front of us a spine-chilling, almost grotesque looking chateau. I noticed a flock of crows circling their way around the building, and my body shivered - the blood in my body running.

For all I knew, the crows were most likely a creature far more deadly than what I thought.

"Welcome to Zybern, Arch Angel." A figure stood forth from the shadows, tall and slender. It took my eyes a few moments to focus, and I took in his ghastly pale skin and coal black eyes and carven cheeks. His robe matched the colour of his orbs, and the shadow the hood cast over his face left an ambiguous aura about him - something almost sinister yet beautiful.

"Arch Angel Raphael." Azriel nodded, and dropped his head in respect.

Arch Angel. He was one of the five.

I couldn't help but notice how different the two Angels were, and why I had always thought they'd be alike. While Raphael's presence, masked by shadows and smoke enrobed in dark felt eerie and ominous, Azriel almost illuminated - exactly like the moon in a night sky, his aura regal and imposing.

Three other people emerged from behind Raphael, all of them with frowns of confusion of varying severity. Like their Arch Angel, they were all pale - as though they had lived away from the sun for most of their lives, and their eyes were two orbs of black and nothing else. It was almost like they were dead.

Well, that would explain them being Angels of Death.

All at once, the Arch Angel and his disciples' eyes turned towards Celeste and I.

Azriel slid one hand into his pocket, and with the other gestures towards Celeste. "Celeste, commander of my armies. I am sure you remember her from our previous meet over dinner discussing affairs." Cool, calculating grace.

Raphael gave Celeste the briefest nod, without saying anything else. Instead, his gaze shifted back to Azriel. "And the other one?"

"We thought it would be best not to bring him." Azriel shrugged slightly, and Raphael's expression seemed to give away that he was relatively pleased with the decision of leaving Julian.

And suddenly, his gaze shifted to me. Pointing forward a long, pale finger adorned with silver rings toward me, he asked "And her?"

I could have sworn my breath hitched in my throat.

Azriel gestured to me. "Ah, this is Adeline. An apprentice within my army. I hope you don't mind me-"

"Bold of you to bring along the very two acquaintances who stole from my land, Azriel." Raphael interjected, and the people behind him glared at us - glared so intensely it felt like their gazes had gone straight through me.

Wicked, cruel - that's what Celeste and I - what Azriel was to these people. Of course we were, the very people they were hunting had shown up to their doorstep.

"I don't believe there is theft in simply taking back what is yours."

The Arch Angel of Death raised a brow, and said carefully, "It looks like you have an explanatory tale to tell."

"Precisely," Azriel shifted his hands into his pockets, a classic motion. "We best go inside."

"Could I interest any of you in a drink to accompany that?" A voice spoke from among the shadows, and from the glass door of the chateau stepped out an unfamiliar woman.

Raphael seemed to know her, and placed a hand on her shoulder, "Aerith, Arch Angelaina of Zybern."

She was stunning, and I couldn't quite comprehend how I had encountered so many attractive bodies in my time here. It was as though they were all individually hand-crafted, moulted carefully to be the perfect version of themselves.

Aerith was tall, perhaps taller than Celeste but stood shorter than Azriel. Like her people, she was pale - but it complimented her carved cheeks and thick lashes. Unlike her people, her eyes were far from a midnight black, and instead were icy blue - heavily contrasting against the other muted tones of her face. Her body was slim, not boney like what I was becoming, and her hair was thick and jet black. The silk dress she wore adorned her body in the most beautiful of ways, accentuating her curves - exactly what I presumed Azriel's type to be.

I couldn't make out who she was, Raphael's wife or his daughter? Or simply another ruler of his capital? I was quick to scan there being no ring on either of their fingers, but they both looked young enough to be married or paternally related.

"Your grace," Celeste murmured quickly, nodding her head in respect for the Arch Angelaina. I figured she recognised the lady, but was not familiar with her presence.

"An honour," Her sweet, plump pink lips carved into a smile which screamed cunning of the highest degree, and it didn't take me long to notice her gaze was fixated on Azriel, "And a pleasure."

Azriel seemed to recognise her stare, and he returned it - cool, swift and calm, "The pleasure is mine."

"And so it is," She murmured huskily. I noticed her dark almond-shaped eyes briefly sweep over the Arch Angel beside me from head to toe before gesturing towards the door. "Do come in."

Tension. I couldn't place my finger on what sort of tension there was between them - whether it was promiscuous, spiteful or otherwise.

My stomach churned at the thought.

We were led into a palace crafted of rock-flecked walkways and walls, windows tall with all curtains drawn as if daylight itself was a threat. Black glass chandeliers adorned with candles provided the only light into the hallway. Servants and courtiers hurried across and around, most white-skinned and clad in loose, black clothing - almost similar to reapers themselves. Their dark eyes beaded towards us as we crossed their path, perhaps aware of our fate, aware we were the hunted individuals their city sought.

I remained a step behind Azriel as he walked at Raphael's side, while Celeste remained within reach and I wondered if she was also to be my bodyguard. Raphael and Azriel had been talking lightly, bland conversation, both already sounding bored.

Aerith, the Angelaina of Zybern, walked close to Azriel.

"I hear you are hosting the annual event for the Blossoming this year," Raphael said to him, looking over to the male on his left.

Azriel took a small nod, "You hear correct." Blossoming? It was an event I didn't recognise - or been informed about.

"I take it you will also be drinking surely, as a host?" Aerith posed to Azriel, her voice sickly sweet such as a berry drenched in sugar, and her body language almost seductive. To that the Arch Angel replied with smooth grace, "I would like to think I will be observing this year, rather than participating."

The corners of the Angelaina's mouth raised - a cunning, immodest smile which felt like ammunition to my eyes, "What a shame, after the amusement and pleasure of last year I would have thought I would see it again."

"You heard His Grace, Aerith." Celeste suddenly interjected from beside me and I noticed a flicker of revulsion across her stern features.

My stare darted from her to Azriel, who avoided eye-contact with Aerith and tactically chose to remain silent. Even Raphael hadn't spoke a word to us in a few moments, and I couldn't decide whether he chose to ignore his Arch Angelaina's vulgarness with Azriel; or simply remained unaware.

Whatever was going on, had I not had the status of Azriel's lapdog in this gathering I would have asked immediately. All I knew was that it left me, and it seemed Celeste, uncomfortable.

Raphael led us into a vaulted room and black oak and brown glass, over-looking the mouth of a mountainous terrain that stretched on forever, and we all seated ourselves around the opium pearl table.

"So, Adeline. How do the lands of Pandaemonium compare to the ones you have seen?" Raphael's eyes slid to me, and slowly he pulled down his hood to reveal his dishevelled coal-coloured hair. An attractive blood-sucking vampire - that's what this man was.

I felt Azriel's gaze on me, and I automatically presumed Raphael meant the fairy lands I had 'originated' from. My hand lifted to release my hair from behind my ear, curtaining my pointed ears - once rounded and human, "Everything in Pandaemonium is lovely, although I have only seen Velastille and Zybern."

Barely. I had barely seen Velastille, and Azriel still hadn't completed the promise he owed to me to visit the city.

Aerith leaned closer to me, as though she was surveying my presence, "And how, exactly, do you fit within Azriel's court?"

A direct, threatening question asked after a roundabout one from what appeared a jealous, curious female—to no doubt get me on uneven footing.

It almost worked—I nearly admitted, "I don't know," but Azriel swiftly said, "Adeline is a member of my Inner Circle; - a warrior who will be fighting alongside my people in the War."

Both the Arch Angel and his...lady took the response as an invitation to return to more important matters, the reason we were here - the supposed theft committed.

"I take it you are aware of what happens to those who steal in Zybern," Raphael said, his tone stern, "It is not daily the individuals being hunted appear at our doorstep." His glare flickered from Celeste to myself.

"Indeed," Azriel shifted in his seat, swirling what looked like fizzing alcohol around in the small glass provided by the palace's courtiers, "And therefore we have come to ask your forgiveness."

Raphael scoffed, amusement laced on his features, "The Arch Angel of the Night Sky asking for forgiveness? Surely you can do better, Azriel."

Azriel sniffed at his wine—and I wondered if he was trying to piss them off by implying they'd poisoned it as he said, "I prefer to resolve things in a civil manner, and with the War upcoming I think you and I both have greater things to focus on."

Raphael raised a steady brow, "Do not dismiss me Azriel."

"It is not a dismissal," Azriel shrugged, "I have brought the very tonics stolen from you in hopes of your forgiveness."

I had to hold myself back from letting my expression demonstrate my surprise. Azriel had not seemed content with returning the tonics the last time we had spoke, what changed?

We all looked towards Raphael, waiting for any response. He held Azriel's gaze, both of them holding a glare so deep it almost made me uncomfortable.

"Very well," Raphael replied, relaxing into his seat. I heard Celeste release an unhinged breath she must have been holding in from besides me. "Present them to me."

With the unbothered wave of his hand the very potions Celeste had stolen from the cave appeared within Azriel's grip. He offered it gently to the Arch Angel across from him.

Raphael obliged, holding each small bottle between his fingers and observing them carefully, "These have not been used?"

"Not even opened," Azriel finally took a sip of his wine, "Just as they took them."

Raphael set down the potions looking mildly satisfied, but Aerith drew closer - her features inquisitive, "I know you, Angel of the Night District. You must have an ulterior motive, something you require from us as a result of you returning the potions so casually."

Azriel tilted his head to the side, letting out a small low chuckle before raising his gaze to challenge Aerith's, "Then you know me better than what I thought you did."

She edged closer in her seat, maintaining eye-contact. A self-satisfied smirk played on her plump pink lips, "I know more to you than just your outside, Azriel."

I felt Celeste shift uncomfortably besides me, and I too felt that familiar feeling of my stomach churning upon her words. What the hell did she mean by that?

"I think it is enough I spare your two accomplices from the bounty placed upon their heads, don't you?" Raphael asked - a complex, calculating question.

"I don't think we should forget who stole what first," Azriel checked his nails briefly, "You're forgetting what you owe us, Raphael."

"And what will that be?"

"A pardon. And then no one has to know that the Arch Angel of Zybern was struggling to supply his own weaponry and so he decided to steal my family's Swords of Michael. You can't hunt me for stealing your potions, but I can behead you right this moment for stealing my parent's swords."

Raphael's eyes grew dark, haunted upon his words, "Do not threaten me in my own home, Azriel. My patience only goes so far."

"It is not a threat," Azriel countered, "It is the truth and you know it."

Raphael fell silent, and all our gazes fell onto him, waiting. He looked helpless, and with a defeated sigh he nodded, "Very well."

"Then I believe my business here is complete," And with that Azriel rose from his seat. Celeste and I mimicked him quickly, not knowing what to do besides follow behind him as he left the room.

As we got into the hallway, Celeste nudged Azriel, "I cannot believe you actually returned the potions."

"I didn't," Azriel smirked, amusement gleaming within his aflame golden orbs, "I gave him replicas."

"As if," I spluttered, and Celeste's eyes threw wide open too, "You crazy bastard."

And then we were winnowed away back to Velastille but instead of focusing on the sensation of my feet coming off the ground, all that occupied my mind was Azriel and Aerith.

****

hello!! I'm back!!

man, it feels good. as I've said multiple times, I've been going through a lot the past couple months but the amount of positive reviews and feedback im getting on Azriel is so crazy! I love it so much!

you guys are the one thing keeping me going. thank you for loving this book so much.

in the meantime, what tf is going on between Aerith and Azriel and wtf is the blossoming?!?!

please remember to drop me a vote if you enjoyed and a comment if you're feeling it! every little helps!

stay happy!

- J xxx

CHAPTER TWENTY FIVE

J ULIAN

Having to remain behind while Azriel, Celeste and Adeline took to duties was not something Julian was not used to. In fact, he enjoyed his moments of solitude - opting to offer a helping-hand in the estate stables or looking to silly little errands around the home.

Today he had decided to head to the library. It had been a while since he'd picked up a book - by a while, perhaps four days, and he was beginning to feel the withdrawals. Soon enough he found himself walking through the corridors towards the family library, and just before he was about to enter through the sliding glass doors he had heard the sound of a book page flipping .

His heart sank.

He had managed to catch the gleam of her reddish-brown hair before he had quickly pressed himself around the corner of the wall in hopes she hadn't seen him. Leave, a part of him screamed, you embarrassed yourself the last time you saw her when you spoke to her drunk.

Stay, another half hushed at him, you know how badly you want to speak to her.

And so he obliged, taking a solid deep breath before slipping through the glass doors and into the library.

"Hello," he murmured softly, and shut the door carefully behind him.

Cirse was reading in one of the lounging chairs, hair fallen in front of her face and a book spread across her lap. Julian's abrupt arrival had taken her by surprise, and she quickly glanced up to meet his gaze. The young male read her expression - she was taken aback, but somewhat glad to see him.

"Hi," She replied, and the sweetness of her voice was like hot honey being poured into Julian's ears. He hadn't heard it in so long, "I thought you had gone out on the errand today?"

"Not me," Julian let out a nervous laugh as he took a hesitant seat across from her, "I think Azriel thinks I'm a bit incompetent when it comes to speaking to other Arch Angels."

Cirse shut her book, leaning forward with an amused yet interested expression upon her fairy-like features, "And why is that?"

So Julian proceeded to tell her about the incident with the Arch Angel of Zybern and steak, to which he had Cirse laughing so much she almost fell out of her chair. It was a sight he knew he could never bore of.

"How has it been - living at the estate with Adeline?" Julian had asked her after the two had finished exchanging laughs back and forth.

Cirse nodded, a gentle and fluid motion. "It's been wonderful so far. I really do like Miss Adeline, and caring for her too. Although, one thing I will say is caring for her means I'm barely able to wander freely around the estate. When she is at training it is usually just a visit to the house library and back for me - I would love to go for a stroll within the gardens without feeling like I have to rush back inside."

Julian blinked a couple times - taking in what the pretty female across from him had said. He didn't think he had heard her speak so much, and in one go, to him ever before.

Smiling faintly, Julian asked, "Well, would you like to take a walk within the garden, my fair lady?"

She seemed so small before him, so fragile compared to the scales of his fighting leathers, the breadth of his shoulders. The wings peeking over them. But Cirse, to his surprise, did not back from him nor shy away as she nodded.

The silver-haired male, graceful as any courtier, offered her his arm and she obliged - and for the first time he felt her soft milk skin come into contact with his. Heat radiated from Julian's face and when he looked down to the lady by his arm he noticed colour bloomed high on her milky-and-honey cheeks.

And with that he led her downstairs and out to the estate garden, sunlight bathing the couple.

****

ADELINE

When we were returned back to the estate, I was in subtle surprise to see Julian and Cirse arm in arm on what appeared like a walk together in the gardens. It had been a while since I had seen the two interact but it warmed my heart - and I couldn't decide whether I was happy for them or was simply jealous of not being able to attain what they had.

Celeste had just walked by and head upstairs without paying much mind to them - a classic move from the dark-haired angel. The two had caught Azriel's eye though, and I had noticed a flicker of disapproval across his features before he too also head indoors.

Why would he not be happy for his second?

Tired from the visit to Zybern, I opted to return to my chamber. Azriel and Celeste had disappeared, to their own affairs I presumed, and I enjoyed the feeling of solitude for the first time in a little while as I wandered down the hallway towards my bedroom.

"Adeline!" I heard a voice call out from behind me, and when I spun around I was faced with Julian quickly pacing after me down the hall, "How was the trip?"

I raised a suspicious brow, "Why aren't you with Cirse?"

I watched, having to bite my tongue to withhold a smile of amusement as Julian's evidently became nervous. "I have no idea what you're talking about, I wasn't-"

"We all saw it," I mused, my tone teasing as I turned back around to continue towards my room - an indication for Julian to follow, "You're not fooling anyone."

From behind me, the silver-haired male raced to keep up with my strides in desperation, "Did she say anything to you regarding me? Does she speak about me in general?!"

I allowed Julian into the bedroom before me, sliding the door shut behind us and supporting my back against it while I stood. Azriel's Second in Command perched himself onto the edge of my bed - his eyes eager.

"Sometimes," I nodded truthfully, "She'll ask me about you sometimes and gets really shy about it. It's so cute."

"Fuuucckk," Julian plopped back onto my bed, his hands behind his head, "She is so perfect."

Make yourself at home.

I gnawed at my lip for a few moments, debating in my head whether it was the right thing to do before blurting out, "Hey Julian, what's the Blossoming?"

I saw the young male's chest pause in movement, before he slowly sat up. His tone was now bleak, "Who mentioned the Blossoming Night to you?"

"Raphael said Azriel is hosting it this year."

"It is just an annual event which takes place."

I raised a suspicious brow again for the nth time, "What does the Blossoming Night celebrate?"

He rubbed his neck, "Well, it is a spring event which takes place following the Winter Equinox. It just has a few strange deep-rooted rituals. You will probably see a lot of females around, a lot of them from other districts too, mostly dressed in...revealing clothing - and sometimes the other Arch Angels are present also."

"Females in revealing clothing?" I almost spat my words, "Is it an event or an opportunity for a private show?"

When Julian failed to reply for a few moments, I made my way over to the bed and plopped down beside him, "Well?"

He shrugged, and I could tell he was struggling to articulate the necessary words. "After the Winter Equinox, which is passing now, a lot of males find their Starmates - the women they have been destined to be with. The bonding between the two must be consummated and this takes place on the Blossoming Night."

Though I tried to ignore it, my chest caved a bit.

"What about the males and females who haven't found their Starmates?"

Julian took a heavy swallow, "Well, that is why a lot of women dress in revealing clothing. There is a lot of alcohol involved on the night, and males can be attracted to the scent of their Starmate which will often lead to plenty of couples to sleep together that night. The clothing is there as another lever for attraction - to attract a male who could be the one."

I hadn't even realised how hard my finger nails were digging into the palm of my hand, and I had to pull back quickly before I drew blood.

Julian, who had probably realised I was uncomfortable, attempted to stand in order to make his way out - but I gripped his arm quick and tight enough to get him to sit again. I had questions dotting within my mind and I needed to ask.

"What's going on between Azriel and Aerith?"

Julian's iced blue eyes snapped towards me, a glimmer of surprise written upon his face. "What do you mean?"

"Oh, you know exactly what I mean, Julian. I know it might not be any of my business but I'm purely curious, is there something going on between them?"

"What makes you think that?"

"Well," I leaned back onto the bed, using an arm to support my weight as I tried to recall the strange occurrences between the two, "She asked him if he was drinking again this year. Her body language was super seductive

- she was basically undressing him with her eyes. She also said something about not only knowing him from the outside - God knows, it was all so weird."

"Ah," He chewed at the inside of his cheek for a few moments, "They have a bit of history."

"History? How so?" I probed.

"They've been sleeping together for a few yearly Blossoming Nights in a row now. I haven't really ever questioned it."

I could have sworn I felt bile and vomit rise in my throat.

"But isn't Aerith the Arch Angelaina of Zybern? That means she is Raphael's mate, doesn't it?"

Julian clicked his tongue and shook his head, "Not really. She was initially the Princess ruling over one of the areas within Zybern. One day we just heard that Raphael had taken her as his lady, and she was now the Arch Angelaina. Most people think she did it for status, not for love - meaning I'm 99 percent sure they are not Starmates, which therefore means she is not a legitimate Angelaina and nor will her offspring with Raphael be."

I blinked, attempting to process the information. So many thoughts, so much confusion, so many questions ran, poked, swirled within my mind. "Is Raphael unaware?'

"Of what? Azriel and Aerith's little affair? Raphael has known since the first Blossoming event it occurred at; almost everyone within the courts know. It happened first at Raphael's own district - he was the host. He has never questioned it, whether it was to Azriel or Aerith. Az is the most powerful Arch Angel to ever walk, being a fallen angel with rich lineage; Raphael would know better than to confront his acts - as vile as they are."

If Aerith and Raphael were not Starmates and she along with Azriel would sleep together every Blossoming Night - didn't that mean he was drawn to her beauty, attracted to her scent, attracted to her.

Didn't that make them Starmates?

My heart sank deep into the pit of my stomach, so far it deemed difficult to be retrieved. When I had been silent for at least a couple minutes in an attempt to gather my thoughts, Julian placed a hand on my shoulder, gave me a small perhaps comforting rub, and then left.

I didn't head down for dinner that night.

Instead I stayed in bed, wrapped between the silk sheets while my thoughts consumed me. Azriel and Aerith together, that was fine - fair enough. I knew we owed each other nothing beyond our promises to work and fight together.

He could still be my friend, my companion - whatever this strange relation between us was. His taking someone to his bed didn't and shouldn't change those things.

In honesty, I guess it had just been a relief to believe that for a moment, he might have been as lonely as me.

****

stop I lowkey feel so so bad for Adeline, she can get on my nerves sometimes but right now I feel so bad :(

and so the secret is revealed.

let me know what you think, and please please don't forget to show your support thru comments and voting for the chapter! I really appreciate it!

love u all too much, thank you.

- J xx

CHAPTER TWENTY SIX

A/N - After the previous chapter, I have had a few questions regarding what I envision Az and Adeline to look like more realistically if they were a person and not through art. Although I think the art I have in my 'Cast' section depicts them with enough space for your imagination, for those of you who wanna know what myself as an author think they look most like then you can find the photos above! (yes azriel is still art bc i just don't think i could find a man who matches azriels features enough to my imagination and yes it's a rhys artwork but he looks similar to how i picture azriel - again, this isn't an ACOTAR fic so they're completely separate!)

ADELINE

I hadn't even realised I had fallen asleep, and so when I jolted awake out of my slumber I had completely forgotten where I was for a few moments.

Moonlight danced upon the mountains beyond my open windows - a feature which failed to give me a hint of the time of day as Velastille was always dark. The utter silence which had fallen around the estate was what prompted me to check the clock on the wall.

Three in the morning.

I had just sat up in my bed when my bedroom door creaked open, and entered Cirse - clutching a book in her hand. She must have returned from the library, excited with a new read.

Upon seeing me awake, her face dropped into a surprised expression.

"You're awake ma'am?"

I pushed my chestnut hair out my face, not failing to realise how much healthier it was starting to feel compared to the brittle, damaged hair I had once arrived to Velastille with, "I suppose so."

"Is there anything I can help you with?" She asked with genuine concern, and I gave her a warm smile, shaking my head.

"It's late, Cirse. Why don't you head to bed?"

"How about a bath? And then you can have something to eat? You did not have dinner - there are left overs in the dining room."

As much as I wanted to pass, the idea sounded far too appealing and so I agreed. Cirse head straight to the en-suite connected to my room and began to run a bath for me.

Once in the tub, I took my time. And behind the locked door, I closed my eyes and appreciated the feeling of the water against my bare skin - almost like a warm embrace, something I had not received in so long. I didn't get out from the bath until the water had gone cold.

Cirse was sat in the window seat in my room, invested deeply in her book. Once she caught sight of me in my towel she immediately stood to tend to me, drying my wet hair into tender waves and applying the lushest, thick lotion to my face and neck. After providing me with a fresh pair of silk, pearl-coloured pyjamas, she retired to bed.

Although it was four in the morning, I couldn't deny the pang in my stomach from hunger and I had to fight myself to head down to the dining room. Walking through the halls of the estate in such bleak silence was so strange to me, almost eerie with the only light source being the moonlight through the windowed walls of the corridor.

And when I entered the dining room, Azriel was lounging on a side sofa in almost total darkness besides the burn of a candle on top of the marble fireplace.

"Shit!" I gasped, quickly reaching to snap the light switch on in order to illuminate the room, "Why the fuck are you sat in the dark at four in the morning?!"

All he did was arch a brow at me, taking a quick sweep of me from head to toe with his gaze. I took one look at his hand behind his head, the long legs draped over the edge of the sofa, and ground my teeth. "What do you want?"

"I was just enjoying myself before you came and disturbed it. What do you want?"

I walked over to the dining table, a bowl covered in aluminium foil catching my eye. "I was hungry. Is there a problem?"

A glimmer of amusement flickered within his burning-gold eyes. "You're so much more hostile than usual. Is something wrong, darling?"

I twisted my face in disgust, "Do not."

Pulling off the aluminium covering the bowl, I revealed a portion of what looked like pasta in a creamy sauce. My stomach almost grumbled at the mere sight.

"I have a problem, Adeline," Azriel announced, massaging the area between his brows.

"And what is that?" I tried to keep my tone neutral, unbothered and inattentive as I grabbed a fork and took a seat at the dining table in a chair facing towards the sofa.

"I seem to feel slight regret for tricking Raphael with the potions. He might have been an asshole for stealing my Swords of Michael, but I like Raphael. Heck, I even like Aerith. I'm feeling like it was a bad idea."

"Well, he doesn't seem to like you if he stole from you." I took a bite, and had to withhold myself from making any sound when I realised how good the sauce was.

"Aerith has mentioned that he speaks a decent amount about strengthening our alliance often, so I'm under the impression he does."

"Oh?" I wasn't even able to swallow my food before the bitter words spat right out my mouth, "That's a strange thing for Aerith to mention while you took her to your bed."

Azriel's eyes immediately snapped towards me, cunning - like a wolf within a snow-raged storm in hunt for food, "What?"

I swallowed and decided I wasn't hungry anymore, so I stood up to put my bowl away - making sure to avoid eye contact at all costs. "You heard me."

From my peripheral vision, I saw Azriel stand - a graceful, slow movement. "So is this why you won't look at me? Because you think I fucked her for pleasure?"

"Why else do you fuck someone for multiple years in a row?"

He came towards me with slow, long strides but I stood my ground, even as he stopped with hardly a hands breath between us. He looked down at me from his height, his aflame eyes melting my olive-green own. "Is somebody jealous?"

"Why would I be? About someone who fucks other people's wives for pleasure?" I challenged.

His snarl was soft yet vicious. "Pleasure? You think I practically sold myself to Aerith for pleasure?"

"What else could it be?" I spat at him.

"Velastille a couple years ago was under threats from Zybern. We were not always alliances - they wanted to invade us, but under the radar so that none of the other districts would find out. I met Aerith at the Blossoming moons ago, we became friends and that was when she told me about Raphael's plan. She also happened to confess she was attracted to me, and said she would happily tell me any insider details about what was going on within the walls of Zybern...if I slept with her. And so I did." He took a step closer to me, and I took a step back. "Do you think I particularly felt good about having to take a married woman to my bed? Do you think I felt good about doing that? Do you know how much alcohol I would have to down before I even did it? Velastille as it is right now, peaceful and calm, the people happy and content - this is why I did it."

"She clung to you like she was expecting it again this year."

"And I am sure," Azriel said, his breathing uneven. "you saw I didn't pay any attention to her. I broke anything we had between us last year and I promised myself that even - even if such a situation was to happen again, I would never put myself in such a low position for a second time."

I stayed silent, opting to keep my mouth shut while he remained merely inches away from me - so close I could smell his sharp cologne scent and the heat of the air from his nostrils. I think he realised the flicker of fear in my eyes, because instantly his features softened and a gleam of that usual amusement came to light.

"So," His eyes flickered down to my lips, then back to my eyes, "Am I safe to assume you were jealous, Adeline?"

This time I chose not to shy away to his gaze, and instead leaned in closer to him - both of us maintaining intense eye contact. Our breath intermingled, and I couldn't deny how hard my heart was drumming in my chest, "Maybe I was."

He raised a brow, a slight smirk spreading on his lips. Nonetheless, his voice remained low and husky, "I knew it would come out at some point."

I rolled my eyes and tore away eye contact, turning to leave - but he had other plans. His one hand immediately snaked around my waist and shoved me against the wall; not hard enough to hurt, but hard enough to make a statement. My eyes flew wide in shock.

"What?" I tried to keep my tone bitter, but I'm almost certain he picked up the slight quiver in my voice.

"Tell me."

"Tell you what?"

"Tell me you were jealous."

I scoffed, giving him a look. "You cannot be serious."

His grip around my waist somewhat tightened, his warm palm on my smooth skin through the silk pyjama shirt. My body shivered at the touch - realising I was so touch deprived. "Tell me."

Azriel's face were merely inches away from mine and I could feel my chest beginning to race at the unfamiliar close proximity of our bodies. His grip was tightening and I could feel myself giving in before-

"I was jealous," I breathed, "I was jealous of you and Aerith."

A satisfied smile grew on Azriel's soft lips, and I almost let out a sigh of relief when I felt his hand on my waist slightly loosen.

"Good girl."

I felt my the breath of air I was taking hitch in my throat.

Azriel took a step back from me, releasing me of all touch. With that he head towards the door, slow strides, before turning around at the last minute to face me - his gaze so piercing I had realised the reason I had been too shy to go against him at all tonight.

"You've been thinking about the tour I promised you around Velastille. Tomorrow evening, then. Stay ready, and perhaps don't wear something that'll distract me."

With that he left me stood disorientated, walking away into the night of the corridor.

And before he left I could have sworn I saw that damn playful smirk on his lips.

****

ahhhhhhhhhhhhh az and ad moment omg as an author writing this I was so damn excited that they're both having a tension moment for like the first time in twenty mf six chapters LMAO.

im so happy im becoming regular with this book again! its mt pleasure to be writing for you guys, and oh my god we are almost at 50k reads WTF? this is insane I love you all so much!

please please don't be a ghost reader! please show your support with a little comment (don't force it!) and a push on that vote button. as an author, nothing motivates me more than you guys. tell ur friends and family (ok maybe not ur family) and get them readinggg!!

how did you find the chapter?

love you all sm,

- Jen xx

CHAPTER TWENTY SEVEN

A DELINE

Following Azriel's promise, Cirse had helped me in getting ready to go down to the city - having ran me a bath and then proceeding to touch up my makeup while I slipped into a florally silk dress which reached above my ankle.

"Have you been down to the city before?" I casually asked Cirse while she puffed a brush padded with blush across my nose.

She shook her head. "I've never really had the chance. I lived on the outskirts growing up - the struggling areas. I've never seen the actual city of Velastille. I hear it's amazing."

I shrugged, "We will see. Why don't you get Julian to take you one day?"

Cirse's eyes flickered towards me before returning back to the brush against my skin. She remained silent for a couple moments before letting out a hesitant laugh, "No..no, I don't think me and Sir Julian are... like that."

A teasing smile picked up on my lips which had been blushed a gorgeous nudey pink colour, "Are you sure?"

"Yes!" She answered almost too quickly, and I let out a small laugh at the sight.

She ran her long fingers through my chestnut hair. We had decided to keep it down today, leave it in its natural form with gentle waves.

"You will need a pin. Let me grab one for you," She suggested, and spun round to head to the dresser. However, as she did something small and silver fell to the ground.

Curious, I knelt to the floor to pick it up. It was a silver- plated necklace, the charm shaped in the form of a feather with what looked like carvings inside it - almost like an emblem or flag. Slowly rising with the necklace in my hand, I asked Cirse, "This fell from you."

She turned around to face me, holding a couple gold pins in her hand - but I noticed how her expression immediately dropped when she saw me holding what was in my hand. As quick as I'd ever seen her, she rushed towards me and almost snatched the jewellery from me, shoving the pins into my hand.

"Sorry," She muttered, shoving the necklace into her pocket again. "I didn't realise."

I blinked at her behaviour, confused. I was curious as to what the necklace even was, but having caught sight of the time behind her on the huge clock which stood in my room - I knew I had to go and meet Azriel downstairs.

"Is everything okay Cirse?"

She nodded quickly, forcing a smile. "Yes ma'am. Everything is fine!"

Still confused at her odd behaviour, I nodded, slowly taking her word as I head to the door. "I will be back before midnight."

Making my way down the marble staircase, I saw Azriel waiting for me by the main door of the estate. His wings were out, dark and big behind him and he was dressed in a casual black button-up and black jeans. He eyed me, his gaze flickering over the silk dress which clung to my body - midnight black, as per Velastillian fashion, then to my hair - natural and long, and then my face.

He hummed, perhaps out of satisfaction at my look as he took a step closer to me. "Kept the hair natural today?"

I nodded.

"I like it."

I held eye contact with his gold orbs before rolling my eyes and looking away, much to his amusement. He casually lifted a hand and swirls of fog and smoke began to engulf us, and I bit my lip to hold in the squeak when I felt my feet come off the ground. It was a sensation I still wasn't used to.

And once I had touched ground again, and the swirls of smokes and mist began to clear I had finally understood why Azriel had called Velastille the most beautiful district of all.

It was unlike anything I had ever seen before. The night sky was crisp, starry - illuminating. The streets were busy, even for seven in the evening - but then again I had to remind myself I was not in the mortal world any longer. There were tea and cake shops with delicate tables and chairs scattered at their fronts, all full of laughing, chattering Velastillians. Little children with miniature wings chasing each other. An old man stood within the corner with a pot of a rich thick, purple liquid attracting a lengthy queue; I had presumed it was some sort of Velastillian wine.

The starlight and the abundance of fairy lights strapped to every wall within the marketplace seemed to be enough to illuminate the city so greatly. I was taken aback.

"Welcome to Velastille," Azriel said to me, "Let me show you around."

And so we walked through the bustling streets of the city centre together. Azriel kept a few steps away, his hands in his pockets as he offered me bits of information about the area here and there. No one avoided him - no one spat at him or whispered about him as we walked past. Instead they gawked and stared at him in awe, those walking past him falling into a slightly bow and curtsy and a "Good Evening, Your Grace" finished with a beaming smile. Azriel just simply returned the warm smile, nodding his head in acknowledgment at them whenever it happened.

I also noticed people's eyes on me - confused, wandering, curious who accompanied their Arch Angel. I just chose to stay silent as I took in the city, offering smiles here and there.

As we walked further into the market place, the sound of music began to entice my ears. My eyes widened.

Music. Musical instruments. I hadn't heard them since I left the mortal realm.

I hadn't even realised I had started to walk somewhat faster towards the sounds too, following the musical notes through the streets and crowds until I reached a central marketplace. By the fountain in the centre stood a few angels, all tall and dark-haired like their people, each with a different musical instrument in their hand. I managed to identify a banjo and a wooden violin.

"This is Melody Square," Azriel explained, appearing beside me. "It is known for the finest music, using the finest musical instruments."

He must have been right. I had never heard anything even similar to the musical pieces they were playing. Upbeat, blood- rushing - it felt like I couldn't stand still.

I was snapped out of my musical trance by a tug on my dress. Confused, I down to meet the sight of three little girls - perhaps all seven and eight in ages. One pointed towards my hair and then another held up a hand which gripped a ton of freshly-picked daisies and chrysanthemums.

"Can we braid your hair, ma'am?"

"O-Oh," I smiled slightly, but then looked toward Azriel - my eyes seeking permission. He raised a teasing eyebrow and I nudged him hard which made him smile which I took as approval.

"Of course you can," I turned back to the little girls, who looked at each other with big, emerald eyes in excitement before gripping my hand and dragging me to the fountain. There I stayed sat and let them play, twisting and braiding and combing my curls while sticking in fresh flowers to seal gaps. I kept a distant eye on Azriel every now and then, who seemed to be distracted by a conversation with a few locals but was still in the area.

"You have such pretty hair! I've never seen anything like it in Velastille!" A girl squealed from behind me. I let out a hesitant laugh.

"Well, I think your hair is just as beautiful!"

"Are you an angel?" Another one asked, "You have pointy ears!"

I swallowed, trying to regain confidence in my voice, "No, not really. I'm a fairy, that's why I have pointed ears and you have round!"

The girls murmured something to each other in excitement but to my relief did not persist in asking anymore questions. After a couple more minutes, one of them suddenly ran off and returned with what looked like a mirror - embedded with midnight jewels around the rim.

"All done!" She held the mirror to my face so I could see my hair. It was twisted into the most beautiful single dutch plait behind my head, adorned with white and purple flowers. Two face-framing strands stayed at either side of my cheeks, and I realised for the first time in so long how alive I looked. From my first day in Velastille, to now - that pale, youthless skin and dead hair were now flourishing; my hair thick and gold and brown, and my face warmer and flushed.

My emerald eyes - for the first time in so long, glowed.

All the chattering from the girls must have caught Azriel's attention because he glanced over at me mid- conversation but then I realised he froze, not even speaking anymore. The locals with him, curious, also looked towards me but I held only Azriel's gaze - confused and shy.

AZRIEL

I stood in thorough conversation with a few locals as we discussed the impact of stocks increasing earlier this year. They had explained to me how they had received bountiful profits as a result, being able to purchase the finest fruits and vegetables for their families back in their homes.

"The upcoming War scares us, Your Grace," the elder of us all said, speaking loud above the music, "The stocks will surely drop again, the profits, the people, this beautiful atmosphere of Velastille - it'll perish."

I had to hold myself back. "And I won't allow that to happen. You are aware of that, aren't you?"

The three of them nodded simultaneously.

"We know what you're capable of," One of the younger locals, Darius, smiled at me. He and I had roamed the streets of Velastille playing together in a time, "I have high hopes for Velastille in the War."

I gave him a nod, pulling my hand out of my pocket to place on his shoulder. "Good, but let us enjoy tonight and drop the sad talk."

They all hummed in agreement, and so Darius cleared his throat. I noticed the same mischievous twinkle in his eyes that he would have as a child. "So who's the lady? A fairy?"

I raised a brow. "I knew you'd ask that. She's a trade deal we made with the fairy kingdom, she's an asset to the military."

"Oh," Darius smirked, "An asset to your bed, more like."

The others laughed, and I rolled my eyes. "Yeah, yeah. Get lost ."

"I will not lie, Your Grace," Xavier, another of the younger locals in our group spoke up, "I didn't really think you had a thing for fairy brunettes."

I gave him a look. "Right, because I don't. Why would I- "

The sounds of little girls squealing and giggling interrupted my thoughts, and I turned my attention and gaze towards them to make sure everything was alright.

But then my eyes froze.

I noticed the locals with me, curious, had also turned to look at what had cut me off. Adeline stood by the fountain, thanking each of the little girls for her hair. I don't know what made me pause - I didn't know why I couldn't simply just look away. It was like I was entranced, had a spell put over me or something.

Her hair was done up with the most beautiful flowers, the white and purple tones making her milk and honey skin glow. Her eyes from a distance met my gaze, and I felt like an absolute idiot for not being able to look away. A twinkle of confusion and shyness flickered across her face, her soft features.

And then I was nudged harshly in the rib.

Tearing my eyes away from Adeline, I looked at Darius annoyed. "The hell was that for?"

The three of them, in a teasing voice simultaneously sang, "You're staaari-iiing."

I rolled my eyes, nudging Darius back in the rib twice as hard before turning to walk over to Adeline.

The music had started to get louder, and I noticed people starting to congregate around the fountain. It got to a point all of a sudden where I was having to slip through people to get to her, but I was finding it difficult to see her.

And that's when the music got louder, and people began to dance - a country dance in groups of two.

I noticed people grabbing others into the circle to dance, and I was just about to reach Adeline when I saw a woman snatch her away into the dance circle.

"Hey, hey, no no!" I scowled, but she was already lost in the dance congregation.

For fuck sake.

I made my way out of the crowd again, back to Darius and the others. "Since when did they start dancing in Melody Square?"

"Every Saturday since you became Arch Angel," Xavier nodded at the crowd.

"Oh."

My eyes searched the dancing crowd, my people happy and joyful. There was no sign of Adeline still and I was starting to get slightly worried - her being human could be scented out at any point, and being in the centre of town for when that happened was not the greatest of places.

"Az," Darius tapped my shoulder, "She's there."

I looked over to where he indicated, and caught her within the crowd. She was being tossed from one person to another, spinning together before moving onto the next. Her freshly braided hair flew behind her, and I saw her face - her smile, the first genuine smile I'd ever seen on her lips.

Through the people she looked at me. I had noticed the crowd had ground sparser, people spreading out more which allowed to more room. I was able to see her clearly and keep her in my view.

She beckoned me over with her hand to join her on the cobbled floor but I immediately shook my head. There was no way in hell I was going down there. She could have been on her knees for me begging and I'd refuse.

Probably.

She pulled a disappointed face at me and I just leaned against the wall behind me, folding my arms across my chest in a way to say 'I'll just watch'.

She rolled her eyes at me, turning her attention back to the people she was dancing with. I couldn't help but notice how truly beautiful she looked - not that she had ever been ugly but the youth and colour returning to her face had made me realise how delicate her features really were.

I noticed how every now and then her eyes would continue to flicker back to me, making sure I was still nearby. I was a protector to her, someone she relied on, was dependant on almost.

I was so caught up in my own damned thoughts that I hadn't even realised Darius had pulled me off the wall, and suddenly I was being pushed toward the crowd.

"Hey, hey hey, no I don't dance!" I tried to dig my heels into the cobbled floor as Darius and Xavier laughed to one another, and before I knew it a lady had grabbed my arm and pulled me into the dance circle.

Fuck.

ADELINE

As I swapped partners for the nth time, my stomach aching from all the laughing of the fast-paced dance, I noticed Azriel had been flung into the crowd.

My mouth almost dropped.

He kept his eyes on me, and me him, and I noticed how both of us tried to reach each other through the dancing crowd. The music loud, the people laughing - the smell of burning fire and ash in the air.

I was pushed closer to him at a point and I held my hand out for him to grab, but was pulled to the side by another person instead. This continued, both of us in massive attempt to try and find each other within the dance when I suddenly lost sight of him again.

I continued to dance, but my eyes didn't refrain from searching the dancing congregation around us. When I hadn't seen him for a couple moments, I started to feel unsettled and anxious.

Suddenly, two hands on my waist and I was snatched away from my current partner and my back was pressed against the chest of someone else. Frowning, I turned my head to see who it was and could have sworn I had never been relieved to see Azriel before that moment.

He took my hand and gently spun me round so I was facing him now, and I locked my arms around his neck, "You get jealous I was dancing with another man?"

He let out a scoff. "I'm not threatened by any other man here, Adeline."

"I didn't think you would be," I rolled my eyes to his amusement.

"You know what I was jealous about?" He asked, and I noticed him bring my body slightly closer to his. I obliged, allowing him control.

"What?"

"You smiling. You smiling so genuinely for all these people, for this music." He murmured, "I was jealous I saw you smile genuinely for the first time, and it wasn't to me."

He took my hand and spun me around, as per the dance move with all the other couples doing the same. I didn't know for sure though, everyone else was a blur. I couldn't even feel the music anymore, my body was numb - all I felt was my heart rise to my throat at his words.

I didn't know what to say, and so I remained silent while we locked hands, spinning into a circle before he lifted me by my waist and tossed me into the air. The music had started to grow increasingly faster, and so did our dances - faster and faster before I felt like I wasn't even dancing on ground anymore. Before I felt the blood rushing through my veins, and could hear my heart pound in my ears. Before I couldn't even control my laughter at the speed we were going at.

And suddenly the music ended. And I found myself pressed against Azriel's chest, my arms again back in starting position around his neck and his hands adorned on my waist. We both panted heavy, trying to swallow to regain air flow into our lungs. Our eyes remained locked, both of us passing each other a reassuring smile, and then a light laugh at our states.

The crowd around us had started chattering again, couples beginning to disperse from the centre of the square. We stayed there. In the exact same position.

I watched as his eyes slower lowered to my lips - and this time it wasn't an action laced with tease or seduction, but instead genuineness. His hands tightened their grip onto the silk dress around my waist and I simultaneously tightened my grip around his neck, our faces drawing closer.

So close I could see his individual long dark lashes, and he could feel the warmth of my breath. So close I felt his top lip brush my bottom, my breathing stifling, before his eyes suddenly flickered back up to me and he blinked - and I could have sworn I saw a glimmer of regret. Almost immediately after that he let go of my waist and stepped back, and I stared at him in confusion but he did not return my gaze.

"A-Are," He swallowed, as though he was trying to regain his composure, "are you hungry?"

As puzzled as I was at his sudden odd behaviour, I couldn't deny the grumble in my stomach after all that dancing. I nodded slightly.

He nodded towards one of the lit cobbled alleyways which I presumed led out of the market square, "That way."

He began to walk, back to his usual stance with his hands into his pockets, and I followed behind him like a mindless puppy. I had to keep my eyes to the ground to avoid the more prominent stares I was receiving now, probably after people had witnessed what had just happened.

I would've been lying if I had said I wasn't just as confused.

***********omg stop the tension the tension the tensionwe were going to get an adriel kiss :(let me know how you found the chapppp, i took some insp from my favourite disney movie tangled of course. i honestly felt it fit the scene so perfectly.also how do we feel about an azriel pov!!!!

also major apologies for such a late upload! i had been busy with celebrations as it was my birthday week! but that's all over now.

i hope you're all okay! please please show your support with a vote and a comment! and thank you so so much for 51k reads!!!! it's so insane to me how fast azriel is gaining reads since i started uploading again and my vision of this book would have simply remained a vision if it wasn't for you all. thank you so much, truly.

love, j xx

CHAPTER TWENTY EIGHT

JULIAN

The fire was roasting away within the dining room, while Julian knocked back his final sip of red wine. Celeste sat across from him, playing about with the remaining green beans on her plate. They had obviously received the news that Azriel would dine with Adeline out in the city, and so they had dinner alone tonight.

"Something I don't understand," Celeste begun out of the blue, placing her fork down, "is why is Azriel treating her like someone special? She's a trade agreement - purely a fighting piece, why is he taking her out to see the bloody city?"

Julian leaned back into his chair. To be fair, even he was clueless as to the reason Azriel was always accompanied by the young mortal woman, and he had never asked.

"I'm not too sure," He shrugged truthfully, "Perhaps he's trying to make her comfortable, settle her in. It's probably hard to leave a whole fairy realm to move to the angel world."

Celeste rolled her eyes, also leaning back into her chair. Her arms crossed against her chest, "Something is strange. The way he acts - I never see him act. He's meant to be training her and instead he's out there running around the city with her?"

Julian raised a brow, "Why does it bother you so much, Cel?"

Celeste looked at him, her stare cold and icey as she barked a laugh, "Me? Bothered? I'm not bothered, Julian. I just don't understand why a boring little fairy who can just about hit a few shots with an arrow is starting to become a part of our Inner Three? Our circle? It took us thousands of years to establish our positions, why did it only take her a couple of months?!"

"It's Azriel's command. Your bitching isn't going to change things, you know."

Celeste raised a perfectly shaped brow at him, her feline eyes sending daggers in her counterparts direction. "We might as well get your little slave girlfriend to join us too."

"I think that's enough," The silver-haired male harshly placed both palms on the table in front of him.

"What?" She seethed, her tone somewhat teasing, "I've seen you, waddling behind her like a forgotten puppy. You're a warrior - Second in Command to the most powerful Arch Angel of all time, and you're infatuated over a girl who's not even equal to a grain of dust on my bare foot?! Ugh, please!"

Julian had already bared his teeth, and before he could snap back in anger they heard the rattling of a couple utensils behind them. Both angels turned round to catch sight of Cirse stood within the doorway, a tray with what looked like rosemary tea poured into tea cups in her hand. Her face was twisted in upset, her ocean coloured eyes filled with salt water- like tears at what she had heard. Quickly placing the tray on a coffee table by the door, she left the room without another thought.

Julian's heart sank at her reaction and his body almost instantly followed after her as though it was a sixth-sense. But before he left, he turned to face his disinterested friend.

"It's been obvious to me for a while that you're just jealous of losing Az's attention and the grip you had on him to someone inferior and your ego is making you a shitty person, Celeste. Grow up."

His words hit her like salt poured directly into an open wound, and she physically almost flinched as he left the room - not forgetting to slam the door behind him.

ADELINE

Despite the chill night, every shop was open as we walked through the city together. I remained a couple steps behind Azriel, reading the names of the shops we passed - jewellers, threaders, cafés. They had everything.

Azriel had not turned round to speak to me since we had left Melody Square, and the tension in the air was suffocating.

Eventually, we entered a small restaurant by the edge of the riverside built under a two- story building. It was beckoned with browns and golds and the smell almost made me salivate instantly. The owner seemed to know Azriel, for he approached him with a smile and gave him a hug - which the Arch Angel surprisingly allowed, and then directed us to a table out on the open balcony of the restaurant, overlooking the river.

Azriel and I walked over to our seats, the starry night crisp above us. No other customers seemed to be out on the balcony but for us, except an elderly couple who had both bowed their heads in respect to Azriel as he passed them.

Menus were already placed down on the table, and so to avoid any awkwardness I picked mine up immediately, pretending to scan the dishes on offer although I knew nothing was going in my head.

The night was cold, Velastille had just come out of winter and so I shivered slightly at the breeze which rustled the garden pots stacked for decor. Azriel also picked up his menu with one hand, then with the other free hand moved his index and middle finger. A small fire log appeared in the middle of a table, and flames of gold and amber began to dance between us.

"Anything look good to you?" Azriel asked, looking over at me. I made sure to keep my eyes on my menu.

"What do you suggest?"

"The roasted hawk is good- with the rosemary potatoes. It's pretty much the only thing I get when I'm here."

Although the idea of a hawk roasted sounded completely absurd to me, I placed my menu down onto the table. "Then I'll get that too I guess."

A waiter rushed over to Azriel as soon as he raised a lazy hand into the air, and bowed at him before asking for the order. Of course, he ordered himself a glass of white wine to accompany his meal and asked me if I fancied any - to which I shook my head.

Once the waiter left, again a couple moments of silence and awkwardness consumed us before Azriel decided to put a quick end to it.

"This is my favourite view of the city," He said, looking out to the breathtaking view we had to our sides. The gushing crystal clear river besides us, with a perfect view of the city of Velastille on the other side. In the far distance, tall grey mountains sprung into the clouds and I managed to catch sight of lights at the top.

"What's that over there?" I pointed.

"The estate," He answered, "Where we live."

"If you love the river so much, why is your house at the top of the tallest mountains I can see?"

A light smile spread across his lips, his eyes still scanning the breathtaking beauties of the view our balcony seat had to offer, "If I had it my way it would be closer to the river, but the estate is very old. My great- grandfather had it built that high and as far from the city as possible on purpose while he was in reign, to make it harder for enemies to attack. And to stop the city residents attacking his home if there was a revolt."

"He sounds like a delight."

Azriel's slight smile stretched into a light laugh, "I know. My father com- pletely changed Velastille during his reign - made it peaceful and what it is today. I'm purely just trying to maintain what he created, and doing anything I can to do that."

I watched the glimmering reflection of the moonlight in the river for a couple moments, mustling enough courage to ask, "What happened to your father?"

He fell silent for a few, tapping his fingers against the table we sat by and I had started to regret asking before he said, "He was killed."

"How?"

"Maximus, King of Ancient Pandaemonium. His brother. At the time Maximus was just the younger brother of the strongest Arch Angel in all districts and he was jealous. Of course he was, why wouldn't he be? He was so jealous, he stole the Angelican Blade my father was crafting - an extremely powerful weapon, and stabbed his brother with it. After that, he stole the Blood Jewel and reclaimed himself King. No one challenged him, no district did - why would they? He held the Blood Jewel in his Crown - something which made him so powerful he could conquer anywhere, any realm, mortal or immortal." He swallowed, "The other Arch Angels had all accepted their fates - it took me years to beg for their alliances in this War. I couldn't physically sit there and let my father's murderer wipe my district clean and make me his bitch."

I fumbled for the right response to the sorrow in his words, but my curiosity consumed me. "So you're not the most powerful Arch Angel?"

"I am," He nodded slightly, "Maximus knows it's only the Blood Jewel which gives him advantage - otherwise I am a threat to him. Without it he is nothing, and he knows that. Hence why he's been after me for so many years, because I am what he wants to be."

"What makes you so powerful? You don't have the Blood Jewel?"

"The fact I am Hybrid. I was born of pure Fallen Angel blood from my father, and the powers of my Goddess mother. They were the first couple to not be of the same specification in history- and both of them being the most superior types resulted in me being the most superior Arch Angel to walk the ground."

I shuddered at the thought - the thought I was in presence of a creature I had no idea half of what he was capable of. It had me taken aback completely.

"I'm sorry for your father." I murmured to him, trying to provide some comfort. He just shrugged, continuing to look out over the city. I couldn't help but watch the slight movement of his side profile, how perfectly crafted he was. An immortal, heavenly being I could never understand - how sharp his jaw was, or how dark his hair was, with traces of midnight blue when hitting the light. Or his perfectly straight nose. His poise, rosey lips, or the lengthy lashes which adorned his bedroom eyes.

I realised a small smirk had started appearing upon Azriel's lips, and that snapped me out of my thoughts. I frowned, confused, "What?"

"You can quit daydreaming about me now."

I felt my body flush with heat of embarrassment. "What? I-I wasn't?"

"You were, Addy."

You're so far up your own ass!"

He turned to look at me, raising a judgemental brow at me with his annoying smirk only widening. "Bedroom eyes? Really?"

My eyes flew wide in a mixture of shock and embarrassment, "You said you can't read my mind?!"

He tilted his head, a smooth graceful motion. "And you really believed me?"

"Well, not anymore but - I, ugh! I hate you so much!" I panicked, watching his set of pearl teeth appear as he laughed into the night as our food arrived to the table.

I had learnt a couple things from tonight's evening with Azriel, but perhaps the most prominent of those were that I surprisingly liked the roasted hawk, and even more surprisingly - I had started to really enjoy the young Arch Angel's company.

***********awhhhhhh my babies! i love them sm.

ALSO ALSO ALSO - i've stressed this before but i'll do it again. this is NOT an ACOTAR fanfic!! i know i may use similar art or methods to describe Azriel, but he is COMPLETELY separate to the Azriel in that book. This story is completely separate as are all my characters. Hope that clears some confusion up!

how did we find the chapter!!!please please leave a vote and a comment!

thank you!

-j xx

CHAPTER TWENTY NINE

J ULIAN

The young silver-haired male had followed the lady-in-waiting down the lit corridors, and upon entering the second floor of the estate he could hear the gentle sobbing coming from the library. He tapped a couple knocks to the door, with the sobbing almost instantly shifting to sniffles, and then entered.

"Hey," Julian murmured softly, kneeling down infront of Cirse while she sat in a chair. Her petite nose was red, and her eyes watery from crying. It broke Julian's heart. "Are you okay?"

She wiped her eyes with the back of her hands, trying to control her sniffles. "I don't understand w-why she is so horrible. What did I do to her?"

Julian used the back of his knuckle to lightly wipe the dampness of her under eyes. "There's nothing wrong with you, Cirse. Absolutely nothing. If anything, you're perfect. She's just jealous."

"Of what? This?!" She ran a hand through her amber hair and forced a laugh, "That's stupid."

"I love it." Julian admitted, "It makes you stand out."

"Whatever," The young lady sniffled in response, wiping her nose. "Why'd you come after me anyway?"

Julian was slightly taken aback by the question, but tried to regain composure. He didn't want to come across desperate, like a dog awaiting his owners return - but he also didn't want Cirse to believe he didn't care.

"Because there's something that draws me to you, Cirse." He murmured, and she looked at him surprised.

"Really?"

"Every time I see you my heart crushes under the pressure of finding you so gentle - so soft. You're what I need in this treacherous world of constant violence which is my brain."

Cirse remained silent, her big blue eyes staring at the powerful male kneeled in front of her. Julian cleared his throat, "I wasn't sure when to give it to you."

The Second pulled the small velvet box from the pocket of his fighting leathers and opened it for her. Cirse sucked in a small breath which left whispers across his skin as she took in the sight.

A silver plated necklace - the amulet blue to match her eyes but designed to show true depth of the colour when held to the light. A thing of secret, lovely beauty.

"It is beautiful," She whispered, lifting it from the box. Her eyes, dreamy, lifted up to meet his. "Put it on me?"

His head went quiet - his thoughts, everything. He took the necklace from the box as she exposed her back, sweeping her hair up in one hand to bare her long, creamy neck.

He knew it was wrong. He knew Azriel would be mad. He didn't even know if he and Cirse were mates, but there he was, sliding the necklace around her. Letting the tips of his fingers brush again her soft sweet skin. Cirse shivered under his touch.

It had never gone this far. They'd exchanged the occasional brush of fingers or link of arms, but never this. Never blatant, unrestricted touching. Wrong - it was so wrong.

He needed to know what her skin tasted like.

She turned around to face him, the amulet hanging low enough to tease his cleavage. He tried to control his gaze, but he was desperate - so desperate for her. Her innocence, her beauty, her grace.

Cirse stepped closer to him as though she had read his mind, pressing her body up against him in a way that could have made his knees buck. Without thinking, his hand slid up her neck, burying in her thick hair. He tilted her face the way he wanted it and watched as her pinkish, plump lips parted - her eyes deeply scanning his before fluttering shut.

Offer and permission.

He nearly groaned in relief as he lowered his head towards hers.

"Julian."

Azriel's voice thundered through him, halting him mere inches from Cirse's sweet mouth. Unrelenting command filled his name, and Julian looked behind him. Azriel stood by the glass door to the library, glowering towards them.

"Front room, now."

Azriel vanished, and Julian was left standing before Cirse. His stomach twisted as he pulled his hand from her hair and stepped back. Forced himself to say, "This was a mistake."

She scanned his eyes, hurt and confusion present in hers. "I'm sorry."

"Don't apologise," He managed to say, "Never apologise. It's I who shoul d.." He stood up, shaking his head. "Goodnight, Cirse."

With that Julian left the room, appearing at the doors of Azriel's front room a couple moments later. Azriel was stood towards the flames burning away in the fireplace, and turned to face his counterpart when he heard his entrance.

The young Arch Angel's face was still, like an emerging storm. Grace. "Are you out of your mind?"

Julian stood firm in his stance, adorning a mask of pure ignorance. "I don't know what you're talking about."

Azriel took a couple enraged steps towards Julian. "I'm talking about you about to kiss Cirse - an angel, may I add, whom has been hired to serve and so we have no knowledge on her. And you were about to do that in the middle of the library where anyone could see you?!"

"Drop it, Azriel," Julian had enough of withholding his tongue, "I have seen you act like this before. You killed my first love in this exact same way!"

"And you think I didn't have a reason?!"

"I think you didn't have enough of a reason!" Julian was now the male to take a step towards his opponent. "You accused her of witchcraft because she had strange healing powers you hadn't seen other angels have?! So you kill her?!"

"I was protecting our people!"

"It just feels like you're protecting your throne and your crown!" Julian's teeth bared - like a silver wolf within a cold-ridden battle. "So what, because you have don't know much about Cirse yet she is in your household you are threatened?! Have you seen the girl?! You think she wants your crown?! You're delusional, Azriel."

"Don't call me that."

Julian stiffened. "I truly think I'm her star mate, Az."

Azriel blinked. "What?"

"The way we feel together, the way we touch - how we look at each other. The undeniable attraction between us, the chemistry, the-"

"Has both of you being mates been confirmed?" Azriel's voice was pure ice, "Have you both witnessed the shooting star together to symbolise that?"

"Well, no, but-"

"There you go." Azriel growled, "And until the confirmation of the stars of your apparent mate bonding, then you will stay away from her and will not risk our household for a girl whom we have no information on."

"You can't order me to do that."

"Oh I can, and I will. If I have to remove her from here then I will. If you're wanting a fuck, Julian, then I suggest a brothel out of Velastille."

Julian snarled, staying silent. Azriel had rarely ever threatened Julian as such or merely implied to pull rank. It had stunned Julian enough to know not to continue.

Azriel jerked his head towards the door. "Out."

And on his way out, Julian made sure to slam the door as hard as he could behind him.

**********A D E L I N E

A couple of days had passed since my trip into the city with Azriel. Surprisingly, I hadn't really seen him around after that. I'd seen a bit of Celeste, but I had come to realise she simply preferred her own space and stuck to training the military or staying in her room within the estate. Julian, oddly, had walked past me every time we'd met in the corridors without much acknowledgment.

I was perched upon my window seat, head buried in a book I had found lying about on a counter in the drawing room when Cirse knocked and entered my room.

"Good afternoon, ma'am," She smiled, her usual soft look although I could very clearly sensed something different about her. Sorrow, perhaps. A forced smile.

I chose not to ask.

I closed up my book and hummed a response, watching as she walked over to my closet and threw it open. Placing my chin in my hands as I watched her, I asked, "What's going on?"

The red-haired maiden looked at me as though I was illiterate and insane, "What's going on? The Blossoming event is being held tomorrow evening and you still do not have an outfit."

Of course. I had completely forgotten about the event or anything to do with it. Just hearing the name had started to make my stomach churn with dislike.

"I can just wear anything, Cirse. It's not the end of the world."

"It is when you are the district holding the event, Adeline ma'am," She clarified, sorting through the gowns hung up. Heck, I didn't even know I had this many gowns. I couldn't even remember the last time I had opened this closet myself.

"How about this?" Cirse pulled out a short, tight, midnight blue dress.

I raised a questioning eyebrow at her, and that seemed to be enough as she slowly put the dress back to its place and began looking again. A couple moments of rummaging later, she revealed a floor-length black dress, spaghetti strapped adorned with materials of lace and silk. It was truly breathtaking.

And then the door swung open. Expecting to see Azriel there, with his on- brand cocky smile and bedroom eyes - I was surprised to be met with Celeste instead.

"What is it?" I frowned slightly, sitting up straight on my window seat, "You can't just barge in when you please, Celeste."

She balanced a rounded hip against the door frame, checking her well-manicured black nails. "Already have. I hear you're both discussing Blossoming outfits?"

I noticed Cirse slowly pull the hanger on which held the dress she had picked for me closer to her body. This, however, seemed to of caught Celeste's attention as her wolf-like snowstorm eyes snapped towards the dress.

"You're wearing that?" she pointed a dainty finger at it.

"Is there a problem with it?" I challenged, my eyes narrowing.

"Yes. The fact it looks like my dress, for starters, and the fact I will simply not let you wear something like that and upstage me at my own event. Change it."

I huffed a laugh. "Your event? And me upstaging you? I didn't realise you were this insecure, Celeste." A teasing tone from me, cool and calculated.

"I said what I said, Adeline." The feline glowered at me, sparks of rage presents within her orbs. "Change the dress, or you'll see how we go about things tomorrow evening."

And with that she left. Cirse looked visibly distraught, confused and concerned but I only sighed - sick of her typical bullying antics and superiority.

"God, she's a bitch." I muttered to Cirse's surprise, who happened to nod and squeak a small giggle in agreement. As she went to put the dress back into the closet, I stopped her.

"I'm wearing that dress, Cirse. Let's see what she has in store for me tomorrow evening then."

**********yay finally an update! sorry for how late it is. i'm moving back to uni this week and with preparation taking up all my time i was struggling to find time to write.

i suggest following me as i post announcements if the chapter has been delayed or disrupted by something happening in my life! x

hope you enjoyed this!! please give me a vote and comment if you did!

lots of love,

-j xx

CHAPTER THIRTY

A DELINE

Preparations for The Blossoming Evening had begun. From the crevice of my room I could hear the frantic sounds of servants within the estate rushing to get all the tasks done before the event tonight.

I had been alone for some time in my bedroom, unknowing of what to expect or what to do tonight. Azriel hadn't spoke to me about the night at all, and I was mildly unaware of what lay ahead.

I was just about to get up to start running myself a bath when my bedroom door flung open, and expecting it to be Cirse ready to get me dressed, I was surprised to see Azriel at the door instead.

He shut it tightly behind him, then rested against it - eyeing me head to toe. "What are you doing?"

"About to run myself a bath?" I answered, pulling a face to demonstrate my confusion.

"I think there's been some miscommunication, Adeline." He spoke slowly, "You're not coming tonight."

I frowned, "And why is that?"

The Arch Angel ran a loose hand through his dishevelled black hair, looking somewhat hesitant, "This is a very... Angel ritual. You being in a room of us is setting yourself up. If someone smelt even the slightest scent on you, we are finished. I won't be risking it."

"That is so unfair. You can't just lock me in here, Azriel."

"I'll do what I must to protect you." He answered truthfully, "So please, listen to me."

"Protect me? You can't-"

He lifted a hand as if to touch my arm - perhaps to comfort me, but lowered it before his fingers could graze the fabric of my tunic, "Stay in your chamber, Adeline."

And with that he disappeared, pulling the door tightly shut behind him.

****

I did as he commanded. Waited for what felt like hours in my room, bored out of control as I looked for some entertainment within the four walls I was confined to. I realised I hadn't even eaten dinner, and the growling of my stomach was becoming more unbearable by the second.

For the past hour Cirse had come and joined me in my room, having not been invited to the event either. We had both talked for a while, but the urge within me to see what was happening was eating me up.

From my window I could see the dozens of bonfires popping up along the far hills, and could hear the classical music and crowd in the Great Hall within the estate. It was a large ballroom I had presumed - a section of the estate I had never visited. I couldn't stop pacing up and down the room, gazing out towards the fires in the distance.

Stay in your chamber.

But a wild voice weaving within the drum beats whispered to me go.

Go and see.

By ten o'clock - only an hour into the event, I could not stand it any longer. I turned to Cirse, taking her hands into mine, "Come on, Cirse. We must go."

She quickly pulled her hands back, hesitant and nervous. "We haven't been invited, ma'am."

"And so? You'd rather sit in here all night and rot?"

"Well, perhaps if I had a nice book and-"

"We're going."

I quickly walked over to my closet, throwing it open to reveal gowns hung up neatly. I selected the lacey black floor-length dress I had liked earlier; and pulled out a gorgeous cream-coloured silk slip dress for Cirse.

We spent the next half hour adorning our hair, glittering our eyes and painting our lips. Straight after, we found ourselves hand in hand hurrying down the empty corridors. The classical music accompanied by drum beats came from far away - beyond the corridor and the palace gardens. To our luck, we came into contact with no servants as we left the estate- noticing the kitchen also empty of staff and food they had been preparing for days as we walked past it.

Rushing down the steps into the gardens, we followed the sounds of the music and distant chattering until we eventually arrived at a separate building still on the plot - I had presumed The Great Hall. It was magnificent, made from what seemed the finest architectural ability.

Concealed by the greenery of the thick shrubs which surrounded the building, Cirse and I gaped at the hundreds of people - all angels, stood about, some spilling out into the gardens. I could have pointed out who the Arch Angels were had I been blind - they all walked with great authority, representing their people and dressed in the finest of clothes.

The familiar faces of Azriel, Celeste or Julian were no where to be seen. Ignoring the tight knot forming in my stomach, I made sure to release my curled hair in front of my ears to conceal them, and then pulled on Cirse's hand - tugging us out of hiding.

"Walk with authority," I murmured to her, "Like you're supposed to be here."

And thankfully, no one looked twice in our direction as we entered the hall - walking past the Velastillian guards dressed in their typical armour of midnight blue and black who guarded at the steel door.

The exterior of the building did no justice for the interior. The Great Hall might have been the work of a God, adorned with colours of cream and white and silver. The glass chandelier which hung in the centre, supported by pillars standing tall caught every person's eye. How could it not, when it glimmered like the reflection of the moon upon a river in the dead of the night. The floor we walked upon was perfectly polished marble to match that within the estate, and provided the perfect base for what led ahead. Leading up a small set of crafted marble steps was a throne - and my breath hitched at the mere sight. It sat alone, made of moonlit crystals and the finest threads of black and gold.

It was the ideal place for a King. The official seat of the Arch Angel of Velastille.

Musicians played upon a stage crafted within the corner, and the people we passed - all angels with authority and purpose, did not look, smile or greet us.

"This is insane," Cirse whispered to me in awe, squeezing my hand, "I am in shock."

All I did was nod in agreement, barely receptive as I took in the grand atmosphere around us.

Suddenly, a man caught my eye - gorgeous in facial nature. He had black hair and the same piercing wolf-eyes I had seen before. I noticed people stare at him, some pausing conversations to watch as he sauntered through the crowd - smug and cocky.

The man looked familiar. The eyes, the facial structure, the body clad in black. He paused at a female, and when I focused hard enough; my heart sank when I realised it was Celeste. She looked pain-stakingly beautiful - what younger me would have imagined a midnight princess to appear as, dressed in a black gown far too similar to mine.

Curiosity got the better of me, and I led Cirse slightly closer to the pair - ensuring we still blended within the crowd.

The man said to Celeste, "Where is he?"

No greeting, nor formality.

Celeste had a noticeable expression of discomfort, perhaps hatred upon her face. Her eyes sent him those same piercing daggers I had experienced time before, "He arrives when he wishes to."

And with that she turned away from him, walking away within the crowd. My eyes still remained halted upon the mysterious male, the familiarity itching my brain the wrong way.

Who was he?

Hesitantly, my attention stripped away from him to survey the banquet tables covered with wreaths of fat, succulent fruit, interrupted with varieties of roast meats and bottles of fine alcohol. It might have made my mouth water, were it not for the fact that no one touched the food - the immense power and wealth within the room allowing it to go to waste.

Cirse nudged me straight in the ribs to direct my attention to another man, dressed in Velastillian fighting leathers, who had stepped onto the platform where the throne sat. He spoke to the crowd in a voice that was clear, dominant and certain. "Your Arch Angel approaches. He is in a foul mood so I suggest any alliance talks are paused until a later date, and those within the Great Hall remain in good behaviour."

And before the crowd could begin murmuring, I felt him.

The Great Hall had hushed, as though no one wanted to become evening entertainment for the predator which approached us. People started to move out of the way, crafting a clear walk way from the door to the throne.

Remembering my position, I stayed hidden among the crowd - my head low.

Julian first appeared at the door, clad in heavy armour and fighting leathers. The Arch Angel's Second - he was armed with two guards at either side as a form of security, for himself and the Arch Angel who followed him.

Azriel then appeared. Adorned in a black tunic laced with gold and iridescent thread, his power filled the hall, the mountain, the world - wherever we were. His posture was tall, his expression bored by the attention he was getting - in need of entertainment, and it didn't take me long to notice what sat upon his dark hair.

A silver crown; which danced with stars made from opal stone.

The face of midnight sky and moonlight. The most powerful Arch Angel to walk.

No wings, no weapons. No sign of his warrior element. Nothing but elegance.

The Fallen Prince.

I made sure to keep a tight grip on Cirse's hand as we stood closer within the crowd, but that didn't cease the fact my eyes remained glued to Azriel like a hawk - as did everyone else's - as we watched him walk through the cleared path and slowly climb the steps to his throne.

Each foot he set down sent a tremor through my spine.

He took a quick, lazy glance around the room - at those gathered before him, watching him. And then he took a seat at his throne - a poise, graceful, effortless movement.

Silence. Such silence I was scared - scared someone could smell my scent within the crowd or hear my frantic heart beat in panic.

Leaning back into his throne, readjusting his hips in a way which almost made mine buck - Azriel made a lazy effort to signal with his finger as if to say 'continue'.

And the second that gesture was received, the musicians begun flooding the hall with the beauty of the instruments they held, and the hall once again became enlightened with the buzz off the chatting crowd.

Cirse and I were still stood hand-in-hand, attempting to process what we had just witnessed. That was when I suddenly felt a cold hand grip my shoulder from behind.

"What in God's hell are you doing here?"

**********thank goodness i'm only a day latesorry! i moved into my new student accommodation so i was settling down with flatmates!

i hope you're all enjoying azriel still! let me know what you think and who you think the mystery man is !!!!

please don't forget to comment and vote x

- j x

CHAPTER THIRTY ONE

A DELINE

I spun around to meet the cold face of Azriel's cousin, Celeste, who started scowling at me even harder when she surveyed the dress I was wearing.

"Seriously?" Her tone was flat, judging but I held my ground regardless and dismissed it, "Why are you here? I don't remember you or server girl being invited?"

"Azriel invited us," I snapped before I could think. Of course, it was a lie - but her supremacist attitude had prodded every part of my brain already.

She looked confused, not buying it but also hesitant to accuse us. Her iced grey eyes ran another look along my dress, and then along Cirse's in what looked like disgust before she huffed, "Just stay out of my way."

With that she turned and merged away into the crowd.

"Why does she always have something up her arse?" Cirse mumbled in annoyance while I barked a small laugh in agreement.

"I wish I knew."

We spent the next hour exploring our surroundings together. The classical music along with all the rich attire created such a regal atmosphere; it was clear Cirse and I stood out like a sore thumb. I had watched Azriel a decent bit of the night too, assessing how he stayed slouched in his throne watching his subjects dance and talk - taking a few moments here and there to engage in conversation with other important looking angels who approached his throne.

I was still surprised he had not spot me.

Cirse and I had caught sight of Julian at the food table, alone. He held an empty plate in his hand, his eyes scanning the platters of food in front of him as if deciding very intricately upon what to get. I took this as a chance to slightly nudge Cirse.

"Go over to him," I whispered, to which her instant answer was to frantically shake her head. Again, I nudged her.

"You're going to regret it if you don't. You look so beautiful."

I watched as her soft face fell into an expression of thought - wondering if it's a good idea, before I shoved her again.

"Cirse, go!"

She pulled a face at me before going over to food platter area, and I almost hummed in delight when I saw the silver- haired male's look towards her in awe.

I was so caught up in watching the couple that I hadn't even realised someone calling my name from among the crowd.

"Adeline!"

I spun round, eyes darting through the people in an attempt to find the source. Again, "Adeline!"

Celeste. What the fuck does she want now?!

I tried to ignore her, pretending as if I hadn't heard anything and was unaware of her calling my name. It wasn't long till she was besides me, again grabbing my shoulder to spin me around.

"Adeline, where were you?!" She asked, a scent of bittersweet in her tone, "Have you tried any of the fruit punch yet? Our chefs crafted it from the finest berries in Pandaemonium."

"I think I am good, thank you." I forced the fakest smile in her direction, but instead the black-haired female grabbed my hand and started dragging me through the crowd. Confused, I attempted to dig my heels into the ground - but it was no use against the slip of the glossy marble floor.

Celeste led me over to drinks table, all of the beverages presented in regal glasses filled with fizz. I noticed how two glasses of a reddish liquid adorned with berries were isolated and set to the side, and she reached over to grab the glass on the left.

"You must try," She edged the glass closer to me, "It's genuinely addicting."

I scanned her expression - the random burst of emotion from her combined with her desperation to get me to try this drink made me nothing less than suspicious.

Nonetheless, I hesitantly took the glass from her hands. Her lips, painted with a bloodied blackberry colour, curved into a smile. Grabbing her glass, she raised it to mine.

"To our alliance."

I waited until she had taken a sip before I felt half as comfortable raising my glass to my lips. I attempted to reassure myself in my head - surely she knew poisoning me would risk her position.

The icey liquid tipped down my throat, a burst of fruity flavour and bubbles along my tongue. I couldn't deny - it was delicious, nothing I had ever tasted before in the human realm. Before I had realised, the glass was empty and I was already asking Celeste to pour me another glass.

That turned into another glass. And another. And another. All within perhaps twenty minutes. Upon finishing each glass in my hand, I felt this undeniable thirst in my throat which beckoned me to ask for more.

I must have had at least nine glasses before I started to realise my vision beginning to double.

Shit.

Attempting to stand straight and still, I realised Celeste was absolutely no where to be seen through the limited vision I had. The crowd around me all doubled, lights from the chandelier aching my eyes and my body struggling to maintain composure.

The bitch drugged me. Fuck.

I needed to grip on to something to hold myself straight, but every pillar within the Great Hall was out of touch due to the number of people surrounding them. I tried to form a coherent thought - look for someone who would help me like Julian or Cirse, but I couldn't make out a single face. Sweat started building up in beads upon my forehead.

I couldn't breathe. I couldn't stand. I was going to pass out; the secret would be out, they'd all know I was human.

Panic.

I fell to my knees, unable to support myself. I noticed the loud chatter surrounding me begin to ease - my heart rate increasing by every second.

And then black boots stopped in my line of sight.

Blinking to try and focus as hard as I could, I followed the body which stood in front of me to be met with Azriel's face.

I failed to register anything until he leaned down, his cold fingers lingering under my chin and lifting it. I felt eyes on me, from the blurs of the crowd surrounding us within the hall. Their gazes burnt into my skin.

Everyone noticed the push of his fingers, the predatory position he stood in as he said, "Come with me, Adeline."

Another tug on my chin, and I surprisingly rose to my feet. He led my through the crowd, my knees bucking in pain from struggling to hold my weight. He held my hand as we climbed the steps to the throne - from what I barely made out. He sat, smiling faintly at his court.

And with a pull on my waist, he perched me onto his lap.

I felt like a mouse being played with by a feline.

Azriel's hand slid along my bare leg through the slit in my dress. Cold - his hands so cold I almost yelped.

I felt his face grow closer to my neck as he whispered to me, "I told you not to come tonight, Adeline."

I wanted to respond but I failed to form even a coherent thought.

"What happened, hm?" He murmured to me, his tone soothing, "Did she put something in your drink?"

All I wondered was how he knew. He wasn't there and I was certain Celeste wouldn't tell him of her wrongdoing. I managed to nod my head to confirm.

His hand continued to stroke my thigh in long, continuous movements. Despite my vision almost being a blur, I could feel the eyes on me - some jealous, some confused.

"When the drug wears off it will lead to drunkeness. Do you want me to get rid of the drug effects?"

I nodded.

"Very well," He clicked his fingers besides me, and I felt my vision almost instantly return. However, now my body felt too loose. It felt too good, a buzz in my brain which fed me serotonin.

I was drunk.

"I like this," I mumbled to him, enjoying the knot of anxiety in my stomach disappear. He hummed in acknowledgement, and I felt his hand slide higher up my thigh - the propriety touch of a male who knew he owned some body or soul.

I noticed Celeste amongst the crowd, who instead of looking infinitely proud of herself, looked disgusted and annoyed. I smirked in her direction.

Karma's a bitch.

Despite how tipsy I felt, I couldn't refrain from listening to the murmurs of the crowd beneath us. His court looked at us with a certain amount of dislike, vulgar comments being passed back and forth between some individuals. I tried to ignore them but being drunk and lacking control of my thoughts didn't help in that.

That was until an older looking man close by to us turned to another male angel on his left and commented, "Looks like Azriel has another whore."

Whore. That's what they saw me as? The Arch Angel of Velastille's whore.

"Would you have it any other way?" Azriel asked me suddenly, his voice low.

"What?" I looked down at him, still sat in his lap, confused.

"You're thinking about the fact he called you my whore," His fingers started running circles on my thigh now, setting aflame wherever he touched, "Don't you like that?"

"H-How did you know I thought that?" I managed to mumble out to which a curve appeared on his lips.

"I have access to your thoughts, Addy."

I blinked, trying to gather myself, "You know what I'm thinking?"

"Most of the time."

"You're a dickhead for lying to me!" I nudged his chest and his playful smirk widened.

Tapping the skin on my thigh now, he said smoothly, "We'll talk more in detail about that when you're sober. For now, let us deal with this imbecile in the crowd."

Before I could reply, Azriel's voice cut through the crowd - silencing the crowd and the music being played simultaneously like thunder through clouds, "Orion."

It was all he needed to summon the ill-speaking elder man who stood in the crowd below us. Orion bowed before his Arch Angel, an undeniable resentment clear on his features as he glanced at Azriel - then me.

"How are you, Orion?" Azriel asked, his tone laced with amusement as he stroked my bare arm with his knuckles.

"Good, my lord." Orion kept his head low, refraining from eye contact with the Arch Angel.

Azriel leaned closer to me, and I couldn't even expect it as his tongue flicked my earlobe. My hips almost bucked in his lap, but I bit down on my lip to keep myself in check, "It doesn't seem that way."

Orion's face flickered with panic, his voice reflecting this as he said, "What do you mean, my lord?"

"Call my guest a whore, do you, Orion?"

"N-No! Of course not, my lord!" the male's voice shook with fear.

Azriel's lips played around my neck, pressing kisses into my skin. My eyes felt as though they were close to rolling into the back of my head from the sheer pleasure.

"What is my title?" Azriel asked Orion, raising a brow at him. The crowd, silent, watched eagerly - switching between us and the older man below us.

"Arch Angel of Velastille."

"So," Azriel checked his nails, before looking at Orion with eyes of intense calm rage, "Do not call me Azriel. You are below me, you will address me with respect. Do I make myself clear?"

Orion nodded quickly, still keeping his eyes to the ground.

Azriel raised his voice slightly now, speaking to the crowd now too as well as Orion. "If I hear anyone, anyone, bark another word about my guest I will not hesitate to break your fingers one by one while you are conscious. Is that understood by the court?"

Silence. Pure silence. Azriel was power - the court shook under his presence.

He pressed a kiss to my jaw, and I tightened my grip around his neck as he dismissively said to Orion, "Bring my 'whore' some wine."

A command. No politeness.

Orion stiffened, but strode off almost immediately. Another kiss pressed to my cheek caused heat to emerge from my body, from between my legs. I was hot - so hot, and I couldn't deny I wanted him. I did so bad, and I couldn't tell if it was the alcohol convincing me.

"Let us give them a show that'll stay engrained in their brains forever, hm?" I felt Azriel murmur, before I felt his fingers playfully stroke towards my inner thigh.

I had never wanted to be somebody's plaything half as bad.

CHAPTER THIRTY TWO

A DELINE

Azriel clicked his fingers, and within seconds the orchestra had begun enlightening the halls with music. The crowd, however, filled with people of grandeur and elegance, struggled to tear their gazes away from us.

I had become the Arch Angel's whore - the wild, dark thing he cradled in his arms.

Azriel seemed to like that thought, as moments later he looked up to me with his gold bedroom eyes glazed with something red-hot. Infatuation, maybe - arousement. We maintained strong eye contact as his hand gradually traced the skin of my thigh - higher and higher. In desperation, I even shifted closer to him - his fingers teasing near the black panties I wore beneath this damn dress.

I had been so cold and lonely for so long, and my body cried out at the contact - at the joy of simply being held and touched and feeling alive.

I felt the tip of his finger arrive at the waistband of my panties; so far from where I wanted them yet so close. My head felt so heavy I was struggling to support it, hence why I chose to drop it to between the dark male's shoulder and neck while he continued to play about with my waistband.

A dirty tease - that is what he was.

And as he did that, I looked to where Orion was standing, watching us, my wine he had been commanded to bring forgotten in his hands.

More, I wanted more so bad.

"More?" The powerful male whispered into my ear, and I jerked my hips at his voice - ignoring the fact he had yet again read my thoughts.

His finger slipped under my panties, my dress covering the scene in a manner where no one could see or make out anything within the crowd. I was flushed - I wanted him so bad. My hand brushed past his crotch, where I felt the firmness in his pants. I realised how much he wanted me back, how bad he wanted to-

He stopped.

Withdrawing his fingers from under my underwear quickly, he readjusted my dress in a way to cover my bared skin. Confused, I stared at him with a look of annoyance clear in my eyes yet he ignored it. A hand under my thighs and another behind my back, he lifted me up.

I felt his lips near my ears. "If I was going to ever make you feel good, Adeline, I would want you to be sober so you could feel every little detail of what I'd do to you."

Shivers down my spine as I clasped my arms around his neck. He carried me down the steps of the throne and then into the crowd, ignoring any stares he received as he did so. I kept my head close to his chest, my eyes shut and my head spinning in ungrateful movements which had me thinking I would vomit at any moment.

My eyes still shut, the sounds of the music and the crowd faded - until all I could hear was the mere clicks of Azriel's shoes down the grand corridor of the estate. I recognised that sound instantly.

"Where are we going?" I managed to mumble, my eyes far too heavy to keep open.

"To your bedroom, Adeline." I heard him reply, laced with that rich regal accent.

After what felt like the farthest walk down the corridor and up a staircase, he finally very gently put me down - handling me with precise care as though I was a fragile object.

Opening my eyes, we were in my bedroom and I couldn't have been more glad. An ache had started to overcome my body and I knew sleep is what I desperately needed. The dress I wore had started to itch my skin and cause me discomfort, and so without a second thought I pulled it over my head.

I watched as Azriel looked away as quick as light, "Holy shit, you could of warned me?!"

"Don't act like- like you're not dying to see," I slurred, poison still injecting my voice even while drunk.

Azriel cleared his throat and opted to ignore my remark as I climbed into my bed, pulling the duvet over me and almost sighing in relief at the comfort. "You can look now."

The young male turned, hesitating to look as if he thought I was fooling him and would still be led upon the bed in pure nakedness. Once seeing me tucked into bed, he relaxed and slowly crouched down besides the side my head rest.

"Are you going to try and get some sleep for me?" He murmured, and I nodded - my eyes already starting to flicker closed. The only thing keeping them open was how stunning he looked - knelt by the side of my bed, his dark hair messy and his crown tilted upon his head. His fiery gold eyes encased by those thick, black eyelashes and his structured features.

"I want to kiss you," I murmured, propping myself up onto my elbows in a way my cleavage was visible without me realising. He kept his eyes focused on mine.

"Do you, now?" A smirk spread across his lips. Those pink lips which looked so so... delicious.

He let out a low chuckle with snapped me out of my thoughts, "Delicious? Do better, Adeline."

"Hey!" I mumbled, my speech slow, thick and heavy as I felt my eyelids grow heavier with each passing second. I have up against the weight of my body and led back down into the sheets. You said you couldn't read my thoughts."

No answer, but instead I felt a press of lips onto my forehead, soft and mellow, "Goodnight, Adeline."

Then pure darkness.

****

I awoke the following morning, my head extremely groggy and my vision blurry. I wasn't sure what went into crafting alcohol for angels, but it was surely some strong ingredients.

Sitting up in my bed, I tried to recollect what had happened the previous night - but everything was fragmented. Bits and pieces of broken memories I was trying to pierce together - before some vivid images flashed through my brain.

Me atop Azriel, moaning - feeding into his ego, his masculinity, him.

Fuck.

I could already feel my cheeks heating up with embarrassment. He had let me do that in front of the courts - I felt like strangling him.

Pushing the covers off me aggressively, I quickly came across my naked body.

Thoughts started to race through my head - negative thoughts, negative connotations of waking up naked without a trace of memory of what could of happened.

My heart was beating far too quick. I didn't like this at all.

A gentle knock on the door, and Cirse - my maid entered. I gathered the duvet and pulled it to conceal myself, my tone frantic, "What happened last night, Cirse?"

She was carrying a tray with what looked like toast, jam and tea for me, but upon seeing my anxious and disturbed state she quickly set it down before rushing over to me. "What do you mean, my lady?"

"What did he do to me?! You must know?!"

"N-Nothing! You were drunk and were sat on his lap within the hall, and-"

"I know that," I snapped, "What happened when he took me back? Did he undress me and touch me?!"

"N-No, I really don't think so ma'am. I really don't-"

"Get him to come to my room." I seethed through my teeth. "Right now."

Panicked to see me this exasperated, the young maid immediately rose to her feet - rushing to leave and fulfil my command.

And I? I remained sat upon my bed, heart racing as I begged the only body I trusted with my soul had not abused me.

Not again.

*********not again? uh oh. what do you think she means by that :) i leave it to interpretation for now but the answer will be revealed soon.

i'm so sorry for such a delay in updates, with uni i am so so busy soi'm trying extremely hard to deliver these chapters to u as quick as i can but i'm falling behind. please bare w me - i haven't forgotten!

please please vote and comment to show your support!!

love u all, J xx

CHAPTER THIRTY THREE

(it's been a while so i'd recommend giving the last two chapters a quick read so you're aware and up to date!!)

ADELINE

I was angry. My skin was hot to touch - like a burning cauldron beginning to overflow.

Within the first few seconds of Cirse leaving my roomI had jumped out of bed - rustling around for some clothes I could wear. A basic sweater and pyjamas pants had to do. Within the same few moments, there was a knock to my bedroom door, followed by it swinging open.

"What is the point of you knocking if you are going to just open my door anyway?!" I snapped, turning around to be met with Azriel. He was dressed in his signature black fighting leathers, a belt of weapons clung around his slim waist.

He looked slightly taken aback at my instant remark, "Why is the honourable young lady so moody?"

"Moody?" I forced a laugh, my eyes sending bullets towards him, "I have one thing to ask you, and one thing only."

He leaned against the door, crossing his arms and jerking his head at me to continue, "I'm listening."

"Did you or did you not rape me last night?"

Azriel seemed to almost lose balance despite being supported by the door. His gold eyes turned slightly darker in shade, "What?"

"My question is clear. Did you or-"

"You are insane." It was the Arch Angel's turn to bark a laugh, "You think I raped you? You must be in-fucking-sane. I couldn't ever do anything of the sort."

"I'm sure you loved me grinding on you last night in front of a bunch of men, like a silly whore! How can I be so sure you didn't take advantage of me when you took me back?!"

Azriel looked lost for words. "Let me show you."

"Show me?" I arched a brow, my tone seething with sarcasm, "And how exactly are you going to do that?"

"Close your eyes."

Skeptical, I glared at him. "Why?"

"Just close your eyes, you absolute headache."

I closed my eyes, uncomfortable and unknowing, immersed in darkness. I waited a few seconds, and I was awfully close to snapping at him until what seemed like a hallucination right before my eyes began to appear. Colours, merging into one to form an image in front of me -

"What's happening?"

"Hush."

An image formed. It was me sat upon Azriel's lap last night, adorned in the same dress I had worn. I looked out of it - completely drunken and lost, but enjoying myself. He looked concerned, perhaps due to the wandering eyes upon me from the crowd. Suddenly, he arose - lifting me up with him. I followed the image as he carried me down the corridor gently, heading toward the direction of my chamber - and I started to feel a knot of guilt arise in my throat when I saw him do nothing but put me to bed.

My eyes flickered open and the image vanished.

Azriel stood by my door still, his features deathly cold and solemn. I quickly tore eye contact from him and looked down into my lap in an attempt to hide the tears building up in my eyes.

Shit, Adeline. You are not going to cry in front of this asshole right now. Stop.

I remained still as I heard the Arch Angel's footsteps come towards me. Hesitantly, for sure, he sat himself down beside me on my bed.

"Are you okay?"

I normally would have snapped at him, telling him to get out of my room or something similar - but the pure concern in his voice seemed to soften me up almost instantly. Regardless, I dared try to speak due to the fear of enticing a breakdown and so I instead nodded.

"Hey," He murmured at me in an attempt to get me to look at him, "Tell me what you're feeling."

Continuing to stare into my lap, I swallowed hard - trying to evade my tears and my pain.

"I was just scared."

My voice came out frail and fragile and it was frankly obvious that I was on the verge of tears. He must have known this, as I felt him shift slightly closer to me on the bed,

"Scared of being touched, Adeline?"

I nodded.

I heard the dark-haired male take a sharp inhale next to me, as if he was attempting to compose himself before I felt the warm sensation of a finger under my chin. He lifted it, forcing my emerald eyes to intertwine with his gold.

"I know you're scared, Adeline." He whispered to me, yet his tone remained firm, "But I want you to remember this. I would much rather - much rather endure a lifetime of being stoned to death with the most painful weapons than let a single scratch touch your body. Do you understand me?"

We maintained eye contact, and I hadn't even realised how my body trembled after his words, my eyes starting to brim with tears to an intensity that I was struggling to control any longer.

A single tear slid down my cheek, and within seconds I was sobbing - shaking uncontrollably with a desire to just be held. And he did that.

Azriel almost immediately pulled me into him, wrapping his arms around me tightly in order to shelter me - shelter me from this cruel, cruel world and its contents.

AZRIEL

She would never know, but my heart ached as I held her tight enough that I could feel the trembles of her small body against mine. This was a frail being who was traumatised from something I didn't have the knowledge on.

Rubbing her back gently as she sniffled into my chest, I hesitantly murmured to her, "You're traumatised, Adeline. Why?"

As I expected, I was met with silence and sniffles. I hadn't anticipated much else and as much as I was intrigued, I chose not to prod her any further. Instead, I just continued to pat her soothingly.

"I was sixteen."

I paused, confused, "Huh?"

The young mortal pulled herself away from my arms, exposing her tear-stained cheeks and blushed nose and cheeks from crying a moment ago. I noticed as she struggled to hold eye contact,

"I was sixteen when I met this boy from the village. His name was Harry," She seemed to have a faint smile playing on her lips as she told me, as though she was reminiscing good moments she may have experienced with this male. Nonetheless, her voice remained shaky, "We became the closest pair of friends very quickly, although our friendship was looked down upon frequently because of him being middle-class and me, poor. He met me at my best though - my most confident in my self, my looks, my personality. I always looked up to him considering he was a couple years older than me, and I was too late to realise when that inspiration had turned into infatuation."

I glowered at her, on-edge as I anticipated where this was going, "You fell in love?"

She used the back of her hand to dry her eyes, " I thought I had, I truly did, until one night." She paused and took in a sharp breath. "We were sat in the fields just by the outskirts of the village. It wasn't anything new or odd to us - Harry would make it a weekly occurrence to steal some alcohol from the market, and I'd sneak out of the house once my father was asleep to meet him and drink. I'd look forward to those nights every week, until one night I noticed his demeanour was off. Instead of drinking himself, he was pressurising me to drink more instead. Instead of listening to my conversations, he was much more focused on making sure I was drinking to the point I was becoming uncomfortable with the force."

I watched her intensely. As much as I didn't want to admit, I found myself with a tight knot in my stomach - a pit of anxiety.

"It got to the point where I became annoyed at his behaviour and got up to try and leave, but-," Her voice cracked, and she followed it up with a quick clear of the throat in an attempt to evade a breakdown, "But he didn't let me. Instead, he grabbed me and didn't let me go. At first I thought it was a joke - I laughed, until I realised it wasn't. He was gravely serious, and before I knew it my clothes were being ripped off of me."

She shut her eyes tightly as though she was trying to avoid the memory forming in her mind. My mind, however, was blank - purely and utterly stunned by shock.

"It took me a few moments to realise what was happening, but when I did I had begged." I watched as her eyes began to well up with tears, her expression painful, "I b-begged so much for him to stop, but he u-used me - again, and again and a-again."

Fuck.

Adeline inhaled another striking breath in an attempt to compose her shaking body and voice. "O-Once he was done with me, I was dumped in the field and left to dress myself and get home myself. When-"

"What about him? What happened with him? Did he pay the price for it?"
I couldn't help but interject - it was as though there was liquid rage seething
through my veins.

Adeline stared into her lap, before weakly shaking her head. "Nothing
happened to him, why would it? He went on to marry a marchioness from
the city and no one ever heard about what he did."

"What?" I rose from the bed, desperate, "What the hell did your father
say?!"

Adeline huffed a sad laugh, as though what I had said was ridiculous. "Papa
was defenceless. Who in their right mind would listen to a poor old man
and his sixteen year old daughter over a middle-class boy?" She continued,
"Papa kept me in the shadows after that, making sure I was safe by never
letting me out his sight - but the isolation stole my personality and happi-
ness with it."

I froze.

The cuts. The headaches. The flashbacks.

Fuck, Az.

ADELINE

Azriel had stayed silent long enough for me to become confused, and when
I looked up at him the gold tan usually present in his skin was instead
ghastly pale.

"Are you okay?" I frowned, slowly standing up to match him.

He seemed to blink himself out of some heavy thoughts.

"Y-Yeah, yes. I'm fine." A hand on my shoulder, before he pulled me into
a tight grasp of a hug. Normally I'd of swatted him away, but I decided to

take advantage of the warm, soothing embrace he offered me - while trying to rid of the disturbing, painful flashbacks my mind kept painting for me, "I'm so - I'm so fucking sorry, Adeline. You didn't deserve that. You know that right?"

I chose not to respond, but he instantly pulled back from the hug and gripped me at my shoulders instead, forcing me to look at him. Pain, confusion, anger - there was a multitude of so many heavy emotions flickering across his features, "You know that right, Adeline? Tell me right now."

I had never seen him like this. The usual cocky, arrogant warrior was but concerned, worried and nervous as he stood before me right now.

"I-I know," I murmured to his relief as he pulled me into his arms again. As much as I hated to admit it, Azriel was right. I did not deserve what Harry had done to me that night, and I had come out so much stronger as a result. I knew I had.

I tightened my grip around the Arch Angel. I had immediately muted my trauma when it had happened and I never got the affection needed to heal me ever, and so I decided I deserved this closeness. This embrace.

Before I knew it, Azriel had his hands under my thighs - indicating to me to jump up to which I obliged. He carried me back onto the bed and sat down with me now on his lap as we remained holding each other tightly, both of us so close it felt our souls could hear one another. It just felt right.

"Kiss me."

His body froze against mine.

CHAPTER THIRTY FOUR

J U L I A N (on the night of The Blossoming)

The young, silver-haired male scanned the array of dishes in front of him, a vacant plate in his hand. The truth was, he wasn't really hungry. After Azriel had placed such restrictions on him from speaking to Cirse, he hadn't had a decent night of sleep thinking about it.

A tap to his shoulder.

Confused, he turned to be met with the face of the maiden from the estate. His hazel-eyes widened at the sight of what stood before him and he couldn't refrain from trickling his eyes down her body, following the length of her milky beige silk dress.

Cirse stood slightly awkwardly, perhaps half shy from the encounter but also feeling the effects of being a misfit in such an event. In her hands were two glasses, both filled with an opaque liquid that had a sheer gold glow.

When he clicked into his senses, he scanned their surroundings quickly. His expression must have dropped - he wasn't in the position to have Azriel or Celeste see him. When he turned back to look at her, she seemed slightly taken aback at his uncalled for reaction.

"I-I can go? I-" She began, but he cut her off by quickly taking her arm and pulling her out the back entrance of the hall - which thankfully happened to be a couple steps away. He had seen Adeline talking to Celeste in the few moments he'd scanned the crowd and was aware their probable, eventual arguing or cat-fighting would keep Azriel occupied.

The open air hit them both like ice glazing over fire. The Great Hall had been toasty, a comfortable temperature, and they had counteracted that by plunging themselves into the gardens of the estate late into the night.

"I'm sorry," Julian spoke before she could question his actions, "I couldn't be seen talking to you in there."

Cirse seemed confused, and cocked her head to the side, "What? Why? Have I done something?"

"No, no, no, of course not," He quickly reassured her, still slightly out of breath by the speed they had left the hall in, "I didn't want to tell you."

Cirse, now becoming uncomfortable and conscious, swallowed hard. "Tell me what?"

"Remember when Azriel had caught us both in the library?" He murmured, starting to massage his temples which had begun to grow sore from the stress, "After I left, I was told to never be seen speaking to you again. He doesn't trust us both together."

The red-haired maiden bit her lip, and Julian wasn't sure whether it was to stop herself from crying or to refrain from saying something negative against the Arch Angel. Either way, he watched as she took a small step back from him.

"I-I'm sorry? I should go. This isn't okay and I truly don't want you to get into trouble with Azriel." Panic dominated her voice.

He took a step in, and reached out his hand to cup her face as a symbol to say 'don't go'. As he did so, some of her hair fell behind her shoulder to reveal her neck - and a beautiful blue diamond adorned upon it.

Julian tried to hold back his smile. "You kept the necklace I gave?"

Cirse blushed, perhaps with the shyness as she murmured, "I have never taken it off since you put it on me."

That was enough for Julian to take both the drinks she still held in her hands and set them down carefully on the grass beside them, before scooping her cheek again and pushing her against the wall of the hall in a manner not to hurt her.

The right hand man was playing a dangerous game - they both knew it, but he couldn't ignore what ignited inside him anymore. Not for anyone, not even his leader.

With another step towards her, he pressed his lips against hers - a strong, passionate movement. The young maiden almost melted against his touch, obliging and opening her mouth when his tongue grazed the bottom of her lip.

She would never know it, but if it was up to Julian he would have her right now - marking her as his and no one else's.

Slowly, Julian pulled away - the pair slightly out of breath from the sudden intimacy they had both shared. Cirse, unlike her usual self, did not pull away from the eye contact once - instead staring intensely into Julian's hazel eyes.

"You look beautiful, by the way," He murmured, pressing a kiss to her nose and then her forehead, before looking over to where he had left the drinks on the ground. "So, are you going to tell me why you were walking around with both of these?"

"Well," She bit her lip to suppress her excitement, "It's a special drink. The barmaid told me it's perfect for people with a headache of a leader."

Silence. Julian didn't do much as shift at her playful remark, and Cirse was just about to panic and apologise for any offence.

But then Julian tipped his head back and laughed, such a loud, joyous laugh as such never reaching her ears before,

"In that case, Cirse, it is best we get drinking."

****

ADELINE

"Kiss me."

I felt his body freeze against mine.

"What?" He murmured, both of us still in an embrace now, albeit stiff and uncomfortable from the shock of my words.

"I said-"

My bedroom door flew open, and the both of us separated from each other as quick as light - startled.

Celeste stood in the doorway, her expression confused perhaps at what she had walked into, but also concerned.

"Azriel, fuck, there you are." She seethed, seemingly out of breath from searching for him. She barely acknowledged me, holding eye contact with

Azriel - but that didn't stop her from throwing a brisk glance of disregard towards me. "You have to come quick."

Azriel cocked an eyebrow, and I shuddered at the tone of apprehension lacing his voice. "Why? What's happened?"

"Aerith of Zybern's here. She's figured out that the potions you returned to them were replicas."

The Arch Angel beside me swiftly rose to his feet almost immediately, expressions of annoyance and tension flickering on his features. "You cannot be serious right now."

And with that the two cousins stormed out of the room without another word or look towards me, the sound of Celeste beginning to debrief the situation to her male counterpart sounding down the glass hallway. I remained sat, trying to process the previous five minutes.

You're right, Azriel. You could not be serious right now.